DEATH DEFYING
ACTS

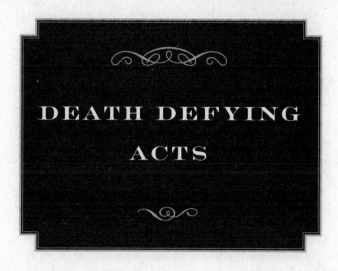

DEATH DEFYING ACTS

A NOVELIZATION BY GREG COX

BASED ON THE SCREENPLAY
BY TONY GRISONI AND BRIAN WARD

Pocket Books

New York   London   Toronto   Sydney

 Pocket Books
A Division of Simon & Schuster, Inc.
1230 Avenue of the Americas
New York, NY 10020

First Pocket Books trade paperback edition July 2008

POCKET and colophon are registered trademarks of
Simon & Schuster, Inc.

For information about special discounts for bulk purchases,
please contact Simon & Schuster Special Sales at 1-800-456-6798
or business@simonandschuster.com

Designed by Mary Austin Speaker

Manufactured in the United States of America

10   9   8   7   6   5   4   3   2   1

Library of Congress Cataloging-in-Publication Data is available.

ISBN-13: 978-1-4165-6079-1
ISBN-10:   1-4165-6079-3

DEATH DEFYING
ACTS

It takes a flimflammer to catch a flimflammer.

— HARRY HOUDINI
Los Angeles Times, October 28, 1924

SYDNEY

CHAPTER ONE

———

1926

THE BODY HIT THE WATER WITH A SPLASH, then disappeared beneath the surface of the harbor.

A collective gasp escaped the wide-eyed throng crowding the docks at Port Jackson. A mob of hundreds, if not thousands, gaped expectantly at the ripples spreading out across the sunlit blue water. Bowler-hatted gentlemen rubbed shoulders with sweaty dockworkers, gray-haired pensioners, and grubby-faced street urchins. Bob-haired flappers and their more respectably attired sisters mingled with the menfolk. Reporters and photographers from all the major newspapers were on hand to cover the spectacle, while roving pickpockets took advantage of their distracted victims.

On this cool autumn day, it seemed as though all of Sydney had turned out to watch the Great Houdini risk death beneath the waves. A brass band played a jaunty ragtime melody, as a busy moving-picture crew captured the historic scene for posterity.

The enthralled members of the audience held their breath, raising hands to shield their straining eyes from the afternoon glare.

At the end of the pier, wrapped in a knitted mohair overcoat, a heavyset Englishman anxiously consulted a stopwatch.

Precious seconds ticked by.

He wiped his sweaty brow with a handkerchief, muttering unhappily to himself. Squinty blue eyes peered out from beneath heavy eyebrows, his trilby hat concealing a receding hairline.

"C'mon, Harry," Morrie Sugarman said. "Don't do this to me again."

Tearing his worried gaze away from the surface of the harbor, Sugarman contemplated the teeming horde packing the wharf. *Quite a turnout*, the middle-aged theatrical manager assessed. *Pity we couldn't charge each of them an admission fee.*

Today's stunt was free of charge, intended to generate publicity, not revenue, although the former would inevitably lead to the latter, provided that Sugarman's distinguished employer survived to make his next theatrical engagement—something that was looking less and less likely every moment that the celebrated magician and escape artist remained underwater.

Acid churned inside Sugarman's substantial gut. Even though he had gone through this hundreds of times before, all over the civilized world, he couldn't help thinking that, just maybe, today might be the day that Harry Houdini finally pushed his luck too far.

At times like this, Sugarman couldn't help wishing that his boss had a less nerve-racking profession. Like taming lions, perhaps, or defusing bombs.

What possessed a man to risk his life day after day for the amusement of an audience? Even after handling Harry's business affairs for over twenty years, Morrie Sugarman didn't pretend to understand what made the Great Houdini tick. Ambition? Ego? That was part of it, of course, but Sugarman had always suspected that deeper impulses were at work.

Why do you do it, Harry? There certainly were easier ways to make a million.

A large industrial crane shared the pier with Sugarman. Brawny stevedores clung to the side of the crane, whose end jutted out over the busy harbor, a thick metal cable dangling from the tip. The Englishman's eyes traced the length of the cable to where it disappeared beneath the dancing water.

A strong breeze blew a salty spray against his face. The sound of shallow waves lapping against the docks was drowned out by the brassy music of the band and the increasingly agitated murmur of the crowd. They had come to witness an exhibition, not a drowning. Seagulls cawed and circled in the sky above them, oblivious to the life-or-death drama unfolding below. Sugarman envied the gulls. He knew just how the restless crowd felt.

Where the hell was Houdini?

At the other end of the steel cable, submerged beneath the harbor, a near-naked figure thrashed violently like a fish on a line.

Heavy chains and manacles bound the man's muscular arms and legs as he sank toward the bottom of the bay. Padlocks clamped the chains tightly around him, as the weight of the iron shackles dragged him ever downward. The muffled ragtime music grew fainter, as did the shimmering rays of sunlight filtering down through the murky water above.

Clad only in irons and long woolen drawers, Harry Houdini struggled to free himself. His wiry, athletic body strained against his bonds. Underwater currents rustled his dark black hair. Piercing gray-blue eyes peered through the salty brine.

Stay calm, Houdini reminded himself. As always, his chief task at such moments was to conquer fear, to retain his wits and faculties despite his alarming circumstances. Even shackled from head to toe, and plunging swiftly toward a watery grave, it was necessary to maintain an absolute serenity of spirit. *If I panic, I am lost. . . .*

He held on tightly to his breath. Years of practice and conditioning had expanded his lung capacity until he could go without breathing for three minutes or more. The cold water leeched the heat from his bones, yet the chill had little effect on him. He routinely bathed in tubs of ice water to inure his body against the shock of a sudden immersion. Indeed, he had become accustomed to a cold bath every morning and seldom enjoyed going without one. Sydney Harbor was not exactly warm this afternoon, but he had attempted this stunt in far cooler waters. Detroit, back in November of '07 ... now *that* had been cold.

Nevertheless, there wasn't a moment to waste. Already air bubbles were starting to involuntarily escape from his mouth and nostrils. First one bubble, then another. Soon a flurry of tiny bubbles percolated up through the depths, taking the bulk of Houdini's breath with them.

FAILURE MEANS A DROWNING DEATH! proclaimed the handbills promoting today's event. The claim was no exaggeration; at least one of Houdini's many imitators had died performing this stunt. But Harry did not intend to visit Davy Jones's locker today.

Moving swiftly and deliberately, he went to work on his bonds.

. . .

Sugarman paced fretfully up and down the pier. Sneaking a peek at his stopwatch, he saw to his horror that yet another minute had ticked by.

The blood drained from his ordinarily ruddy complexion. Another surge of acid scalded his innards. This was taking too long, even by Houdini's famously reckless standards. Sugarman had known his employer to deliberately delay his ascent just to prolong the suspense and milk every last iota of drama from the performance, but he had been underwater for nearly four minutes now. Harry had to be running out of air. Not even the Great Houdini could hold his breath forever. . . .

The crowd was growing restive, too. The assembled

spectators and reporters stared anxiously into the depths, fearing that something had gone terribly wrong with this afternoon's entertainment. Frantic cries and exclamations reached Sugarman's ears, echoing the awful doubts and dilemmas clamoring inside his own cranium, until finally he couldn't take it anymore.

"Up! Up!" he shouted at the stevedores manning the crane. "Get the bleedin' thing up outta the water!"

Black smoke belched as the crane's engine roared to life. The hanging steel cable snapped taut as a motorized winch hastily reeled the cable in, not nearly fast enough for Sugarman and the other onlookers, who watched the churning surface of the harbor with extreme apprehension. A ghastly image, of Houdini's lifeless corpse tethered to the end of the rising cable, flashed through Sugarman's distraught mind. He could already see tonight's newspaper headlines:

THE GREAT HOUDINI PERISHES IN FINAL STUNT!
DEATH CLAIMS FAMOUS MAGICIAN AT LAST!

Just as Sugarman had begun composing Houdini's obituary in his head, Harry Houdini rose victoriously from the foaming water, balanced nonchalantly atop a heavy block and tackle.

Houdini flashed a captivating smile and waved to the crowd as the crane hauled him high into the air. Water streamed from his head and shoulders, his slick black hair plastered to his skull. Sunlight shone down upon his glistening musculature. Linked chains and padlocks dangled beneath him. In the distance, the half-completed structure of the Harbour Bridge, looking like an enormous steel coat hanger, provided a dramatic backdrop as Houdini posed for the cameras.

A god. A hero. Death's conqueror!

The crowd went wild, clapping and cheering ecstatically. Hats erupted into the air, some blown into the harbor by the errant breeze. Grown men embraced each other, perfect strangers slapping their neighbors on the back ... awestruck lads gaped in openmouthed wonder at the magnificent figure hanging boldly in the sky ... ladies waved their handkerchiefs above their heads—all for him. The band struck up an enthusiastic fanfare. Magnesium flash powder went off like firecrackers. The reporters hastily scribbled in their notebooks before scurrying away to hail the news of Houdini's latest spectacular feat to their respective papers.

On cue, a biplane swooped low over the harbor, trailing a long cloth banner that proclaimed in giant letters, *HOUDINI IS IMMORTAL!*

Tell me about it, Sugarman thought. He sagged against the rusty base of the crane as the adrenaline drained from his body, turning his legs into rubber. His pounding heartbeat slowly subsided. *You cocky son of a bitch,* he thought, laughing uncontrollably. *You did it to me again!*

Amidst the deafening applause, the Great Houdini took a bow.

EDINBURGH

CHAPTER TWO

———

. . . AND AS THE GREAT HOUDINI ROSE TRI-
umphant from the waves, it was as if the very Heavens opened, and the
Gods of the Sun, the Four Winds, the Sea, and the Stars all bowed
down before him and made him their King. Not since Captain Cook
conquered the New World has Sydney's harbour witnessed a spectacle so
thrilling and dramatic.

Her name was Maura Evelyn McGarvie, but everyone
called her Benji because they said she had her father's eyes.
The girl's grubby finger traced the words in the luridly il-
lustrated comic book as she squatted on a stoop down by the
Leith waterfront, across the street from the pawnbroker's
shop. The squalid neighborhood had definitely seen better
days. Broken glass and other refuse littered the rough, un-
even cobblestones. Sunlight fought its way through the
smoky haze of countless wood fires. Empty barrels were
stacked haphazardly against sooty stone walls. A nearby alley smelled of piss.

Only eleven years old, going on fifty, Benji looked like a

street urchin straight out of a Dickens novel. A newsboy's cap covered her mousy brown hair, her dirty knees protruded from beneath a hand-me-down pair of boy's short pants. A worn brown jacket and a woolen sweater barely protected her scrawny frame from the autumn chill. A profusion of improvised patches held her tattered garments together, and her heavy, black galoshes were one size too large. With her dressed like Oliver Twist, only close inspection revealed her actual gender. Her face needed washing.

Benji didn't care.

She eagerly flipped the pages of the comic, momentarily escaping her dingy surroundings. Houdini's miraculous feats seemed too fantastic to be believed, yet she couldn't stop reading about all of his amazing stunts and illusions. According to the comic, Houdini had escaped from locked jail cells, sealed milk cans, sturdy wooden crates, a Russian prison wagon, a riveted steel boiler, tarred ropes, and all manner of handcuffs and leg-irons, even when stripped naked and wrapped in chains. He had been tossed off bridges into icy rivers. He had wriggled out of straitjackets while hanging upside down from the tops of skyscrapers. He could walk through solid brick walls in front of thousands of witnesses. He had been sewn up inside the carcass of a dead sea monster. He had been strapped to the mouth of a loaded cannon, escaping just before the fuse burned to the end. He had been chained to the spinning blade of a Dutch windmill. He had been buried alive beneath the earth and had stayed submerged in an underwater casket for over an hour and a half. He had even made a five-ton elephant disappear onstage.

Really? Benji wondered. She wanted to believe that such marvels were actually possible, that a man truly existed who could perform all these wonders, but her short life had already taught her to take nothing at face value. The world was full of crooks and cons, and gullible fools easily misled by a little smoke and mirrors. That's what her mam always said, and Mam knew what she was talking about all right. But part of Benji still prayed that there was more to life than false hopes and trickery. *What if Houdini really is magic? What then?*

"Benji!"

A cross voice disturbed her reverie. Benji looked up to see her mother emerge from the pawnbroker's. Mary McGarvie was a handsome woman, still in the prime of life. Lustrous black curls peeked from beneath a somewhat battered cloche hat. Her shapeless brown overcoat failed to entirely conceal her voluptuous figure. Dark clothing showed off her ivory complexion, while her vibrant brown eyes regarded the world with suspicion. Slender fingers hung on tightly to her purse. Her black cotton skirt rustled as she briskly strode down the cobblestone street.

"Head in the clouds again!" she barked at her daughter. "We've got work to do, girlie!"

Her nose still in the pages of the comic, Benji rose like a sleepwalker from the step. A garish drawing of Houdini escaping from an ancient Egyptian sarcophagus held her attention as she drifted along in her mother's wake.

They headed south toward Edinburgh proper, navigating a maze of narrow alleys and quays. Leith had officially been absorbed by the larger city six years ago, but many residents still considered the port a separate community. Run-down warehouses and shipyards blocked their view of the harbor.

"That's the wedding ring back in the window again, is it?" A lanky ruffian, leaning against a weathered stone wall, called out to Mary as they passed by. Stubble carpeted the man's chin, and his bleary eyes and a florid red nose suggested a predilection for drink, hardly a novelty in this neighborhood. Greasy hair dangled on his forehead, and he was missing a front tooth. His sleeves were rolled up to display faded nautical tattoos. Rumpled clothing looked as if they'd been slept in, perhaps in an alley somewhere. He took a puff from a clay pipe and blew the smoke in their direction; meanwhile he ogled Mary brazenly, undressing her with his eyes, licking his lips. Benji wrinkled her nose in disgust.

"Only good use I ever had for it," Mary snapped.

Drinking and whoring, that was all Benjamin McGarvie had ever shown a talent for, at least according to Benji's mother. The girl barely remembered her father, a third-rate carnival mentalist who had often showed up dead drunk for his performances. Formerly his "beautiful assistant," Mary had kicked him out years ago and taken over the act to support herself and Benji. Nobody had laid eyes on the Amazing McGarvie in years—most believed he was dead.

Benji sometimes wondered what had really become of him.

Now the would-be Romeo sidled up to Mary and

slipped a grimy hand around her slender waist. He reeked of whiskey and cheap cologne. "Mary McGarvie," he cooed in her ear. "A dream come true."

"Not for you." She kept on walking, not letting the man's unwanted embrace throw her off her stride. Her chin remained elevated. Her heels rapped decisively against the cobblestones. She glanced impatiently at her lagging off-spring. "Benji!"

Without warning, she snatched the comic from Benji's grasp and cuffed the girl round the ear with it. Benji yelped and clutched the side of her head, which stung like the dickens. Mary grabbed Benji's hand and dragged her along. Scowling, the girl scrambled to keep up with her mother. She lunged at her comic, hoping to reclaim it, but Mary kept the tantalizing pages out of her reach. *Give it back*, Benji fumed. *I was reading that!*

A window squeaked open, one story above their heads. A haggard-looking woman, with a shriveled face and hair like a haystack, leaned out the window and shouted stridently at Mary, "Leave my man alone, ya Gypsy strumpet!"

Like my mam would want your worthless layabout, Benji thought. The ill-tempered hag and the leering ruffian deserved each other. Her mother no doubt felt the same, since she roughly shoved the unkempt Casanova away from her and hastened down the alley.

"I wouldn't have your hand-me-downs if you paid me!" Mary shot back over her shoulder.

"Pavement princess!" the other woman shouted after her.

"Frigid old piss-pants!"

It took the hag in the window a second to come up with a suitable retort. "Floozy!"

Hell, I can do better than that, Benji thought. "Bloody circumcision!"

The window slammed shut indignantly. The rejected swain beat a hasty retreat, no doubt wondering how he was going to make peace with his aggrieved spouse. Momentarily nonplussed, Mary paused in her tracks and gave her daughter a quizzical look. She arched an elegantly plucked eyebrow.

Benji shrugged. "It's in the Bible. . . ."

Mary rolled her eyes and let out an exasperated sigh. Then she tightened her grip on Benji's hand and resumed their energetic march through the waterfront.

To the southwest, above the soot-covered roofs of the surrounding shops and warehouses, the great stone battlements of Edinburgh Castle could be glimpsed climbing toward the sky. The imposing medieval edifice, perched upon the rocky crest of an extinct volcano, loomed over the city below. Its ancient grandeur only made the seedy port seem all the more dismal, at least as far as Benji was concerned.

In days of yore, she recalled, the fortress had held countless prisoners in its infamous dungeons. Could Houdini escape from the sunless vaults beneath the castle? Benji hungrily eyed the precious comic in her mother's hand. She had just been about to read about his legendary escape from Scotland Yard in London when the thrilling pages had been plucked from her grasp. Frustrated, she lifted her gaze toward the castle's impervious stone walls.

I'll bet he could do it, she thought. *If anybody can.*

. . .

McTavish's Palace Music Hall was a once extravagant Victorian pile now rather gone to seed. Traces of its former glamour still clung to its crumbling Moorish facade, which faced out onto a bustling street in a working-class corner of the Old Town. A fresh layer of bright red paint disguised the crumbing plaster and mortar. Peeling yellow trimming mimicked gold leaf. Curvy moldings and arabesques gave the building a faintly oriental flair. A string of electric lights outlined the marquee, which proudly advertised THE BEST OF VAUDEVILLE—FOR ONE WEE SHILLING! Gaudy canvas posters ballyhooed an impressive-sounding panoply of acts, including acrobats, jugglers, comedians, dancers, vocalists, and even "Six Genuine Wild Indians!" Enticed by the poster's extravagant promises, customers queued up at the ticket booth in front of the entrance. Tinted-glass panes offered a peek at the lobby inside.

A horse and cart clopped down the street in front of the theater, not nearly fast enough for the impatient driver of the motorcar stuck behind them, who honked his horn in a futile attempt to hurry things along. The swaybacked nag showed what she thought of the horn's intrusive beeping by lifting her tail and dropping a load of stinking manure directly in the automobile's path. The motorist's curses provoked laughter from the blue-collar crowd queued up at the box office. A few pedestrians joined in the hilarity before continuing about their business. The reek of the horse dung mixed with the auto's exhaust to form a stomach-turning miasma that made Mary gag at the stench. Not for nothing had Edinburgh acquired the nickname of Auld Reekie.

Ah, the sophistication of big city life . . .

She stared across the street at the music hall's future customers, discreetly examining them as keenly as a fortune-teller perusing some tea leaves. No detail escaped her scrutiny: a rolled-up brolly, an open wallet, a toy in a lady's hand, a snot-nosed child squirming in his mother's arms, a cad slyly slipping his wedding band into his pocket. Tuning out the general hubbub of the street, Mary caught snatches of conversation between the various patrons in line for tickets to tonight's show. All potential marks, every jack and jill of them.

So who are the most likely prospects today?

Benji fidgeted beside her. She juggled a trio of billiard balls, a hobby she had picked up backstage at various music halls and dime museums. Mary glanced down to make sure the girl was also giving the queue a good once-over, just as Mary had trained her to do. Two pairs of eyes were better than one, even if one of those pairs belonged to a mere slip of a girl who didn't yet fully realize that life was a deadly serious business, one that would grind you into mincemeat if you didn't keep your wits about you. *All the time with her head in the clouds and barely a lick of common sense,* Mary lamented silently. *Just like her shiftless, no-account father . . .*

"Pay attention," Mary whispered. "Your supper's riding on this, too."

Satisfied that she had set the girl's head straight for the time being, Mary returned her attention to the box office, just in time to see an apple-cheeked redhead ride up to the curb on a bicycle. As the lass dismounted the bike, Mary caught a glimpse of shockingly scarlet knickers.

Well, aren't we the daring one?

Arms akimbo, the redhead confronted a raffish young blade whom Mary assumed to be her beau. "Didn't I know I'd find you here, Sean MacDiarmid?" she accused him. "About to waste our hard-earned wages on a show."

"Aw, come on, Rose," he pleaded. He was a strapping youth with a good deal more natural charm than the scruffy wharf rat who had accosted Mary down by the docks this morning. Sean flashed the redhead a devilish smile. If nothing else, he still had all his teeth. "A shilling won't break the bank."

"This bank was broke a long time ago!"

Embarrassed by the public display, Sean lowered his voice in hopes of getting Rose to do the same. He cozied up to her and whispered something in her ear. Judging from the way she blushed and giggled in response, Mary guessed that Sean was well on his way to overcoming his sweetheart's objections. *I'll be seeing both of them at tonight's show,* she predicted. *I'd bet a crown on it.*

Unable to eavesdrop on the couple's conversation any longer, Mary shifted her gaze to another likely prospect. An older gentleman, his shoulders stooped as though laboring beneath a heavy load, caught her eye. A keen observer of the human animal, Mary noted that, unlike the other eager ticket-buyers, this individual appeared both hesitant and sad. His doleful mien, his defeated carriage ... everything about him suggested that he was burdened by some hidden woe. Mary's shrewd brown eyes studied his frayed shirt, the slightly askew tie, the rumpled trousers, the dandruff on his shoulders. *Who let him out in such a sorry state?* she wondered, etching the salient details in her memory. *Or is he simply past caring?* He peered at the theater posters through a pair of smudged glasses. The telltale flash of a gold watch-chain called out to her.

Mary watched carefully as the gentleman bought a single ticket for tonight's performance. Looking down, she was gratified to see that Benji had picked the man out of the crowd as well. *Maybe there's hope for the girl yet,* Mary thought.

As though sensing her mother's eyes upon her, Benji glanced upward. Their eyes met in a moment of silent communion. There was no need for any words; they both knew what needed to be done. Mary nodded, almost imperceptibly, and Benji slipped away down the sidewalk.

Be quick about it, Mary thought. *And careful as can be.*

．　．　．

"You'll be after your usual posy of violets, Mr. Robertson?"

The old gent had paused in front of a corner flower stall. Fresh roses, begonias, azaleas, rhododendrons, heather, and other colorful blossoms spilled over the edge of the wooden stall, their mixed fragrance wafting across the intersection. Mr. Robertson sighed heavily as he inhaled the bouquet of the violets. He dabbed at his eye with a handkerchief.

"They were always her favorite."

The flower vendor nodded knowingly, as though she had heard this many times before. She gave Mr. Robertson a sympathetic smile as she carefully wrapped the posy in clean white paper. Benji quietly approached him from behind, then audibly sniffed some flowers to get his attention. Watery eyes, shadowed by heavy bags beneath them, took notice of the elfin figure that had seemingly materialized at his side. Benji smiled up at Mr. Robertson angelically, the very picture of childish innocence. Her sunny countenance brought a feeble smile to his careworn face. Her gleaming blue eyes shone almost as brightly as the gold pocket watch hanging on a chain from his waistcoat.

Easy as pie, she thought.

It wasn't exactly an elephant, but this was one disappearing act she could manage all on her own.

. . .

Moments later, Benji placed the pocket watch in Mary's outstretched hand. But the ticking timepiece wasn't all that the young scamp had acquired during her foray; Mary noted with amusement the bright red carnation now adorning her daughter's hair. She permitted herself a rare smile before flicking open the lid of the watch. Inside she found a faded portrait of a tall, graceful-looking woman posing amid a lush flower garden that showed every indication of being lovingly cared for. Directly opposite the portrait was an inscription.

" 'To Charles, with never-ending love,' " Mary read aloud, wincing slightly at the unrealistic sentiment. " 'Your Violet.' "

She nodded in approval. *That will do for a start*, she mused. *Now I just need to do a little digging before the curtain goes up.*

Taking Benji firmly by the hand, she made haste to the next stop on their itinerary.

. . . .

The Hall of Records was located on the second floor of the city library. Shelves stacked with over a century's worth of dusty volumes rose up like the cliffs below Edinburgh Castle. Cobwebs gathered in the corners. Dust motes danced in shafts of sunlight beaming down through sooty windows that were placed high overhead. A musty atmosphere hung over the all-but-deserted chamber.

Mary knew the chamber well, as well as the resident librarian.

Unfortunately.

"Deceased: Violet Robinson," Mr. Fettes recited, pointing to a handwritten notation in the heavy tome lying open on the counter before him. The librarian's cadaverous appearance was more appropriate for a morgue; his pasty white skin looked as if it had never felt the sun's touch. A few lank strands of hair were combed over his pate in a failed attempt to disguise his baldness. Hollow cheeks and sunken eyes added to his ghoulish visage. Spectacles pinched his nose. He affected a cultured tone, but Mary could hear the slums of Glasgow beneath his posh accent. "Died of heart failure."

Mary's hand covered her mouth to stifle what she thought was a fairly convincing gasp of despair. She leaned over the counter, trying, without being too blatant about it, to get a better look at the entry in question. *Does it say any-*

thing about the husband? she wondered. *His full name and profession perhaps? Any other next of kin?*

The librarian drew the tome back before she could decipher the upside-down writing. Mary resisted an urge to curse out loud as he snapped the book shut. *Bloody hell!*

"You're quite the unfortunate one," Fettes observed archly. "It was your long-lost uncle a week ago, was it not? And now poor Mrs. Robinson . . ." His smirking tone made it clear that he did not accept her explanations at face value and had not for some time, yet he was willing to go through with the charade nonetheless. "My most sincere condolences, Mrs. McGarvie."

Filthy weasel, Mary thought irritably, even as she choked back another sob. "You're so kind."

"You'll be wanting to examine the records, no doubt." He peered over the top of his spectacles at the rolling ladder leading up to the higher shelves. A lascivious smile crossed his face. "The information you need may be on the *fifth* shelf."

Same as always, Mary thought wearily. *The dirty-minded bugger can't wait for a peek up my skirts.* Well, she could play that game if she had to. She met his leer with a knowing smirk of her own. "Or even the sixth."

Swallowing hard, Fettes moved aside to let her step behind the counter. She squeezed past him quickly, before he could work up the nerve to get too bold with his hands. His lewd regard was irksome enough; she wasn't about to let him take any further liberties with her person. She didn't need a closer look at the records *that* much.

"It's the details of our dear departed that one later cherishes," she observed as she set foot on the lower rung of the ladder. It quivered slightly beneath her weight. "Don't you think?"

Breathless with anticipation, the librarian hurried over to hold the ladder steady. His hungry eyes followed her ascent, treating themselves to an illicit survey of her nether regions. " 'Cherishable details,' Mrs. McGarvie," he echoed her, licking his lips. Mary didn't need to glance down to know that his myopic eyes were all but popping from their sockets. She suspected there was yet more bulging going on farther down. "How right you are."

She plucked a thick tome from the shelf and blew the dust off its leather binding.

This had better be worth it, she thought.

CHAPTER THREE

GARISH POSTERS ADORNED THE LOBBY OF McTavish's Palace Music Hall. The gaudy signs touted the myriad attractions awaiting tonight's patrons as they trampled through the lobby toward the auditorium beyond. The featured performers included such notables as:

MADAME GIRELLI'S
PERFORMING MONKEYS!

REX BRODIE:
THE SINGING COMEDIAN!

THE CAMDEN BROS.!
MIDAIR JUGGLERS AND FUNAMBULISTS!

THE HILARIOUS HOOLIGANS!
LOADS OF LAFFS!

MISS MEGAN ROWLING:
THE VOICE OF THE HIGHLANDS!

Only a few customers lingered briefly to savor the posters themselves, with their lurid colors and bombastic promises. Those of the male persuasion paused slightly longer in front of one particular poster, which depicted an exotic, raven-haired beauty clad in a wispy oriental outfit that scarcely concealed her womanly curves. Kohl-lined eyes and sinuous limbs evoked the forbidden pleasures of some desert potentate's harem. Mata Hari herself could not have been more alluring.

All but unnoticed by the poster's admirers was the additional element of a brown-faced child wearing a golden turban, depicted at the painted enchantress's side. Flamboyant lettering extolled the pair by name:

THE TANTALISING
PRINCESS KALI
& HER DUSKY DISCIPLE!

PSYCHIC EXTRA ORDINAIRE!
RISQUÉ! BAFFLING! MOVING!

FAREWELL PERFORMANCE TONIGHT!

"You hear that? 'Risqué.'" An acne-scarred youth nudged a companion with his elbow. He smacked his lips loudly. "That's worth a shilling, I wager."

His friend ogled the scantily clad woman in the poster. "Ya think that's what she really looks like?"

"Only one way to find out, bucko."

They winked at each other before hurrying inside to

await the fleshly incarnation of the seductive vision on the poster. After all, they didn't want to miss her "farewell performance."

.   .   .

Looks like a rowdy crowd in the cheap seats tonight, Mary thought, peering out at the audience from around the corner of the flimsy proscenium arch. A paltry orchestra labored heroically, but failed to drown out the raucous uproar coming from the gallery, where the barbarian hordes drank, caroused, and quarreled with abandon. An usher walked down the aisle, spraying perfume water from a huge brass pump in a hopeless attempt to dispel the fetid odor of too many unwashed bodies crammed together in one space. A fight broke out between two drunken louts, and a beefy bouncer (who had once found employment as a circus strongman) was forced to intervene, dragging the offending lummoxes out by their ears. Rubbish pelted the stage, occasionally raining down on the heads of the customers in the respectable midrange seats below. The unlucky patrons protested vociferously, but to no avail. Overripe tomatoes, bananas, and other produce continued to bombard the stage and orchestra pit. They splattered upon the boards, spraying juice and seeds in all directions. The battle-hardened musicians kept playing despite the deluge of refuse.

Not that Mary entirely blamed the trash-flinging critics. The act currently occupying the stage was truly dreadful. Mary watched, aghast, as a clumsy fool, wearing a striped yellow waistcoat, a bowler hat, and a pair of ridiculous-looking fairy wings, chased a dwarf around the

stage, while wielding an oversize butterfly net. His wee target ran circles around the hapless pursuer while tooting a
kazoo. A painted backdrop identified the pair as THE HILARI-
OUS HOOLIGANS! The larger man bore a slight resemblance to
Charlie Chaplin, but lacked any trace of Chaplin's gift for
comedy. Mary shook her head in disbelief. She'd seen some
dubious acts in her time, but this unfunny spectacle was in a
class all its own. *Words fail me*, she thought. *And yet I'm being
dropped from the bill?*

Red-faced and puffing, the larger of the two performers
made one last lunge at his diminutive cohort. But the dwarf
nimbly eluded capture by bouncing onto a convenient
trampoline, which propelled him high above the stage.
Tooting from both ends of his stunted frame, he farted a
cloud of thick green smoke.

Only a handful of customers laughed.

Red velvet curtains swished shut, mercifully bringing
the excruciating performance to a close. Instead of applause,
jeers and catcalls erupted from the audience. An empty bottle arced through the air before crashing down onto the
stage. From her vantage point in the wings, Mary watched
the dwarf and his partner beat a hasty retreat. The little
man's emerald emission hung in the air for a moment before
dispersing backstage. A faint chemical smell irritated her
nostrils. She wrinkled her nose in distaste.

I don't even want to know how that gag is done.

Undaunted by the irate crowd, McTavish himself
strode out onto the stage. The theater owner, who doubled
as the master of ceremonies, was decked out like a Highland

dandy, complete with a tartan kilt, sporran, and feather-crested bonnet. His lean, vulpine face was heavily rouged and powdered, his dyed-black hair slicked back with pomade. A waxed mustache resided above his upper lip. If the audience's hostile reaction to the previous act concerned him, he gave no sign of it, strutting about the stage like the Cock o' the North. An airborne banana came hurling at his head, but he deftly snatched it out of the air.

"Aha! Courtship!" He waved the banana back at the mugs in the balcony. "Who's the baboon?"

A mutton-faced gent stuck his head out over the rail of the battery. "Who you callin' a baboon, ya wee poof?!"

McTavish brandished the banana like a professor wielding a pointer. "Are you a mammalian primate, or the *Papio ursinus*?" The audience oohed at the emcee's highfalutin vocabulary. They may not have known what it meant, but it certainly sounded impressive. McTavish pursed his lips as he slipped back into the vernacular. "Give us a kiss, ma wee marmoset!"

The audience roared with laughter.

"Enough monkey play!" Changing the mood, McTavish assumed a more conspiratorial tone, lowering his voice to a stage whisper. "This evening, ladies and gentlemen, I have something a little titillating. A little, dare I say it, *risqué*. . . ."

The audience straightened up in their seats. From the wings, Mary spied Mr. Charles Robertson making his way down the aisle toward the pricey seats up front. Murmuring apologies, he squeezed past several grumbling audience members to reach a seat in the third row. He settled down into the empty seat and wiped his brow, looking slightly out of breath. A bowler hat was deposited upon his lap.

About time he got here, Mary thought. She had been starting to fear that she had endured the librarian's loathsome attentions for nothing. But things were definitely looking up now. Perhaps, if she put on a really first-rate show tonight, that backstabbing tosser, McTavish, would reconsider and keep her in the show?

She knew full well why she was being let go after tonight's "farewell performance." McTavish had already booked a competing mentalist, Duncan, the Scottish Swami, who, rumor had it, was already sharing McTavish's flea-infested bed. The sheer injustice of it galled Mary's soul. She had caught Duncan's act at a carnival sideshow a few years back. On his best day, he wasn't half the "psychic" she was . . . as she was determined to prove any minute now.

Who knows? Maybe a talent scout or slumming theatrical impresario was in the audience? All she needed was just a lucky break to hit the big time and leave dumps like McTavish's Palace behind. *It's possible*, she told herself. Stranger things had happened, although seldom to her.

She made a few last-minute adjustments to her costume, then took her place behind the moth-eaten curtains as McTavish began to wind up his spiel. She glimpsed the front of the stage through a crack in the curtains.

"No juveniles among us, I trust?" The dapper emcee made a show of scouting out the audience for any underage patrons. He twirled his mustache. "No Free Ministers, no Soldiers of Temperance or Mrs. Grundys?" Saucy audience members hooted derisively at those avatars of pious morality; McTavish's Palace didn't exactly draw the family crowd, although it was still a few steps up from burlesque. Men shifted impatiently in their seats. McTavish stepped back and grandly threw out his arm. "Then here's your last chance to see . . . the Tantalizing Princess Kali and Her Dusky Disciple!"

The orchestra attempted a Middle Eastern air. The houselights dimmed and the curtains parted. Clouds of scented incense billowed out across the seats in the front rows. A hush fell over the audience, aside from a few yahoos who clapped and whistled in anticipation. A spotlight danced around the theater, weaving in rhythm to the music. Hanging Chinese lanterns lit up the cherry-red walls of the auditorium. A pair of shining bronze censers descended from the flies. Teasingly, the incandescent beam darted over the walls and across the empty boards before finally exposing to view a pair of delicate feet in high-heeled golden sandals. Sharp intakes of breath could be heard all throughout the auditorium.

With agonizing slowness, the spotlight rose, widening to reveal a statuesque woman dressed like a vision out of an erotic fever dream. Her voluptuous body was generously exposed by a gauzy costume that might make a belly dancer blush. A sequined brassiere scarcely contained her full white breasts. A thin swath of golden silk clung to her hips, preserving what little remained of her modesty. Diaphanous harem pants offered veiled glimpses of her supple legs. Pearls and gemstones glittered all over her skimpy attire. Bangles adorned her bare arms and fingers. Polished turquoise gleamed in the jeweled diadem crowning her bewitching countenance. Kohl created enticing black shadows around her deep brown eyes. A sparkling ruby (or a glass replica of same) nestled in her navel, surrounded by a scandalous expanse of taut white skin.

Rather than a mere music hall performer, Mary McGarvie seemed like a houri out of some sensual Arabian paradise.

Every man in the audience, from callow lads to doddering grandfathers, gaped openly at Princess Kali's near-naked splendor. Their womenfolk either chuckled in amusement at the men's stupefied reactions or else raised their chins in jealous challenge. Not a few of the ladies smiled wistfully, perhaps imagining themselves as seductive femmes fatales.

Do I know how to make an entrance or don't I? Mary smiled to herself, gratified by the audience's rapt attention. She framed her head between her palms, a pose she had picked up from a Theda Bara movie. *Look at their goggle-eyed faces. I've got them eating out of my hands and I haven't said a bloody word yet.*

"Kali, Kasbah," she intoned solemnly, as if in a trance. Behind her, a painted backdrop depicted the pyramids of ancient Egypt. In the foreground of the painting, a camel trekked toward an inviting desert oasis. "Magicaram!"

The audience hung on every syllable, until some joker

recalled that the undraped goddess before them was made of real flesh and blood. An appreciative whoop set off a chorus of wolf whistles and stamping feet. Mary decided it was time to get on with the act, before she lost control of the crowd altogether. *Where's that daydreaming offspring of mine anyway?*

Turning her head to present the audience with a profile out of an Egyptian hieroglyphic, she spotted Benji loitering in the wings. Greasepaint darkened her daughter's face and arms, a golden turban capped by a bright red feather hiding her light brown locks. A rainbow-striped sash girded the waist of a burgundy-colored tunic that smelled as if it hadn't been laundered in recent memory. Billowing golden trousers and pointed slippers completed the ensemble. All Benji needed was a magic lamp to pass for Aladdin himself. Instead she fiddled with a pasteboard lute while Effie O'Reilly, the resident seamstress, stitched up a tear in her costume. *She ripped that outfit again?* Mary thought irritably. *And right before we go on?*

Thankfully, the old crone worked quickly enough. In less than a minute, she bit off the thread and shoved Benji onto the stage. "At least that's one of you decent," Effie muttered, casting a disapproving look at Mary's revealing attire.

Judgmental old prune, Mary thought. *You're just jealous that nobody wants to see your shriveled carcass.*

Benji hastened to Mary's side. The tardy "disciple" gave her mother a sheepish look before bowing low before Princess Kali. Mary lifted one hand to her brow while holding out the other to silence the unruly crowd. She waited until the enthusiastic whistles subsided, then closed her eyes to commune with the spirits.

"I am receiving a message," she proclaimed after a dramatic pause.

"About time, eh?" a heckler jeered. "I sent it a week ago!"

A hint of frown creased Mary's face. She did her best to ignore the gibe. If she played this right, the crowd would soon be too spooked to interrupt.

"I see a flower." She opened her eyes and stared out across the auditorium. "Is there anyone here named . . . Rose?"

Hands went up throughout the audience. Mary didn't immediately spot the redheaded bicyclist from this afternoon. Had Rose ultimately persuaded Sean to save his shillings instead? That would certainly throw a spanner in the works. *I might have to improvise here.*

Benji's keen young eyes came to her rescue. "Gallery, middle, third row," she whispered urgently.

Mary followed Benji's directions. Sure enough, the redhead was right where Benji said she was, waving her hand above her head while Sean grinned like a loon. Mary decided that maybe Benji wasn't a total liability after all.

A wooden runway extended the stage past the orchestra pit. Clamshell-shaped footlights illuminated the pathway before Mary's feet. Moving slowly, she strode out onto the narrow platform until she was halfway out into the audience. Her finger pointed out her chosen target.

"That's a lovely pair of red knickers you're wearing to-night, Rose!"

Sean howled along with the rest of the audience. Rose blushed scarlet, but was clearly lapping up the attention, the shameless hussy. Feigning modesty, she shook her head in denial.

"Prove her wrong, hen!" shouted a voice that sounded suspiciously like that annoying heckler from before. This time Mary didn't begrudge the loudmouth his laugh. The whole theater rocked with merriment.

Having gotten the audience on her side, Mary prepared to usher them into deeper waters. Her voice took on a more somber tone as the music struck an eerie, ethereal chord. A separate spotlight fell upon an unsuspecting patron in the third row. Mr. Charles Robertson, recently bereaved, stirred uneasily as all eyes turned toward him. A hush descended over the audience once more. Benji mimed a haunting melody upon her lute, while the orchestra played along.

Mary began to sway to the music. Her rounded hips rolled languorously while her slender hands and bangle-bedecked arms caressed the incense-laden air. Long, lissome legs wriggled like twin serpents rising from a snake charmer's basket. No madcap Charleston or rumba this, the medium's dance was a slow and sensuous performance that mesmerized every man in the audience, and not a few of the women as well. Her limber body undulated slowly before the crowd.

Three rows in, Mr. Robertson gulped and furiously polished his glasses. He need not have been self-conscious, though; for the moment, not a soul in the theater was watching him. Even the ushers paused to take in Mary's show.

Mary's painted eyelids fluttered. Her bare flesh quivered as she gasped out loud, trembling as though on the verge of rapture. She tilted back her head and clasped her hands above her heart. Full red lips parted, and the captivated audience leaned forward in their seats, straining to hear her message from beyond.

"Oh . . . I see someone now. She's waving to us. Such a graceful lady, so like a queen!"

Mr. Robertson froze. You could have heard a pin drop in the packed auditorium, so quiet and expectant was the crowd. Even the brawlers and slatterns in the balcony had fallen silent, their puny imaginations seized by the unearthly occurrence transpiring before their eyes. Tremulous females tightly gripped the arms of their male escorts. Benji stood attentively at stage right, arms crossed atop her chest. Mary's solemn voice rang across the theater.

"She's in a garden, a beautiful garden. Lush and vibrant. Indeed, she is like a flower herself. Not a rose." She cast a glance at her previous victim, whose flushed features were now quite pale. Beside the redhead, the stalwart Sean appeared utterly transfixed. "More a deep blue flower. No, not blue," she corrected herself. "*Violet* . . ."

Mr. Robertson clutched his heart. The name had obviously struck home.

"Violet is all alone," Mary proclaimed. "But there is a space beside her. She is waiting for another, one left behind in *this* sad, material world." A tinkling laugh escaped her lips. "For a second I saw a funny wee man in a bowler hat," she explained. "It's Mr. Charlie Chaplin!"

The audience automatically applauded the world-famous comic, all save poor Mr. Robertson, who continued to gaze at Mary with undiminished intensity. His myopic eyes searched the smoky stage around the nubile medium, as though hoping for a glimpse of his late wife's shade. Mary felt a twinge of sympathy for the gullible old gent. *Who knows?* she thought. Maybe tonight's performance would grant him a measure of peace by letting him know that his beloved Violet was waiting for him in a better place. And if not . . . well, a girl had to make a living somehow.

"No," she announced. "Not the Little Tramp. Another Charles . . . Charles Robertson."

Tears welled up in the stricken widower's eyes. He fumbled awkwardly for his handkerchief.

Mary recalled the oh-so-respectable-looking matron in the photograph as she slipped into character. Her voice, which had been hushed and reverent, assumed a more prim and proper tone.

"Charles! Charles!"

Mr. Robertson lurched to his feet, suggesting that Mary's impersonation of the Dear Departed had been right on the money. His hands shook visibly as he wrung the brim of his battered bowler hat. The audience tore their collective gaze away from Princess Kali to pay closer attention to the seeming object of the spirit's visitation. They stared at the thunderstruck widower.

"I'm sorry, Charles." Mary went back to her own stage persona, not wanting to push her luck by aping the dead woman any longer. "Violet says you're not looking after yourself. Those cuffs are frayed, and that tie of yours is never straight."

Bursts of nervous laughter broke the tension, but Mary could tell that the audience still desperately wanted this to be real. No doubt they were all too eager to believe that their own deceased loved ones were still around in some conveniently intangible fashion. That was the beauty of a spook act: the punters did half the work by conning themselves.

"Violet?" Tears streamed down Mr. Robertson's face. His voice was hoarse with emotion. Unconcerned by the spectacle he was making of himself, he threw his arms out toward the stage. His plaintive eyes beseeched Mary for yet more proof that his beloved was truly among them.

"She wants to say something," Mary said gently. "She says . . . she's sorry that her heart"—just for a moment, Mary risked channeling Violet's prim voice again—" 'was nae stronger.' Do you understand what she means, Charles?"

"Her heart failed her." Sobs racked his debilitated frame. He needed a second to compose himself. "That's how she went!"

Thank you, Edinburgh Hall of Records, Mary thought, not at all surprised by the gent's tear-jerking revelation. The engrossed audience, on the other hard, looked and sounded suitably agog. *Just as they should be.*

She undulated before the crowd, swaying languidly as though being carried away by some invisible ectoplasmic current. She uncoiled one arm in an ecstatic gesture that blended the sexual with the spiritual. Her eyes closed as she seemed to slip into a trance. Her mouth opened and a bizarre new voice emerged, high-pitched and uncanny, like the wail of a banshee.

"Ticktock, ticktock, who's the one who lost his clock?" An outstretched finger pointed at the overwrought widower, who shrank back instinctively. "Have you lost something, Charlie?"

Robertson was momentarily taken aback by the unexpected query. He fumbled through his pockets. "I . . . I lost my gold pocket watch."

All right, Benji, Mary thought. *Time to earn your keep.*

Putting aside her prop lute, the girl held out a large, tasseled cushion. Mary heard light footsteps on the gantry above the stage and knew that, safely hidden from view, Effie O'Reilly was leaning over the railing with the pilfered pocket watch in one hand. She hoped the seamstress's aim was as good as her needlework.

"It comes!" Mary emoted. "From another world, it comes!"

Effie dropped the watch. An alert percussionist crashed his cymbals. Benji darted to the right, just enough so that the falling timepiece landed squarely atop the plush cushion. *Good catch,* Mary thought, grateful for her daughter's quick reflexes. The gag wasn't nearly so effective if the spir-it's offering crashed with a thud upon the boards.

The audience gasped out loud, then burst into furious applause.

Benji reverently lifted the watch from the pillow. She pretended to examine it for the first time. Mary snuck a peek at Mr. Robertson; to her relief, he didn't seem to recognize the "dusky disciple" as the irrepressible street urchin he had encountered at the flower stall several hours ago. He was too caught up in his poignant reunion with his dead wife to even think of peering past the greasepaint blackening Benji's face.

Just like all the others we've pulled this bunco on.

"There is an inscription, O wise one," Benji declared in a cod East Indian accent. She held out the watch for Mary's inspection.

"No, no, do not tell me!" She recoiled from the prof-fered watch, averting her eyes lest her mystic insights be adulterated by more worldly evidence. "I see it! 'To Charles, with never-ending love. Your Violet.' "

Weeping openly, Mr. Robertson nodded in recogni-tion. Nevertheless, Benji offered the watch to a prosperous-looking chap in the first row. He carefully inspected the watch beneath the floodlights before turning to face the rest of the audience.

"That's what it says," he confirmed.

A murmur of voices arose as awestruck patrons turned to their companions, breathlessly discussing the miracle they had just witnessed. From the sound of things, there wasn't a single skeptic left in the audience. The houselights flickered ominously and all eyes turned back toward the stage, where Mary decided it was time to call it a night. *Always leave them wanting more,* she thought. *Especially when you've got no more tricks up your sleeve.*

"There's a chill wind in the garden now." She shivered and hugged herself against the imaginary cold. "Violet has to go." Once more her voice assumed the guise of the late, lamented Mrs. Robertson. " 'Until we meet again. Good-bye, Charlie. Good-bye. Good-bye . . .' "

The voice trailed off until only silence remained.

"No!" Mr. Robertson staggered forward, crestfallen. "No, Violet . . . please!"

For a second, Mary feared he would rush the stage. "Don't cling to her, Charles. Be patient . . . until you meet in the next world."

Emotionally exhausted, the man sagged back into his seat, sobbing as though his very soul had been torn asunder. Mary experienced an unwelcome twinge of guilt as helpful hands passed the pocket watch back to its blubbering owner. The lights came back up. The orchestra attempted to lighten the mood by segueing into a ragtime number. Princess Kali and her disciple took their bows.

Mary waited for the applause to die down a bit, then held up her hand.

"Ladies and gentlemen," she called out. "I'm getting one last message. I owe Rose over there an apology. She isn't wearing red knickers. Truth is, she isn't wearing any knickers at all!"

McTavish's Palace Music Hall dissolved into hysterics.

Green-farting midgets, my ass, she thought. That's *how you end a show!*

CHAPTER FOUR

—

A STONE ANGEL WATCHED OVER THE DECREPIT cemetery on the outskirts of Edinburgh. Chipped and weathered by the elements, St. Michael himself stood guard over a rambling spread of crumbling monuments and head-stones. Weeds clotted the swards between the tombstones, many of whose inscriptions had long since been worn to il-legibility. Bouquets of withered flowers testified to the re-membrances of the occasional mourners. In the distance, an ugly brick gasworks marred the scenery. Towering smoke-stacks belched thick black fumes into the sooty atmosphere. Darkening storm clouds presaged rain. A stiff wind whipped up the fallen leaves and flower petals littering the grounds of the cemetery. The sinking sun cast twilight shadows over the melancholy setting.

When she was younger, the eerie graveyard had fright-ened Benji. Now it was just a familiar shortcut to town. She and her mam hurried along the cemetery path on their way to see *Ben-Hur* at the picture show. Two days had passed since their last performance at McTavish's Music Hall, and, to Benji's surprise, Mam had actually consented to a night at the movies. *Guess even Mam needs a bit of escape now and then,* Benji thought. *Can't hardly blame her, after getting axed and all.*

Benji's nose was buried in an issue of *Film Fun* she had picked up for a halfpenny. Trailing behind her mother, she chuckled at the slapstick antics of Ben Turpin and Charlie Conklin. *Watch out,* she thought, as Charlie leaned over to peek down an open manhole. Sure enough, Ben kicked his cartoon cohort in the posterior, sending him tumbling headfirst down the ink-black hole. Benji giggled out loud.

"What have you got to laugh about?" her mother said crossly. Thunder rumbled overhead, and Mary peered warily at the sky. "We're out of a job, girlie! Comics and tomfoolery won't fill your stomach!"

Benji looked up from the pages. "It's just a wee bit of fun, Mam!"

Mary snorted derisively. "You sound like your father. 'Just a wee bit of fun, hen!'" Thunder boomed once more, louder and closer than before. The first few drops of rain splattered against their faces. Mary's frown deepened. "And all of a sudden, there was you!"

Benji winced at her mother's harsh words. Did Mam really regret having her so much? The accusation stabbed her straight in the heart, provoking an all-too-familiar pang, but Benji kept her mouth shut, afraid that her mother would change her mind about going to the movies. Benji had been looking forward to the show all day and didn't want to do anything to spoil things. *Is* Ben-Hur *as exciting as they say?* she wondered. The big sea battle was supposed to be spectacular, not to mention the chariot race.

The rain started to come down harder, a torrential downpour that threatened to soak them to the skin. Cursing under her breath, Mary grabbed her daughter by the hand and dragged her down the increasingly muddy path. Benji tucked the comic book beneath her jacket, hoping to keep it dry, and tried to keep up with her mother. To her relief, they were still running toward the movie theater, and not back to their chilly cottage on the other side of the graveyard. If they hurried, they could still catch the cartoon, serial, and newsreel at the beginning of the show.

Benji couldn't wait. More than ever now, she needed something to take her mind off her troubles. She just hoped that the movies would improve her mam's mood as well. It seemed as if her mother was angry and bitter all the time these days. Benji couldn't remember the last time they had been truly happy together. Maybe before Mam kicked her father out . . .

Rain ran like tears down the face of the stone angel.

. . . . .

Drenched and out of breath, Benji and her mam found an empty pair of seats just as a Buster Keaton short was ending. Steam rose from their sodden clothing as they settled in for the show. Puddles formed beneath their feet. Benji basked in the warmth of the crowded movie theater, especially compared to the deluge they had just escaped from. She clutched a torn fragment of her movie ticket as she savored her surroundings.

Darkness concealed the faces of the other patrons. Dust motes danced in the flickering beam from the projectionist's booth. An organist provided a musical accompaniment to the black-and-white images on the screen before them. Seated bodies rustled in the shadows, and low voices whispered to each other. The floor beneath Benji's feet was wet and sticky with spilled soda pop. The tantalizing aroma of hot, buttered popcorn made her mouth water. She wondered if she could talk her mother into some candy and popcorn during the intermission.

Too bad we missed the short subject, she thought. *Maybe we can stay and catch the beginning of the next showing?* She suspected Mam might be amenable to the suggestion. *Any excuse to stay out of the rain.*

The newsreel began. Eager to experience the pagan splendors of *Ben-Hur's* ancient Rome, Benji waited patiently as the glowing screen gave the audience a firsthand look at current events. Gertrude "Trudy" Ederle became the first woman to swim the English Channel. Buckingham Palace celebrated the birth of little Princess Elizabeth. A military coup seized power in Poland. Hindus and Muslims clashed in Calcutta. Mussolini survived yet another assassination attempt. In America, over a hundred thousand weeping fans lined the streets of New York City to witness Rudolph Valentino's funeral procession. Benji knew how the grieving women felt; she still couldn't believe that the legendary screen idol was really dead, and of a perforated ulcer no less. He had been so young . . .

An illuminated title card instantly drove such morbid musings from her mind:

HARRY HOUDINI WORLD TOUR!

Houdini? Galvanized, Benji sat up straight in her seat. *What about Houdini?*

On the screen, the world's most famous magician waved to a cheering crowd in St. Peter's Square. A tailored dark suit flattered his trim figure. Bushy black hair was parted down the middle. A boyish smile contrasted sharply with his piercing eyes, which seemed to rivet Benji to her seat. He had the confident carriage and easy manner of a born star.

Moments later, the news footage showed him hanging upside down from the cornice of a tall stone building, at least sixty feet above the pavement. A canvas straitjacket, boasting an intimidating accumulation of heavy straps and buckles, confined his arms as he writhed at the end of a thick steel cable. The Eiffel Tower provided a dramatic backdrop to the terrifying spectacle. His entire body convulsed violently as he struggled to escape the jacket, like a newborn butterfly still trapped inside a silk cocoon. Benji's heart pounded in sympathy as she tried to imagine herself in such a perilous predicament. Escape seemed impossible and yet . . . there it was! First one arm, then another, wriggled free of its restraints, then went to work on the remaining straps and buckles. Sweating from sheer exertion, Houdini tugged the jacket down over his head until it slipped off him entirely. The defeated jacket dangled from one hand as he waved it triumphantly at the teeming mob of Parisians gathered below. Only organ music echoed inside the small Edinburgh movie theater, but Benji could practically hear the jubilant cheers and applause in her mind. All around her, in the darkened auditorium, her fellow patrons gasped in amazement. Even Mam seemed impressed.

"Not a bad show," she murmured, "provided he doesn't break his fool neck someday."

More titles flashed across the screen, one after another:

ROME! PARIS!

MELBOURNE! SYDNEY!

"What's it say, Mam? Tell us the story."

Benji could read the titles herself, naturally, but she suddenly felt like being babied, like when her mam had told her bedtime stories when she was just a wee bairn. It had been a long time since her mother had read to her.

"*Ssssh!*" Mary hushed her.

The newsreel cut to another occasion, where an equally multitudinous crowd gathered on wooden docks and piers to watch Houdini being wrapped in heavy chains by a team of serious-looking locksmiths. They piled so many links on the unresisting escape artist that Benji was surprised that he could even stand up, let alone grin at the audience. Pad-locks snapped shut, binding Houdini from head to toe, yet he looked remarkably unperturbed. A further title card spelled out the enormity of what lay ahead:

THE GREAT HOUDINI DICES WITH DEATH!

A thrilling shudder coursed through Benji. She snuggled up to her mother, still wanting to recapture a bygone sense of warmth and security. Sniffling, she wiped her nose on her sleeve. "Oh, go on, Mam," she pleaded. "Read to me!"

Mary let out an exasperated sigh. "It just says what's in the picture."

That's not the point, Benji pouted.

Putting aside her disappointment, Benji tried to concentrate on the newsreel instead. On the screen, a sky-high crane swung Houdini dangerously out over Sydney Harbor. A close-up caught a grim smile on his face as he was dropped like an anchor into the depths. Benji could almost feel the icy water swallowing him up.

HAS THE MASTER OF ILLUSION MET HIS NEMESIS?

Both hands clasped over her mouth, to stifle a gasp of fear, Benji held her breath until, at last, Houdini burst to the surface, standing atop the block and tackle in his white woolen drawers. The organist played a triumphant march, while a veritable army of Australians silently cheered their hero. An eruption of hats saluted the victorious escape artist. Benji was tempted to throw her own cap into the air. The movie audience applauded Houdini's feat, with Benji clapping as loudly as the rest. Mam shrugged and joined in, as a show of respect for a fellow performer.

The spontaneous applause died down as the organ music took on a more melancholy air, all but tugging tears from the eyes of the crowd. Benji's throat tightened involuntarily as the scene shifted to a view of Houdini, his head bowed in sorrow, laying a bouquet of fresh roses on a solitary grave. An impressive monument, chiseled from polished black marble, loomed over the gravesite. A sculpted stone urn crowned a tall obelisk towering above the other nearby tombstones. The name WEISS was carved into the base of the obelisk. A lengthy title card placed the tragic portrait in context:

HOUDINI STILL GRIEVES FOR HIS MOTHER

" 'On her deathbed,' " Benji read aloud from the subtitles, " 'Houdini's beloved mother spoke her last words to the great man himself.' "

A striking theatrical poster materialized upon the screen. DO SPIRITS RETURN? the poster asked above a portrait of the Great Houdini. Ghoulish wraiths and hellish flames danced in the background, along with a magician's lovely assistant. The bob-haired brunette wore a skimpy two-piece costume that looked like something Princess Kali would wear. The grim reaper's skull-faced countenance grinned out from the poster.

" 'Do spirits return?' " Benji echoed the portentous query. " 'Houdini says prove it!' " Benji heard her mam sit up at attention. The celebrated Princess Kali was taking a greater interest in the newsreel, as did her unemployed disciple. Benji's eyes narrowed in concentration. " 'Now, famous psychics try to discover those secret words.' "

A montage of unearthly images played out before the audience's transfixed gaze. Ectoplasm, a vaporous white substance, supposedly composed of metaphysical energy, spewed from the open mouth of a turbaned medium. Somber men and women held a séance in a darkened chamber, their hands linked atop a sturdy-looking table. A brass bell and trumpet levitated above the table, seemingly untouched by mortal hands. A tarot card depicted the hooded figure of the grim reaper himself, wielding his deadly scythe. A ghostly apparition was captured by "spirit photography." A medieval woodcut etched a macabre dance of death. Houdini himself, taking part in yet another séance . . .

Grim-faced, Houdini joined hands with the other sitters. He sat to the left of a dignified female medium clad in long, flowing robes. A crystal ball rested atop a pristine white tabletop. The woman stiffened as she seemingly came in contact with the Great Beyond. Her eyes rolled upward until only the whites were visible. Her lips jabbered silently while all the other attendees, save Houdini, stared at the possessed psychic in wonder. Their eyes widened farther as the seemingly solid table suddenly bucked and lifted beneath their hands. Startled exclamations formed upon their lips. They truly seemed to be in the presence of some unruly spirit. . . .

Until Houdini leapt to his feet and switched the lights back on. With a showman's flourish, he yanked the tablecloth aside to reveal the hidden mechanism beneath the table. The medium's bare foot, which had furtively slipped free from her shoe, rested upon a concealed lever built into the floorboards. Her crystal ball crashed onto the carpet, rousing the phony psychic from her "trance." Exposed, she glared murderously at Houdini.

FRAUD MEDIUMS EXPOSED! a poster read.

I knew she was a fake, Benji thought smugly. *On her worst days, my mam can do a better spook act than that.*

HOUDINI'S CHALLENGE!
$10,000 FOR MOTHER'S LAST WORDS!

Mary leaned forward, her gaze glued to the screen. " 'Ten thousand dollars . . .' "

Before their eyes, Houdini scooped up a great heap of American dollars and fanned them out between his fingers, manipulating the paper money as deftly as he might a pack of playing cards. It was more cash than Benji had ever seen in her whole life.

" 'Ten thousand American dollars,' " Mary repeated in a hushed tone, " 'for whoever transmits his mother's last words to him.' " She shook her head in disbelief at the incredible offer. "No one could pull off that one, could they?"

Benji looked up at her mother. "How much is ten thousand dollars?"

It certainly sounded like a fortune.

Before her mother could answer, one last title card flashed onto the screen. Mary's jaw dropped in astonishment. Benji glanced back at the screen, anxious to see what had affected her mother so. A moment later, her own mouth fell open as well. All thoughts of *Ben-Hur* fled from her brain.

NEXT STOP EDINBURGH,
ATHENS OF THE NORTH!

Benji couldn't believe her eyes. She tugged on her mother's sleeve in excitement, barely remembering to keep her voice low. It was like a miracle, the answer to all their prayers.

"He's coming here . . . to Edinburgh!"

Mary and Benji turned toward each other in unison. Their eyes met in the lambent glow of the movie screen. Neither of them needed to say a word. They both knew what the other was thinking.

This is our chance!

CHAPTER FIVE

———

THE ROLLS-ROYCE PHANTOM LIMOUSINE honked its horn as it rocketed past the verdant Scottish countryside. Bleating back at the car, woolly sheep scattered and got out of the way, abandoning the paved roadway for the safety of the open fields. The sleek black limo cruised onward, flanked by a pair of goggled outriders on motorcycles. Flags affixed to the cycles flapped in the breeze. The flags bore a stylized logo that was also emblazoned upon both sides of the customized "H.H." Rolls-Royce, as well as upon the moving trucks following closely behind the limo and bikes.

The polished sheen of the Phantom's black exterior flashed in the sunlight. HOUDINI was spelled out in cursive type upon its hood. The powerful six-cylinder engine purred like a tiger on the prowl. Fresh off the assembly line, the pricey vehicle was the latest thing in automotive engineering. Only the best for the Great Houdini, who understood the importance of making a splashy entrance.

Its pennants unfurled, the convoy sped past green, grassy fields and meadows. Purple heather dotted the gentle slopes of the lowlands. Small farms and villages marked off the miles to the capital up ahead. Edinburgh Castle, looking like something out of the Middle Ages, dominated the horizon, rising proudly in the distance.

Within the plush interior of the Rolls-Royce, Harry Houdini dozed against the genuine-leather seat cushions. Drawn blinds shielded him from the glaring sun outside. His hand twitched fitfully, as though trying to catch hold of some elusive nightmare specter. His eyelids fluttered, his lips mouthing indecipherable words. Houdini's sleeping body gently rocked with the smooth motion of the limousine. An ivory-headed walking stick rested against his knees. A tiny golden key dangled from his watch chain.

He was floating upside down inside a glass coffin. Bubbles clouded the turbid water surrounding him. A wrinkled face, wreathed in white lilies, floated toward him. Silver hair drifted freely. A wispy shroud trailed behind the ghostly figure. Pennies covered her eyes. Shriveled hands reached out for him. A thin voice echoed through the water.

"Ehrich? Where are you, Ehrich?"

Harry awoke with a start. His heart pounding, he reached instinctively for the key, checking to make sure it was safe. Momentarily disoriented, he took a couple of seconds to get his bearings and remember where he was. He shook his head to clear the cobwebs from his mind. He forced a smile at Sugarman, who was seated across from him. The middle-aged manager looked up from his newspaper.

"Still here?" Harry asked.

Sugarman smiled wryly. "Where else?"

True enough, Harry thought. They had been inseparable for more than twenty years now, ever since Harry had first hired him to manage his theatrical bookings. They had met in London back in 1900, where Harry had just arrived in hopes of making a name for himself; in those days, American audiences only took you seriously if you were already a smash in Europe. Without an agent or a booking to his name, Harry had made the rounds of the London theatrical establishment, getting nowhere until he'd met Morrie Sugarman, a hungry young agent who saw potential in the ambitious Yank. Sugarman managed to get Harry an audition at the Alhambra, one of London's most prestigious theaters, which led to Harry's now legendary escape from Scotland Yard. The rest was history, and Sugarman had been his personal manager ever since.

Harry pulled himself together, straightening his jacket. He leaned forward to check out his reflection in the glass partition separating the two men from the limo's chauffeur. The tinted glass showed him a dark-haired man in his early fifties. Shadows under the reflection's eyes hinted at many sleepless nights. The pained, drawn expression testified to years of demanding physical abuse, not to mention the rigors of endless days and nights on tour. Travel by sea had never agreed with Harry; he had lost ten pounds on the arduous voyage to the British Isles. Although he still possessed a full head of hair, he had started to go gray at the temples. He slicked back his mussed hair with his hand.

"You look fine, Harry," his manager assured him.

Harry sank back into his seat. "I look like shit, Mr. Sugarman."

Born Ehrich Weiss, he had been the Great Houdini for thirty-five years now, risking his life twice a day, three times on Saturdays. He had toured the world many times over, from imperial Russia to Down Under, performing before both packed houses and the crowned heads of Europe. He had escaped from countless prisons and death traps, produced and starred in his own moving pictures, become the first man to fly an airplane in Australia, written numerous books and articles, founded his own magazine, exposed dozens of frauds and con artists, testified before Congress on the evils of phony mediums, and outdone every rival magician and imitator that had dared to challenge him at his own game. But his weary bones and aching flesh kept a painful record of every battle he had waged over the last three-plus decades.

Harry fingered the tiny golden key. Sometimes he wondered how much longer he could keep on doing this.

Until I find the answer . . .

Leaving the rural countryside behind, the limo and its escorts entered the city limits of Edinburgh. Harry raised the blinds to get a better look at the Scottish capital. Poised atop Castle Rock, Edinburgh Castle seemed to grow larger by the moment, looming over the thriving city below. The convoy roared east on the Royal Mile, past the City Chambers, St. Giles Cathedral, Moubray House, the Tron Kirk, and other landmarks of the ancient thoroughfare, possibly the oldest in the city. Gray granite buildings rose several stories above the pavement. Just off the cobbled main road, a warren of hidden wynds and closes dated back to the Middle Ages. A few blocks north of the Mile, the sooty black peak of the Scott Monument pointed a Gothic finger at the sky. Harry couldn't help remembering his friend and fellow magician the Great Lafayette, who had died in this very city fifteen years ago, when the old Empire Theater caught fire. A body had been identified as that of Lafayette, until a second body turned up wearing the same charred costume. The first body was ultimately revealed to be that of a double whom the real magician had employed in some of his illusions. Harry liked to think that the Great Lafayette, who had once been the highest-paid illusionist in vaudeville, before Houdini came along, would have been amused by that final bit of posthumous misdirection. He hoped he would have a chance to visit his friend's grave while he was in Edinburgh.

The motorcade took a right turn on Lothian Road, abandoning the cramped confines of the old city for the open spaces and elegant Georgian architecture of the New Town. Constructed in the eighteenth century to allow the wealthy and well-to-do to avoid rubbing shoulders with lower classes, the New Town was the city's richest and most exclusive neighborhood, as well as home to its most expensive hotels.

Or so they say, Harry thought. He looked forward to enjoying the first-class accommodations—if they ever got there. He yawned out loud, still feeling fatigued. His catnap in the limo had done little to refresh him. *Where is this stupid hotel anyway?*

As the convoy finally neared its destination, the unmistakable sound of drums and bagpipes, as well as the muffled roar of a crowd, penetrated the interior of the Phantom.

The limousine pulled into the forecourt of the Scottish Lion Hotel. WELCOME HOUDINI! read a large red-and-white banner draped across the second floor of the elegant Georgian facade of the building. Party-colored bunting hung above the marble archways that graced the hotel's regal front entrance. Brightly colored banners and bunting hung from the upper stories. The Union Jack flew proudly atop the domed roof of the hotel, flanked by the St. Andrew's cross and the Lion Rampant of the Royal Standard. The flags flapped patriotically in Edinburgh's famously stiff winds.

A fifty-man pipe band, in full Highland regalia, enthusiastically greeted Houdini's arrival. Bagpipes blared as the drum corps beat out a staccato march. Teeming fans, barely held back by the hotel's security staff, cheered and applauded. They jostled and elbowed each other as they competed to get a better look at the limo and its world-famous passenger. Dozens of miniature flags, all bearing Houdini's handsome profile, were waved by the cheering multitude. Avid star-watchers scaled the lampposts to get above the crowd. Newspaper reporters and photographers waved their press credentials in the air like mystic talismans as they shoved their way to the front of the mob. Autograph seekers clutched albums and publicity photos.

Harry slicked back his hair one more time. He pasted on his most charismatic smile as he prepared to meet his adoring public. It wouldn't do to betray any hint of weakness or infirmity before the giddy throng outside. He was the Great Houdini, after all.

Here we go again, he thought. *Showtime!*

. . .

Among the zealous horde spilling onto the forecourt was an eleven-year-old tomboy perched atop a parked truck belonging to a moving-picture company. A cameraman, filming the momentous proceedings, shared the roof of the vehicle with her. His bulky box camera whirred in Benji's ears as she guarded her post as stubbornly as Greyfriars Bobby. A towheaded pretender tried to usurp her place, but she kicked the presumptuous urchin in the face without mercy or hesitation. Yelping in pain, the youth tumbled back into the crowd, leaving Benji still in sole possession of a grandstand view. As far as she was concerned, she had the best seat in the house, and she wasn't surrendering it to anyone, let alone some underaged Johnny-come-lately.

He's here, she thought. *He's finally here!*

Lifting a hand to shield her eyes from the sun, Benji leaned forward precariously, tempting gravity in her eagerness to catch her first glimpse of Houdini. Plus, she knew her mother would want a full report on their target's arrival. The famous magician was more than just Benji's idol; he was also a potential gold mine for her and Mam. Part of Benji wished that her mother were here to share the excitement of the moment, but she knew that Mam was busy elsewhere. Mary McGarvie had her own role to play in today's proceedings.

The gorgeous black limo pulled up to the curb right in front of the hotel's front entrance. A red carpet stretched from the arched portico to the end of the walk, awaiting the great man's tread. Velvet ropes guarded the carpet from the hoi polloi. Benji held her breath, taut with anticipation, as the passenger door of the Rolls-Royce swung open and Houdini himself bounded onto the red carpet. Benji recognized him instantly from the comic books and newsreels, but the legendary magician looked twice as impressive in real life. He held aloft a snazzy ivory-tipped cane as he greeted the crowd, who burst into a deafening roar of welcome. A pair of watchful bodyguards, clad in long black overcoats, emerged from the front seat of the Rolls-Royce. Exhilarated by his boisterous reception, Houdini tossed his cane to the nearest bodyguard and vaulted effortlessly onto the roof of the limousine. The unexpected move, executed with feline grace and agility, elicited another round of cheers from the crowd. Visible to everyone in the vicinity, Houdini waved at his fans, who were driven into a near frenzy by his presence. The crowd surged forward, men and women alike shrieking in adoration, flash powder exploding as the gentlemen of the press sought to capture the historic moment on film. The wild scene was almost frightening. The crazed fans were so in love with Houdini that Benji half-expected them to tear the famous magician limb from limb.

Her apprehensions were obviously shared by the stout, middle-aged man who emerged, virtually unnoticed, from the limo behind Houdini. Lugging a briefcase, the man wore a brown, three-piece suit large enough to accommodate his considerable girth. Benji recognized him as Mr. Morrie Sugarman, Houdini's longtime manager; she had read about him in her comic book. An anxious expression upon his face, Mr. Sugarman nodded at the burly guards, who moved quickly to get between Houdini and his impassioned admirers. Their heavy overcoats added to their bulk as their forbidding visages warned back the crowd. The hulking bodyguards reminded Benji of the bouncer at McTavish's. She briefly wondered if Houdini had recruited either of them from a strongman act.

She forgot all about the bodyguards, however, when Houdini delighted the crowd by doing a handstand atop the Rolls-Royce. Bouncing back onto his feet, he strolled along the length of the limo's roof, giving his fans a good look, before diving into the midst of the crowd, who gladly hoisted him up onto their shoulders. Mr. Sugarman looked aghast at his reckless client. The two bodyguards shrugged their shoulders, acknowledging that there was nothing they could do if their charge insisted on literally throwing himself into the company of his ardent fans. Benji doubted that anyone on earth could keep the Great Houdini from doing whatever he pleased, no matter the risk to his person. That's what made him so astounding.

Buoyed upon the shoulders of the crowd, Houdini waved to his worshippers. Flash powder exploded repeatedly, causing bright blue spots to dance before Benji's eyes. Scoop-hungry reporters competed to get the magician's attention.

"Mr. Houdini!" they shouted, their pens poised above their notepads. "Mr. Houdini!"

At his direction, Houdini's bearers lowered him to the ground. His feet touched down on the red carpet. A pair of freckle-faced teenage girls, wearing tartan skirts, shoved past the reporters. "We love you, Mr. Houdini!" They clutched photos of Houdini to their breasts. Tears streamed down their cheeks as their shrill voices hurt Benji's ears. "We love you!"

He graciously accepted the photos from the hysterical lasses. Using Sugarman's shoulder as a writing desk, he scribbled his autograph onto the photos before handing them back to the beaming girls, whom he also treated to a smile. They squealed in ecstasy. Benji felt an unaccustomed stab of jealousy. Why should he waste his time on those silly bints?

An intrepid cub reporter, wearing a tan overcoat and fedora, stole Houdini away from his adolescent admirers. The youthful journalist looked like a mere boy next to the veteran performer. "Welcome to Scotland, Mr. Houdini."

"Thank you, son." Houdini's deep voice held a distinctly American accent. "So, I believe there's a famous monster hereabouts."

"That'll be Nessie, Mr. Houdini," the reporter replied, referring to the mythical sea serpent said to reside in the depths of Loch Ness. Benji recalled that years ago, in Bos-

ton, Massachusetts, Houdini had been sealed inside the preserved corpse of another sea monster, one that had recently
washed ashore nearby. Although shackled from head to foot
and locked inside the dead beast by heavy chains and locks,
he had eventually escaped from the stinking carcass, just
like Jonah from the whale.

Maybe he had in mind a repeat performance?

"Uh-huh," Houdini said. "Well, you tell Nessie that
Harry Houdini's gonna tie a knot in her tail and fling her
into the Scottish ocean!"

Laughing, the reporters jotted the outrageous boast
down. They were loving this, and so was the onlooking
crowd. *I'll bet he could do it, too,* Benji thought. *He looks fit enough
to wrestle his way out of anything.*

A second reporter stepped forward. "What about that
ten thousand dollars, Mr. Houdini?"

"You psychic, son?" Houdini replied. "Put me in touch
with my dear, departed mother, and it's all yours." He raised
his voice to address everyone within earshot. "Never met a
reporter yet that didn't know the truth before it happened!"

The assembled journalists took the gibe with good
humor, chuckling knowingly to themselves while scribbling madly in their notebooks. Benji had to admire the
way Houdini worked the crowd and the press. If only
Princess Kali and Her Dusky Disciple could garner such
publicity!

Angry protests from the crowd interrupted the impromptu press conference. Benji watched from her elevated perch as a beefy, potato-faced boxer muscled his way through the mob, over the vocal objections of those who had gotten there first. Fully kitted out in padded gloves and long johns, the scowling intruder ignored the complaints of the other spectators, barging forward until he was only a few yards from Houdini and the dense pack of reporters. Smelling a good story, the journalists and photographers stepped aside to let the pugilist pass. He was an ugly cuss, whose flattened nose and cauliflower ears bespoke his profession. Sandy brown hair had been cut short. A sweaty towel was draped over his shoulder. He held his gloved mitts up in front of him, as if he was spoiling for a fight. A heavyweight, he was at least 175 pounds, if not more. All of it muscle.

A scrawny, balding gent followed in the boxer's wake, looking like an ugly gnome compared to the muscle-bound boxer. Breathless and sweaty, the gent laid a possessive hand upon the fighter's bulging biceps. Benji figured him to be the boxer's manager. "Still in good shape, Mr. Houdini?" he called out.

"Never better!" Houdini answered confidently.

Mr. Sugarman sidled up to his client. He eyed the newcomers suspiciously, looking more worried than ever. He grimaced and clutched his chest. *Heartburn*, Benji speculated, *brought on by nerves?*

"They say you can take a punch from any man, Mr. Houdini," the gnomish promoter stated loudly. He glanced around to make sure the entire audience was listening. Benji, for one, couldn't wait to see what happened next. She remembered an illustration in her comic book, of Houdini standing tall while an assailant's fists pounded uselessly against the magician's gut; Houdini had supposedly conditioned his body to withstand any blow. Was she now to witness this astounding feat firsthand?

If Benji was excited at the prospect, Mr. Sugarman looked positively alarmed. "Elbow these freeloaders!" he barked at the diligent bodyguards, who converged on the boxer and his promoter. The surly-looking fighter bobbed and wove as they approached, throwing jabs at the empty air. Clearly, he wasn't about to leave quietly.

"You scared of my boy's punch, Mr. Houdini?" the grinning promoter challenged. This was a win-win situation for him. Either Houdini backed down from this encounter or his boy got to take a shot at the famous celebrity. Either way, the unknown boxer would make a name for himself, perhaps at Houdini's expense. *Apparently Mam and I aren't the only ones trying to take advantage of the Great Houdini's visit to Edinburgh,* Benji thought. She hoped the ugly lummox wasn't about to steal their thunder.

Mr. Sugarman looked at Houdini and shook his head. "Watch yourself, Harry," he whispered, just loud enough for Benji's keen ears to overhear. He stepped between Houdini and the boxer. "This mob can smell blood."

Houdini paid his apprehensive manager no heed. He gestured to the bodyguards, instructing them to back off, and calmly approached the sneering boxer. The challenger was at least a head taller than Houdini, and significantly heavier and younger to boot, but Houdini did not appear concerned. He looked the boxer over, appraising him as he might a prime piece of livestock. Nodding, he made his decision.

"I'll take your punch, Hamish."

Mr. Sugarman groaned and buried his face in his hands. Benji gulped.

Houdini took off his jacket and handed it to Mr. Sugarman. The boxer lumbered forward, but Houdini held up his hand. An expectant buzz rose from the crowd as Houdini turned away and took a moment to prepare himself. He inhaled deeply and threw back his shoulders, firming his stomach muscles beneath his tailored white shirt. Mr. Sugarman opened his mouth to protest once more, but Houdini silenced him with a look.

The gauntlet had been thrown. What else could he do but pick it up?

Houdini turned back toward the boxer, his jaw set so tightly he couldn't speak. He gave the impatient pugilist a nod. He beckoned silently with his hands. *Do it!* Benji put her hands over her eyes, not entirely sure she wanted to see this. She watched intently through her fingers.

The boxer didn't need any further encouragement. He bobbed upon his heels, closing in on the smaller man, then let go with a real slammer to Houdini's gut.

Pow!

Benji winced along with the rest of the crowd. That had hurt just looking at it.

But Houdini did not stagger or collapse beneath the fearsome blow. Instead he looked about with a mystified expression on his face.

"You done it yet?" he finally inquired.

The crowd went berserk, hollering and hullabalooing. The reporters guffawed as the dumbfounded boxer stared at his fists in obvious bewilderment, as if he still wasn't sure what had just happened.

Jeers and laughter followed the boxer and his promoter as they eventually slunk away in defeat. Mr. Sugarman looked overcome with relief, while even the stone-faced bodyguards cracked smiles. Houdini clasped his hands over his head like a champion. Unruffled by the incident, he flashed the crowd one last smile before strolling down the red carpet into the hotel. Waving flags saluted his exit.

Up on the truck, Benji cheered wildly along with everyone else below. All the stories about Houdini were absolutely true, she realized. His reputation wasn't all hype and ballyhoo. The Great Houdini was just as remarkable as everyone said he was. So overjoyed was she to discover something genuinely wonderful in the world that she almost forgot why she was here in the first place. It wasn't until Houdini disappeared into the hotel that she grasped the drawback to the great magician's seeming invincibility:

How on earth was Mam going to trick a man like that?

.   .   .

Houdini's initials were embossed in gold upon the bulky steamer trunk being wheeled on a trolley through the opulent lobby of the Scottish Lion Hotel. Reinforced with sturdy straps and buckles, the trunk looked like a prop from his show, but it was actually more important than that. There were no sliding panels or hidden compartments in this trunk; it was built to keep its precious contents safe and secure.

A straining bellboy pushed the trolley across the carpet, following Houdini and his entourage. Harry paused long enough to appreciate the posh decor of the lobby. Ornately carved antique furniture rested atop carpets of thick wool sporting traditional plaid designs. Marble columns supported the high ceiling. Potted plants and vases of flowers added a softer touch to the imposing architecture. A welcoming fire roared in a large stone fireplace. A grand staircase, with sweeping wrought-iron railings, led to the mezzanine. The luxurious five-star hotel was a far cry from the seedy tenements and flophouses he had bunked in back in the early days of the act, when he was still playing beer halls, dime museums, carnivals, and medicine shows. There had been times when he hadn't known where his next meal was coming from, let alone his next booking. In his bleakest moments, he had even considered throwing in the towel, giving up show-biz for good and going back to work in that same miserable sweatshop he had started out in, cutting ties for a living. That was before he realized that *escapes*, not old-fashioned sleight-of-hand tricks, were his ticket to stardom. Any second-rate carnival conjurer could produce a pigeon out of thin air or manipulate a doctored deck of cards, but a man who could liberate himself from any prison or bonds? Only the Great Houdini could escape from any challenge, anywhere in the world. And the public couldn't get enough of it.

I've come a long way, he reflected. *With how much longer to go?*

The manager of the hotel, who had introduced himself as Mr. Wallace, walked backward before Harry and his party. The man was practically falling over himself in his determination to welcome the Great Houdini to his establishment. "We call it the Suite Royale, Mr. Houdini. The very best we have. It's such a honor to have you with us."

A heavy thud interrupted his obsequious babble. Harry glanced behind him to see that his trunk had slipped off the trolley onto the floor. "Hey!" he barked at the hapless bellboy. Tight-lipped with anger, he clenched his fists at his sides. It was all he could do to keep from grabbing the clumsy oaf by the collar and shaking a little consideration into his empty head. Didn't he have any respect for other people's private property? "Careful with that trunk, you schmuck!"

The butter-fingered bellboy went pale. Flinching from the tongue-lashing, he looked as if he wanted to sink into the floor and disappear. Unfortunately for him, he was nowhere near the magician that Houdini was.

Where did they find this idiot?

Harry resisted a temptation to take custody of the trunk himself. Forcing himself to look away, he turned his back on the petrified flunky. Wallace glowered at the bellboy, who would be lucky to still have a job by nightfall, as Harry walked briskly past the mortified hotel manager.

Sugarman strove to smooth the waters. "Mr. Houdini's very tired after his journey." He signaled James Vickery and Franz Kukol, their ever-vigilant bodyguards, to make sure Harry was not disturbed by any of the wide-eyed guests and hotel employees milling about in the lobby. He needn't have reminded them; the burly watchdogs were already on their toes.

Let's just get to this famous suite in one piece, Harry thought irritably. Sugarman wasn't lying when he said that Harry was exhausted by the trip. That performance in the fore-court had taken a lot out of him. *Who the hell invited that gorilla with the boxing mitts?*

Thankfully, the rest of their trek through the hotel proceeded without incident. A short elevator ride later, they were ushered into the Suite Royale. Harry stalked past Wallace without a word. Ignoring the lavish furnishings and decor, which the hotel manager was only too eager to point out, Harry marched straight to the palatial bathroom. Behind him, he heard the chastened bellboy deposit the trunk upon the carpet with an excess of care. Sugarman tipped the schmuck for his efforts.

"A real dollar bill!" the bellboy exclaimed, his mood instantly improving. He gaped at the crisp green bill as though he had never seen one before. "Thank you, sir! And thank Mr. Houdini!"

"I'll do that," Sugarman promised, before hustling the youth out the door with all deliberate speed. Wallace started to step inside the suite, no doubt intending to give them the grand tour, but Sugarman blocked the startled manager with his bulk, then gently shut the door in his face. "Thank you. That will be all."

Houdini was less diplomatic. He slammed the bathroom door behind him.

Out of sight at last, he coughed and doubled over in pain. Gritting his teeth against the agony ravaging his throbbing torso, he savagely tore off his jacket and shirt. The discarded clothing landed in a heap upon the floor. Torn buttons rolled across the spotless porcelain tiles. A ribbed corset girded Harry's waist. Purple and yellow bruises, both old and new, discolored his chest and abdomen. Every breath sent a fresh spasm of pain across his ribs. His golden watch and chain glinted amidst the fallen clothing. Wincing from the effort, he bent over and retrieved them from the floor. He gripped the chain tightly in his fist as he leaned over the porcelain sink, letting the marble countertop support his weight. Damn, this was a bad one.

"Harry?" Sugarman was knocking at the door. "You all right, Harry?"

Harry was in too much pain to reply. He coughed again. Blood splattered the sink and swirled down the drain. He gasped out loud as a tormenting convulsion racked his body. Years ago, while escaping from a heavy canvas bag in Detroit, he had ruptured a blood vessel in his kidney. At the time, a doctor had warned Harry that he wouldn't last a year if he continued performing his strenuous escapes. The Great Houdini was still proving the doctor wrong nearly fifteen years later, but not a day went by that his injured kidney didn't torture him. And getting punched in the stomach by a headline-hungry prizefighter didn't help any. *But what was I supposed to do?* he thought. *Let the whole world think that Harry Houdini was afraid of some meatheaded Scottish bruiser?*

"Harry?" Sugarman knocked insistently at the door. "Harry, let me in, will ya?"

Hold your horses! Harry thought. The pain gradually subsided, just as it always did. He knew this goddamn routine by heart now. As the excruciating spasms gave way to merely a steady ache, he dropped wearily down onto the toilet seat. Loosening his grip, he opened his fist to discover that the tiny golden key had pressed its imprint into his palm. Just as the memories it provoked were etched irrevocably into his soul. Wiping the blood from his lips, he closed his eyes and let his head sag backward. His ragged breathing slowly settled back into its normal rhythm. He sighed in relief. It felt as if the worst was over, at least for the moment.

About time.

By now the knocking at the door sounded positively frantic. "For God's sake, Harry! Let me in!"

"I think I can wipe my own ass, Mr. Sugarman, thank you!" Harry hollered back through the door. He lumbered unsteadily to his feet.

The knocking ceased, replaced by an indignant silence from the other side of the door. Harry mustered a wry smile as he visualized his manager's characteristically exasperated expression. *You know,* he thought, *if I wanted to be nagged all the time, I would have brought my wife along on this tour.* But Bess had tired of showbiz years ago and now preferred to hold down the fort back in their ritzy New York brownstone. *Probably just as well. I'm not fit company these days for anyone not on my payroll.*

"It's okay," Harry assured his worried manager through the closed door. Sugarman acted sometimes as if he expected Houdini to drop dead just as Valentino had a few weeks ago. "Nothing to worry about. The golden goose is still laying."

For the time being, anyway.

CHAPTER SIX

——

TWILIGHT FELL OVER EDINBURGH, BRINGING a smoky evening fog that spread through the well-kept streets and squares of New Town. A light rain dampened the sidewalks outside the Scottish Lion Hotel. The neighborhood lamplighter went about his duties, igniting the streetlamps with his pole. The lambent gaslight cast long shadows over the forecourt.

Rufus Montgomery, the night concierge, was glad to be snugly indoors on a night like this. As he manned a desk by the front entrance, he anticipated a quiet and uneventful evening. A clock on the wall gave the time as five thirty. Mr. Houdini and his party would be departing for the theater soon, in preparation for tonight's debut performance, and the unruly horde of fans and reporters who had greeted his arrival had long since dispersed. *And none too soon,* Montgomery thought. Despite the favorable publicity to be gained by hosting such a prestigious guest as Harry Houdini, there was something to be said for maintaining a certain degree of order and decorum. The guests and staff of the Scottish Lion were entitled to nothing less. *This is a hotel, not a circus.*

The revolving door spun round to admit a stranger to the lobby. Montgomery's attention was instantly riveted by the breathtaking vision striding confidently into the hotel. An elegant brunette clad in a silk and lamé evening coat sauntered into view. An impressive sable stole was draped over her regal shoulders, and a cloche hat protected her head from the cold. Tasteful pearl jewelry shone upon her ears and fingers. The doorman, Collins, saluted her smartly as she entered.

Oh my, Montgomery thought. *What have we here?* He didn't recognize the woman, and he was quite sure that he would have remembered such a striking beauty had he ever encountered her before. She clearly belonged in this exclusive locale, however; her exquisite poise and carriage were those of a woman well accustomed to a life of wealth and luxury. She strolled across the spacious lobby as though she owned the place. The concierge hastened to greet her.

"Madame . . . ?"

She dismissed him with a regal wave of her hand, sauntering past him with barely a sideways glance in his direction. Montgomery discreetly admired her figure from behind. His appreciative gaze ran down her legs, then did a double take at the unexpected sight of a pair of shabby brogues. The obviously run-down footwear clashed starkly with the glamorous and affluent impression the nameless woman was attempting to present. Montgomery realized at once that he had been hoodwinked.

The nerve of the woman! He had no idea what the impostor was doing, but she was undoubtedly up to no good. A common whore or gold digger, he suspected, out to land one of the many well-moneyed gentlemen staying at the Scottish Lion. *Not if I have anything to say about it!*

Irked at being so easily deceived, he snapped his fingers and nodded in the woman's direction. Two alert employees, Gray and Jenkins, hurried to intercept the intruder before she reached the elevator. But the woman was too quick for them. She darted into the waiting lift. The elevator doors slid shut, cutting her off from her pursuers. Montgomery swore as the lift ascended before his eyes.

"Bloody hell!" His eyes tracked the indicator arrow above the elevator entrance. "Don't just stand there!" he barked at the security guards. "Go after her! Take the stairs!"

Jolted into action, Jenkins and Gray ran up the nearby staircase, racing the rising elevator. Unable to bear the suspense, Montgomery chased after them, taking the steps two at a time. He caught up with the men on the third floor, where they stood waiting outside the elevator entrance. An arrow indicated that they had indeed beaten the elevator to this floor. Red-faced and panting, the concierge joined his subordinates before the entrance. Judging from their surly expressions, Gray and Jenkins hadn't enjoyed the exhausting sprint up the stairs any more than he had. They rolled up their sleeves in anticipation of the woman's arrival. "I want that woman removed from the premises," Montgomery insisted. "And you needn't be too gentle about it."

"Not to worry, sir," Gray assured him. "We'll deal with her."

See that you do. The concierge had no doubt that the two men were more than capable of handling one overambitious tart. *She'll think twice before showing her duplicitous face at this establishment again.*

A bell chimed above the doorway, signaling the elevator's arrival on the third floor. Montgomery assumed his sternest expression and stepped back to allow the other men to take custody of the troublesome slattern. He hoped that she would not raise too much of a ruckus on her way out. It was embarrassing enough that she had already penetrated so far into the Scottish Lion's rarefied preserve. He wouldn't want her enforced departure to disturb any of their highly respectable and eminent guests.

The doors swished open. Montgomery looked forward to seeing the woman's chagrin when she realized she had been caught. To his surprise, however, the impostor was nowhere to be seen within the empty elevator. All that remained of her was a discarded fur stole lying crumpled on the floor.

What the devil? Montgomery exchanged baffled looks with the other two men. Stepping inside the elevator, he bent down and lifted the fur stole from the floor. The only tangible evidence of the mysterious beauty's existence, it seemed to mock him by remaining behind after its lovely owner had seemingly vanished into thin air. A whiff of some exotic perfume still clung to the fur, which, upon closer examination, was patently fake. Montgomery spied a label pinned to the inner lining of the deceitful garment. The simple cardboard tag read, "Costume Department. McTavish's Palace."

Oh, dear Lord, he thought, chilled to the bone by the obvious implications. The vanishing lady was no ordinary tramp or social climber. Alas, the truth was something far worse. *Heaven help us*, the humiliated concierge lamented. *She was an* actress!

He might never live this down.

. . .

Harry posed in front of an ornate framed mirror as he dressed for tonight's performance. An impressive stack of mail rested atop a mahogany, three-drawer chest below the mirror. Harry had found the correspondence waiting for him upon his arrival at the hotel. He sorted through the mail while putting on his tuxedo. Sugarman fussed around him like a knight's squire.

"Listen to this," Harry said, reading aloud from one note. " 'Madame Clare de Lune, Psychic EXTRA ORDINAIRE, respectfully accepts Mr. Houdini's psychic challenge.' "

"Clare de what?" Sugarman asked. "Clare de who?"

Houdini smirked. "Get yourself an education, Mr. Sugarman. Clare de Lune. It's French."

"I got an education," Sugarman insisted, "sweeping floors on the London stage. University of Hard Knocks."

"I majored at that college," Harry admitted. His father, Mayer Samuel Weiss, had been a rabbi and a respected Talmudic scholar in his native Hungary, but young Ehrich, as

the son of struggling immigrants, had never been able to af-
ford a formal education. Instead Harry had set off on his
own to make a living at the tender age of twelve. In memory
of his father, though, he had always attempted to compen-
sate for his lack of higher learning by studiously educating
himself. He read omnivorously on a wide variety of sub-
jects, often traveling with an entire bookcase worth of reading material. Indeed, he had been known to buy out the
contents of entire bookstores just to satisfy his thirst for
learning. His brownstone back in Harlem was so packed
with rare books and playbills that he had been obliged to
hire a full-time librarian just to keep his collection orga-
nized. He liked to think that his father would approve.

He put on a pair of flashy golden cuff links, then scrutinized them in the mirror. They seemed a bit much. "What
do you think?" he asked, holding up his cuffs for Sugarman's
inspection. "Think I look like a fruit?"

"A fruit?" Sugarman shook his head. He glanced at his
pocket watch, obviously wanting to get going. "Harry, you
look beautiful."

Harry wasn't so sure. He examined the cuff links in the
mirror before making his own assessment. "I look like a
fruit."

"They've got class," Sugarman assured him. "I like
them."

So what? Harry thought. Sugarman was his manager,
not his dresser. He undid the cuff links and lobbed them at
Sugarman. "You wanna look like a fruit, you wear them!"

Sugarman caught the cuff links and deposited them

atop the chest of drawers. Aiming to hurry the process along, he flattened down Harry's stiff collar. Despite the manager's impatience, Harry continued to peruse his mail. He scanned one letter, tossed it aside, then picked up another.

"As it happens," Sugarman said with wounded dignity, "I have got an education, thank you very much. In Law and in Business Management."

Harry was unimpressed. "So go figure out how we can take a percentage outta the gross."

"Out of the gross?" Sugarman scoffed at the very notion. "Oy, I should be so lucky." He peered dubiously at the stack of mail from "Madame Clare de Lune" and her fellow clairvoyants. "Harry, it's like you said: everyone's a fake. Soon as you scratch the gold leaf, all of these so-called psychics and mediums are just made of lead. It's all just mumbo jumbo, hocus-pocus!"

Houdini adjusted his black bow tie. "So what?"

"So why waste our time?" Frustration tinged Sugarman's voice. He clearly didn't understand why this latest challenge was so important. They already had the number one act in the world after all. Why mess with a good thing?

"You think I want to be remembered for a bunch of dumb stunts?" Harry replied, trying earnestly to get his manager to look past the daily receipts for a minute. "Hangin' off a building by a thread, dropped like an anchor to the bottom of the ocean?" He tugged on his suspenders, his impassioned voice growing more heated by the moment. He gestured at the heaping pile of mail. The $10,000 reward was attracting plenty of takers, all right. "For once, it ain't about friggin' chains and padlocks. It's about . . ." He groped for the right words. "It's about *science*, it's about proof, it's about . . ."

His twisted suspenders refused to cooperate with him. He wrestled irritably with the recalcitrant straps. "God-damn this tangle!"

A coughing fit hit him and he doubled over in pain. Beneath his starched white shirt, he felt the tight corset constricting his ribs, making it harder to breathe. He grabbed on to the edge of the chest to support himself.

Sugarman winced in sympathy. "You've been pushing yourself too hard, Harry." He reached out to assist his stricken client.

Harry shrugged off the other man's hand. The Great Houdini could manage on his own. Inhaling deeply, he straightened up and brought the coughing under control. He had never let any sickness or injury stop him before, and he'd be damned if he was going to let anyone treat him like an invalid now. Overcoming pain was all about mind over matter. Hadn't he always said so? At his lectures, he sometimes drove pins through his cheek just to demonstrate how pain could be conquered by a disciplined mind.

The return address on an envelope caught his eye. He snatched up the letter and waved it in his manager's face. "See this, Mr. Sugarman? This is from *Scientific American*." He repeated the name of the prestigious magazine with reverence. "*Scientific American*! My psychic experiment is science!"

Harry had first joined forces with the magazine a year

ago, when he had been invited to take part in an investigation of the alleged psychic abilities of the celebrated Margery, aka Mrs. Mina Crandon of Boston, Massachusetts. Harry had been the only professional magician on a committee composed primarily of distinguished academics and scientists. It was a source of no little pride to Harry that it was *he* who had seen through Margery's cunning tricks and illusions and not any of the more educated members of the committee. *Scientific American* had come close to endorsing Margery as a genuine psychic—before Harry exposed her as a fraud.

Sugarman shrugged. He gently untwisted Harry's suspenders. "Showbiz is showbiz, Harry. It ain't about 'science.' It's about nickels and dimes."

Harry was disappointed by the other man's lack of perspective. Didn't he realize that they could be on the verge of a major breakthrough here? Sure, most of the psychics out there were con artists just out to make a quick buck, but what if they could find the real thing? Suppose it really was possible to communicate with the Other Side? What if he found the Answer at last? *Just one genuine miracle, that's all I'm looking for.*

He brushed Sugarman's hands away from him. "Yeah, well, you look after the nickels and dimes, Mr. Sugarman, and I'll look after the science!"

No matter what it took.

. . .

A plain black dress and a white cap and apron suggested that the woman pushing the trolley down the hall was simply one of the Scottish Lion's many chambermaids. But looks could be deceiving. Mary smiled to herself as she approached the Suite Royale. So far nobody had given her a second look, not since she had given the concierge and his flunkies the slip. She wondered if McTavish had noticed yet that the bogus fur stole had vanished from the music hall's costume department.

Serves him right, the penny-pinching git, she thought. *Maybe old Effie can stitch him a new one if he collects enough dead squirrels from the side of the road.*

Her timing appeared to be perfect. The door to Houdini's suite swung open just as she neared the end of the corridor. The magician and his manager emerged from the suite, engrossed in conversation. "We got two hours to check the tank," Morrie Sugarman said, consulting his watch. "Boys will be set by the time we get there. Curtain's at eight."

Houdini graciously held the door open for the "maid." Mary smiled and curtsied. Glancing back, she saw the two men step into the elevator. Neither paid any attention to her. From the sound of things, they had more urgent matters on their minds.

"How's security?" Houdini asked.

"Like Mrs. Clam with a headache," Sugarman answered.

"That tight, huh?"

The elevator doors swished shut, cutting them off from Mary's view. She glanced up and down the corridor to make certain that she was unobserved, then followed the trolley into Houdini's suite.

"Good Lord."

Mary gaped in astonishment, and not a little envy, at the sheer luxuriousness of Houdini's temporary quarters. The Suite Royale more than lived up to its name. Consisting of a bedroom, living room, dressing room, and bathroom, the suite could easily have housed several struggling tenement families. Sheepskin rugs cushioned the floor. A marble fireplace housed the embers of a dying blaze. Ornate plaster moldings added an elegant touch to the decor. Cashmere blankets were heaped atop a bed the size of a circus trampoline.

Fluffy white towels, still lightly steaming, had carelessly been dropped onto the floor of the main bedroom, which was practically larger than the entire backstage area at McTavish's. Macassar oil and a greasy comb rested atop a polished chest of drawers, next to a pair of gaudy cuff links that probably cost more than her entire wardrobe. The palatial suite made the crude stone cottage she and Benji lived in seem like a prehistoric cave by comparison. *All this for breaking out of milk cans and handcuffs?*

For a moment, the sheer unfairness of it all, that she and Benji had to squat in a hovel while the Great Houdini lived like a king, left her speechless and shaking her head in disbelief. Then she pulled herself together and got down to business.

Look at me, she thought scornfully. *Wasting precious time woolgathering, just like that daydreaming daughter of mine.*

Eyes narrowing in concentration, Mary scanned the suite for whatever personal relics might be on hand. She briefly considered pocketing the expensive cuff links, but, no, this evening's outing wasn't about lifting a few pricey gewgaws. She was after information, not prizes for the pawnshop. If she did this right, Houdini would never even know she was here.

She moved briskly through the suite. In theory, the magician and his entourage would be gone for hours, but why take unnecessary chances? Mary wanted to be on her way as soon as humanly possible, after gleaning whatever choice tidbits of biographical detail she could from Houdini's things. She rifled through the wardrobe, but found only two new shirts. The chest of drawers yielded only socks and neatly piled undergarments. She seethed in frustration.

Her gaze alighted on a framed photograph propped up atop a dresser. The portrait showed a petite blond woman smiling demurely at the camera. Small and childlike, the woman struck Mary as distinctly unglamorous; a chaste Mary Pickford type. She tried to imagine the other woman wearing Princess Kali's revealing costume and failed utterly. *Probably couldn't play the vamp if she tried*, Mary thought disparagingly. *And, from the look of things, not enough curves in the right places.*

A handwritten message was scrawled across the photo. Mary read the inscription aloud:

" 'I am with you, my Harry, even in dreams. Your Coney Island sweetheart, your little darling-wife, Bess.' "

Mary rolled her eyes. " 'Little darling'?" She sneered at the saccharine sentiment and put the portrait back where she found it. Moving on, she spied a large steamer trunk resting on the floor at the foot of the bed. Sturdy straps and locks protected the trunk's unknown contents. The massive piece of luggage was practically the size of a coffin.

Hmm, Mary thought. *This looks promising.*

Her senses tingling with expectation, she approached the trunk. She fingered the golden initials H.H., embossed upon the scuffed black leather. What intimate secrets did the mysterious trunk contain? She tugged on the straps, releasing them, but the lid of the trunk refused to budge. Mary scowled and muttered beneath her breath. She was on to something here, she knew, but how was she supposed to get the damn thing open? Her fingertip explored the lock, tracing the outline of the keyhole.

Maybe she could pick the lock somehow . . . ?

A sudden noise sent a jolt through her system, so that she practically jumped out of her skin. Her hands came away from the trunk as though scalded, and she hurriedly picked the damp towels off the floor. She heard footsteps approaching and busied herself straightening up the bedchamber. An indignant chambermaid appeared in the doorway.

"What's this?" the aggrieved maid demanded. "He's *mine.* I do Mr. Houdini."

I'll bet you'd like to, Mary thought. *Bossy trollop.*

"Just who do you think you are?"

Mary chose to brazen it out. "Who do I think I am?" Her annoyed tone matched the other woman's. "I'm the girl doing all the bloody work around here!"

With her nose in the air, she marched defiantly past the

dumbfounded maid, leaving the hijacked trolley behind. She knocked the maid's hat off on her way out, just for good measure.

So much for this fishing expedition, she thought. She hated leaving the sealed trunk and its secrets behind, but there was no point in pushing her luck. *Time to make a hasty retreat.*

She hoped Benji was having more success on her foray.

CHAPTER SEVEN

———

THE THEATER ROYALE, WHERE HOUDINI WAS booked in Edinburgh, was to McTavish's Palace what the Taj Mahal was to the run-down graveyard next to the gasworks. Houdini's dressing room alone was twice the size of the changing rooms Benji was accustomed to. She marveled at the incandescent lights outlining the mirror before the dressing table . . . the enormous bouquets of roses and "Good Luck!" cards filling the room, in honor of opening night . . . the velvety, red floral wallpaper covering the interior of the dressing room. A Tiffany lamp and lit candelabra provided more than enough light to apply one's makeup by. An entire bloody grand piano occupied one corner of the chamber. Outside, an excited crowd chanted the star's name as they waited eagerly by the stage door.

"Houdini! Houdini! Houdini!"

The fervent cries echoed inside the theater. Sneaking about on her tiptoes, Benji peered at the opulent dressing room through the cracked-open door. A star on the door bore Houdini's name, but, as far as she could tell, the chamber was empty. She guessed that the Great Houdini had not yet arrived at the theater.

Which made it the perfect time to poke around a little.

Grinning at her own stealth and cunning, Benji slipped into the dressing room. She snooped efficiently through the drawers and cupboards. As her mother had taught her, she took care to make sure that she put everything back precisely where she'd found it. So far she hadn't discovered anything that her mother could use in their act, but Benji wasn't ready to give up yet, not with ten thousand American dollars at stake.

That much money would change our lives forever. Mam wouldn't have to be so cross and worried all the time. We could be happy again.

A mouthwatering aroma lured her to a tray resting on a nearby counter. A pristine white cloth covered the tray, but failed to entirely contain the delectable smells coming from underneath the fancy linen. Benji eagerly whisked the cloth off the dishes, exposing a veritable feast of fresh lobster, poached salmon, and thick sandwiches bulging with meat, cheese, and mustard. A plate of oatcake crackers and orange marmalade offered a lighter repast. Dundee cake and shortbread stood ready to satisfy the magician's sweet tooth. Tea and ice water were on hand to wash the food down; Benji had read that Houdini never consumed alcohol, due to the extremely hazardous nature of his stunts. He maintained a clear head at all times.

Benji's stomach rumbled like a poorly oiled piece of stage machinery. She and her mother had been subsisting on a meager diet of kippers and skirlie since losing their engagement at the music hall. Unable to resist, she reached out for one of the sandwiches. Before she could claim the tempting morsel, however, a heavy hand descended upon her shoulder. She yelped in alarm and tried to make a run for it, but her captor kicked the door shut in her face. It banged loudly against its jamb.

"You little thief!" Mr. Sugarman accused her. His meaty fingers dug into her shoulder, refusing to let go. Benji squirmed, but could not break free from the manager's grasp. She was trapped!

"I was just looking!" she protested.

A new voice came to her defense. "That's our audience you're kicking in the pants, Mr. Sugarman."

Benji recognized the deep voice and American accent instantly. Harry Houdini emerged from the shadows behind his rotund manager. Distracted by all the food, she hadn't even heard the two men enter the dressing room. She silently cursed herself for her carelessness. How was she ever going to explain this to her mother?

"Mr. Sugarman has a diploma in Business Management," Houdini said, smirking as though at some private joke. He winked at Benji. "What's your name, kid?"

Overwhelmed at suddenly being in her idol's presence, Benji was unable to speak. Her mouth dropped open, but no words emerged. She gazed mutely at the Great Houdini in the flesh, standing only inches away from her. A tailored Savile Row suit gave him an elegant appearance. He knelt down to look her in the eye.

"Lost your voice, huh?" He seemed amused by her dumbstruck reaction. "Where'd you last hear it? Wait a minute, I know."

A tiny voice emanated from the top pocket of his jacket. "Help! Help! I'm in here!" His lips never moved, but the comical voice was as clear as day. Houdini peered into the pocket with a quizzical expression on his face. He dipped his hand into the pocket and brought it out as a fist. Now the voice seemed to come from the closed fist. "Help! Help!"

Mr. Sugarman sighed and rolled his eyes, unamused by the performance. His grip on Benji's shoulder loosened, but the enthralled girl wasn't going anywhere. She was familiar with ventriloquist acts, of course, from her days before the footlights. Yet the simple trick seemed magical when performed by Houdini himself—he was simply a natural at captivating an audience.

He held his fist out in front of Benji's lips. "Open up," he instructed her. "Come on, open up quick!"

Benji laughed out loud, delighted to be sharing a carefree moment with her hero. Houdini mimed tossing the voice into the girl's open mouth. "How's that for size?" He gestured toward the tray of refreshments. "Wanna sandwich?"

She finally managed to speak. "Yes, please, Mr. Houdini."

"The voice fits!" he enthused. "A little gummed-up still, but it works." He stepped aside to let her get at the food. His eyes looked her over in a friendly fashion. "What else can you say?"

She wolfed down a bit of the sandwich. The thick roast beef and fresh cheese tasted like heaven. Forgetting her etiquette, she spoke with her mouth full. "Name's Benji, Mr. Houdini."

" 'Benji Mr. Houdini,' " he parroted, assuming a thoughtful expression. "Hmm, well, I'd drop the second part. Just plain Benji sounds good to me."

" 'Just Plain Benji' isn't much of a name either," she pointed out.

Houdini chuckled in response. "A comedienne! Got a comedienne here, Mr. Sugarman. A regular Fanny Brice. Maybe she can do the warm-up."

The manager's sour face showed what he thought of Houdini's joking suggestion. Mr. Sugarman stood by silently while Benji polished off her sandwich in record time.

"I'm not a comedienne, Mr. Houdini," she volunteered.

He eyed her curiously. "So what do you do for a living? Rob banks? Train fleas? Dance the Highland fling?"

"Steal from dressing rooms?" Mr. Sugarman added acidly.

"I'm no thief," Benji insisted, which was true enough in its way. She'd never stolen anything that hadn't been returned to its original owner eventually. "I'm a psychic . . . well, more a sort of disciple."

"A psychic's sidekick, huh?" Houdini sounded intrigued. Mr. Sugarman just looked more suspicious than ever.

Benji was serious now. *No more kidding around*, she told

herself. This wasn't exactly how she and her mam had intended to approach Houdini, but now that she had his attention, Benji knew she couldn't let this opportunity go by. *This is it. Our shot at the big prize.* Reaching into her jacket, she solemnly retrieved one of the last of her mother's professional visiting cards. The gaudy piece of cardboard, framed by Egyptian hieroglyphs and printed in three colors, had cost them a pretty penny. *Here's hoping that pays off for us tonight.*

Houdini graciously accepted the card. He read aloud from the embossed type. " 'The Tantalising Princess Kali and Her Dusky Disciple.' " He glanced at Benji's notably undusky features. "That's you, right?" Benji nodded. " 'Psychic Practitioners.' "

"We were top of the bill at McTavish's Palace," she bragged.

Mr. Sugarman snorted derisively, but Houdini shot him a warning look. The world-famous magician, who wouldn't be caught dead in a dump like McTavish's, pretended to be impressed and signaled his manager to do the same. No fool, Benji knew he was just humoring her, but she appreciated his consideration nonetheless. Unlike Mr. Sugarman, he was going out of his way to avoid hurting her feelings.

He tucked the card into his front pocket. "Well now, I think I've a little something for you, too." He reached behind Benji's ear and produced a large yellow ticket. Benji's eyes gleamed at the sight of the precious pass. "Tonight's performance," he said. "Don't be late!"

I wouldn't dream of it, she thought, starry-eyed. Wild

horses couldn't drag her away. She greedily clutched the ticket. "Thanks, Mr. Houdini!"

Mr. Sugarman tried to herd her toward the exit, but Benji wasn't done yet. She wasn't so excited at scoring the ticket that she had forgotten what really mattered. She turned back toward Houdini. "My mam does *nae* do tricks, like," she told him. "It's *real*, Mr. Houdini. It's no jiggery-pokery."

She felt bad lying to Houdini, especially after he had treated her so gentlemanly and all, but what else could she do? Ten thousand dollars was too tempting a prize to pass up. *Mam's depending on me.*

"Solid gold," Mr. Sugarman murmured dubiously. "Course she is."

His hand pressed against her back, pushing through the door out into the hall. Benji dug in her heels long enough to pop her head back into the dressing room for a parting shot. "It's true, sir. She's got 'the gift.' "

For the first time, Houdini seemed to take her seriously. He stroked his chin as his piercing blue-gray eyes looked into her own. Benji thought he seemed interested in her claims. She almost expected him to call her back in, holding her breath in anticipation.

It's working, she thought. *He's starting to fall for it.*

She opened her mouth to continue her spiel—

Mr. Sugarman slammed the door shut.

· · ·

The Hall of Records was practically deserted tonight. Mary had the silent chamber all to herself. The light from an electric lamp spotlighted her as she sat at a long oak table, poring over a voluminous file of newspaper cuttings. Her overcoat was draped over the back of an uncomfortable wooden chair. Having shed the maid's cap and apron, she wore only the plain black dress that went with the costume. A chilly draft made her wish that she hadn't discarded the bogus fur stole back at the hotel.

Spread out before her on the table, visible beneath the glow of the lamp, was the entire life of the Great Houdini, as chronicled by innumerable newspaper headlines. The articles were pasted onto the pages of a cumbersome, oversize scrapbook. Mary silently thanked the nameless archivist who had so painstakingly assembled the library's file on the legendary "Self-Liberator," as Houdini liked to bill himself. As every good "psychic" knew, advance research was the real key to a successful visitation from the spirit world. Before she attempted to scam Houdini, Mary intended to learn everything there was to know about the celebrated magician.

Already she had acquired the basics of his life to date. Harry Houdini, née Ehrich Weiss, had been born in April 1874, the third child of Rabbi Mayer Samuel Weiss and his wife, Cecilia. A middle child, he had four brothers and one sister. One of his younger brothers, Theodore, was also a professional magician, going by the stage name Hardeen, although Theo had never quite achieved the stature of his legendary sibling. Rabbi Weiss had died in 1892, when Houdini was only eighteen, leaving his widow with six children to look after . . . or to look after her, depending on your perspective.

Six children, Mary marveled. She thanked her lucky stars that her own husband had only left her saddled with Benji. *We could have been much worse off if I hadn't wised up and kicked his sorry arse out the door right away.*

Houdini met his future wife, Wilhelmina Beatrice Rahner, while performing at Coney Island, New York, in 1894. "Bess" had been part of a singing duo billed as the Floral Sisters. Houdini married her just three weeks after meeting her for the first time, and she promptly joined the act as his lovely assistant. Houdini was Jewish. Bess was Catholic. *That can't have gone over well with their families*, Mary guessed. *Wonder what Houdini's mother, the rabbi's wife, thought of her new daughter-in-law?*

Could her last words to Houdini have regarded his marriage?

Something to consider, Mary mused. She jotted the thought down in her notepad.

The Great Houdini had hit the big time around the turn of the century, once he started specializing in his trademark escapes and challenges, and had been a headliner ever since. City after city, nation after nation, had been conquered by Houdini's death-defying feats. A sheaf of banner headlines charted his stellar career. Mary flipped through the yellowed news clippings. Black-and-white photos and theatrical notices recorded a slew of memorable moments in Houdini's remarkable life:

Nearly naked, his impressive physique clad only in iron chains and manacles.

Tied to a chair by heavy ropes, tugging on the knots with his teeth.

Climbing into a galvanized-iron milk can, which would soon be filled to overflowing with water before being padlocked shut with Houdini still inside.

Practically nude once more, this time being locked inside a Siberian Transport Cell, an intimidating armored wagon that looked like a safe on wheels.

Shackled and standing on a waterfront pier, only seconds before being tossed into the frigid waters of the Erie Canal.

Sitting in the cockpit of his very own biplane, after his historic flight over Australia.

Hanging upside down above Broadway in New York City.

Pulling a string, threaded with a dozen silver sewing needles, out of his open mouth.

Speaking at a war rally, to raise vital funds for the troops.

Standing side by side with Theodore Roosevelt.

Posing onstage with a rearing elephant, which would soon vanish into thin air.

Seated at a typewriter as he composed a bestselling book on magic and mediums.

Battling against a fearsome mechanical man in a scene from one of his popular movie serials. Being pursued by bloodthirsty cannibals in another movie.

I'll give the man this, Mary thought. *He's a true showman, probably the best since Barnum.* As a fellow professional, she had to respect his savvy and stagecraft. It remained to be seen whether even the Great Houdini could have the wool pulled over his eyes by a clever woman. *And why not?* she mused hopefully *He's still only human.*

Flipping through the clippings in chronological order, she came to the meat of the matter. A series of headlines from 1913 seized her attention:

HOUDINI'S MOTHER DIES

HOUDINI IN MOURNING—SHUNS PUBLIC

According to the articles, Houdini had immediately canceled his current tour after his mother's death and had not returned to the stage until several months later. Mary couldn't help being strangely moved by the newspaper accounts of the magician's all-consuming grief. *Would Benji mourn me the same way?* she wondered. *I'm not so sure.*

She turned the pages more slowly now, studying the various clippings more carefully. A subsequent article offered her a degree of encouragement:

HOUDINI FINDS HOPE IN SPIRITUALISM

He wasn't the only one. As Mary knew better than most, spiritualism was all the rage now. Throughout the civilized world, thousands of otherwise sensible people, including many prominent authors and philosophers, were obsessed with trying to communicate with the dead via mediums and séances. Although the spiritualist movement was said to have begun in the late 1880s, after a pair of American sisters claimed to have made contact with the spirit world, it had experienced a tremendous resurgence in the years following the Great War. *All those many thousands of war dead*, Mary reflected, *and all those bereaved loved ones left behind*. No wonder the spook racket was a boom business these days. Almost all had lost someone they desperately wanted to hear from again. The whole world craved some assurance that death was not the end.

Even the Great Houdini.

But the cunning magician had proven harder to fool than the average punter. Mary frowned as she contemplated the next few headlines:

HOUDINI TURNS AGAINST PSYCHICS
"IT'S ALL FAKE," SAYS HOUDINI

For the last few years, it seemed, Houdini had launched a full-scale crusade to expose and discredit phony psychics and spiritualists. He had attended hundreds of séances, often in disguise, only to reveal exactly how the so-called mediums had achieved their "supernatural" effects. Photos showed him whisking aside a curtain to expose a hidden slide projector, or uncovering the concealed electronic transmitter inside a "talking" trumpet or teakettle. Another photo, of Houdini seemingly conversing with Abraham Lincoln, proved just how easily double exposures could be used to create "spirit photography." Onstage, before a laughing audience, Houdini conducted a mock séance, keeping the lights on to demonstrate how to ring a bell or shake a table while pretending to be in a trance. His book, *A Magician Among the Spirits*, asserted his belief that most practicing psychics were simply greedy charlatans and con artists. Mary made a mental note to look for a copy of the book. *Better safe than sorry.*

Only last year, she read, Houdini had made headlines by exposing a noted Boston medium, known only as Margery, as a fraud, despite that Margery had already fooled a blue-ribbon panel of experts. In revenge, the disgraced psychic had predicted that Houdini would be dead within a year. So far the fatal prophecy hadn't come true.

A quote from the man himself caused her concern:

I am prepared to reproduce any signal or bit of legerdemain mediums may employ, no matter how unearthly it may seem to the untrained observer.

Mary's frown deepened. Fooling this man was going to be trickier than hoodwinking the credulous and inebriated audiences at McTavish's Palace. Could she succeed where even the notorious Margery had failed?

I have to, Mary thought vehemently. *A fortune depends on it.*

Conquering her doubts, at least for the moment, she continued to peruse the clippings. A small article from a noted tabloid looked promising:

THE UNKNOWN HOUDINI
A VERY PRIVATE MAN

Mary scanned the article, scribbling down notes on Houdini's personal life. He and Bess were childless, she observed, even after thirty-plus years of marriage. Houdini had once thrown a lavish party in Hollywood to celebrate their twenty-fifth anniversary. In lieu of children, they doted on their pet dogs. When not on the road, which was seldom, he resided in a four-story town house in Manhattan. Houdini's mother and sister had lived there as well, prior to Cecilia Weiss's death thirteen years ago.

Turning the page, Mary discovered a grainy photo of Houdini's late mother: a small, silver-haired old lady in a black dress standing in a garden. *Not unlike Mrs. Violet Robertson,* Mary noted. *What is it with old women and gardens?* In another picture, Houdini posed with the frail old woman, his arm draped protectively around her shoulders. Mrs. Weiss looked proud of her son, the greatest magician alive. HOUDINI PICTURED WITH HIS BELOVED MOTHER, a caption read.

What had that mother whispered to her son, Houdini, on her deathbed? The answer was worth $10,000. Mary's eyes lit up as she examined the two photos. *Now these I can use,* she thought victoriously. She took hold of the page in question. *No one will ever miss an article or two.*

"Another tragic bereavement, Mrs. McGarvie?"

Mr. Fettes, the lecherous librarian, crept up behind her. Mary felt his sour breath upon her neck. He leaned closer, his pointy chin nearly resting on her shoulder. He nodded in the direction of the rolling ladder. "I'm always happy for you to probe the higher shelves." His impertinent fingers climbed up her arm, making Mary's skin crawl. "For those 'cherishable details.' "

Mary coughed hoarsely, loud enough to cover the sound of her ripping the article out of the scrapbook. If luck was with her, the purloined photos were her passport to a brighter future, where she would never have to put up with the likes of Mr. Fettes again. She furtively hid the newspaper cutting beneath her skirt.

"I have all the details I need!"

She got up abruptly, practically knocking Fettes onto his ass. He gaped at her with indignation and frustrated desire as she marched out of the Hall of Records, hopefully never to return. *One more show,* she thought, *for one very special customer, and Benji and I can retire in luxury.*

Harry Houdini wouldn't know what hit him.

CHAPTER EIGHT

———

WATERY REFLECTIONS SHIMMERED ACROSS the rich gold-leaf plaster moldings on the ceiling of the Theater Royale. Benji sat up in one of the plushy uphol-stered fauteuil seats, only a few feet away from the edge of the stage. The gilded proscenium towered above her. A hand-painted ceiling, depicting the phases of the moon and entire constellations of stars, vaulted high overhead. Behind her, over two thousand patrons had crowded in the theater's commodious stalls, boxes, balconies, and galleries. Benji was dimly aware that she looked out of place in the grand circle, alongside dozens of formally attired swells, but that wasn't enough to dampen her spirits. She had a front-row seat for the biggest show in town.

"Fellow Travelers. My dear friends," Houdini ad-dressed the audience. He stood solemnly upon the stage, before a pair of closed curtains. A long, purple dressing gown gave him the appearance of a medieval wizard. His initials were inscribed in large illuminated letters upon the floor of the stage. "Science tells us that Life had its beginnings in the gloomy depths of the ocean."

The curtains lifted to reveal a tall mahogany tank with transparent plate-glass sides. The upright tank was filled to the brim with clear water. A plain aquamarine backdrop did not distract from the forbidding appearance of the infamous Chinese Water Torture Cell. Two grim-faced men in long, black overcoats, whom Benji recognized as Houdini's bodyguards, flanked the stage. Each man gripped daunting wreaths of iron chains and padlocks. The orchestra played an eerie, ethereal tune.

"Our own little lives are but a brief gasp," Houdini declared, "before we plunge back down into that dreamy darkness from which there is no return." He paused dramatically. "Or *is* there? Is Death final, or will Life triumph?"

Along with the rest of the audience, Benji watched in hypnotized silence. The Chinese Water Torture Cell was said to be Houdini's most dangerous escape; none of his legions of imitators had ever dared duplicate the feat. Benji couldn't believe that she was actually going to witness the trick with her own eyes—and from one of the best seats in the house, no less.

"I, Harry Houdini, shall discover the Truth—for all of us!"

He threw out his arms as his assistants approached him from both sides, bearing their heavy loads of chains. Wooden stocks, with riveted metal bindings, descended from above. The stocks were held in place by a mahogany frame that matched the timber skeleton of the Torture Cell. They hung above the stage, suspended by four coiled metal cables.

"Naked, we emerged from that sea of the unconscious," Houdini stated. "Lights, please! For the sake of decency!"

The stage lights went off, casting the area beneath the proscenium into utter darkness. Among the whispered murmur of the audience, Benji heard Houdini's velvet robe rustle to the floor. The rattle of chains and the metallic clang of locks snapping shut echoed through the vaulted auditorium. The orchestra played softly in the background.

Benji leaned forward in her seat. She strained her eyes in a futile attempt to penetrate the darkness cloaking the stage. *What's he up to now?*

Abruptly, the spotlights came back on—to reveal Houdini hanging upside down from the wooden stocks, which were clamped tightly about his ankles. Chains and padlocks held the stocks shut. Handcuffs bound his wrists together. His black hair hung down from his scalp. A pair of white woolen drawers protected his modesty.

Benji blushed at the sight of his undraped form, then scolded herself for such a juvenile reaction. *Ain't nothing you've never seen backstage in the dressing rooms.*

Despite his inverted position above the stage, Houdini had no difficulty projecting his voice. "Ladies and gentlemen, I entreat you. Do not attempt to hold your breath in emulation of me." He called out to his assistants. "The winch!"

Heavy machinery swung into position above the open tank. His assistants produced a pair of stepladders from the wings, which they placed on either side of the vertical Torture Cell. Climbing the ladders, they made certain that the wooden frame holding the stocks was directly above the tank; Benji realized that the frame would form the lid of the tank once Houdini was lowered into the water. The ladders were withdrawn and his aides resumed their positions at either ends of the stage. They now held fireman's axes, to be employed in the event that the Great Houdini required a last-minute rescue. But would they be able to smash open the Torture Cell fast enough? From where Benji was sitting, the glass panes looked to be at least an inch thick.

The music came to a sudden stop. Upside down above the waiting tank, Houdini looked out at the audience. His face and voice were grave. His cuffed hands rested atop his chest as though he were already in his grave. Benji felt as if he were looking right at her. Goose bumps broke out across her skin.

"God guide me . . . and have mercy on my immortal soul!"

A lever was released and Houdini plunged headfirst into the Chinese Water Torture Cell. Liquid gushed over the rim of the tank, flooding the stage, before the heavy mahogany lid sealed the tank shut. Through the clear glass, Houdini could be seen submerged entirely inside the Torture Cell. His loose hair swayed like drifting seaweed. His striking blue-gray eyes gazed out from the watery death trap.

Heavy burgundy drapes fell over the tank, concealing it from view.

Dead silence reigned over the packed theater. Despite Houdini's admonition, Benji had started holding her breath the moment he was dropped into the tank. So did everyone else. An elderly gentleman, seated to Benji's right, was timing Houdini with his pocket watch. The second hand ticked by relentlessly.

.   .   .

Inside the tank, hidden from the audience, Harry writhed and convulsed his body, all but dislocating his ankles before finally kicking his feet free of the stocks. This escape required careful technique as well as physical dexterity; Harry had broken his ankle performing this trick in Albany. Remembering that excruciating ordeal, he made certain never to make that mistake again. Once was more than enough.

He sank to the bottom of the tank, then went to work on the handcuffs. Bubbles escaped his lips and nostrils. Pressing his fingers against the sides of his throat, he forced himself to regurgitate the small metal lockpick he had swallowed while the lights were out. *Thank you, Okata-san,* he thought as he spit the pick into his right palm. Harry had learned this trick from a Japanese acrobat he had performed with in a circus years ago; the young Houdini had spent hours practicing, first with bite-size pieces of potato, then with a small ivory ball, until he could swallow and regurgitate tiny objects at will. This talent had proven singularly useful in his later career as a jailbreaker and self-liberator. Harry had quietly been providing Mr. Okata with a small pension for some years now.

Houdini hesitated, pick in hand. He knew he should free himself from the cuffs immediately; this trick was too risky to take any unnecessary chances with. But he couldn't resist lingering in the dimly lit liquid for just a few seconds more. It was strangely still and peaceful here in this watery tomb. The lack of oxygen was making him light-headed, but not unpleasantly so. Floating here in the silence, cut off from the noise and tumult of the outside world, was perhaps as close as any mortal man could come to the eternal tranquillity of the world beyond, if such a realm truly existed. He peered into the shimmering shadows, waiting expectantly for . . .

A vision came to him, more real than anything he could imagine. A wizened face, wreathed in funeral lilies, floated out of the gloom toward him. Silver hair swirled in the underwater currents. Copper pennies covered her eyes. A wispy white shroud billowed around her. Fragile hands, spotted with age, reached out for him . . .

Harry sat frozen at the bottom of the tank. He didn't move a muscle, even as a flurry of bubbles escaped from his mouth. His air supply was running out, but, for the moment, he was too transfixed by the unearthly vision to care.

Mama? Is that really you?

.   .   .

One after another, the purple-faced audience members could hold their breath no longer. They gasped for air, surrendering to the primal imperative to fill their lungs with fresh oxygen. Her cheeks bulging like a chipmunk's, Benji had held on so far, but she knew she couldn't last much longer. She peeked at the watch of the gentleman next to her. Barely more than minute had passed, yet already most of the audience had given up. The orchestra began playing "Asleep in the Deep." The mournful melody, about sailors drowned at sea, struck Benji as far too apropos to Houdini's present circumstances. The familiar lyrics came unbidden to her fretful brain:

Beware! Beware!
Many brave hearts are asleep in the deep.
So beware! Beware!

Over two thousand pairs of eyes watched the drape-covered tank with increasing anxiety. Worried voices grew louder and louder, unconcerned who heard them. Several men consulted their watches urgently. On Benji's left, a pious grande dame clasped her hands in prayer, beseeching the Almighty for Houdini's deliverance. Nervous gentlemen wiped telltale beads of sweat from their brows or else gulped down a restorative nip from a flask. Ladies fanned themselves to keep from swooning. "Somebody do something!" a panicky voice blurted several rows behind her. "Help him!"

Benji's face was as crimson as the wallpaper in Houdini's dressing room. She felt faint from lack of oxygen. Darkness encroached on her vision. Her lungs were burning. *I can't hold on anymore,* she thought frantically. *I have to breathe!*

Her pent-up breath exploded from her mouth. She greedily sucked down the perfumed air of the theater. Her vision cleared as the creeping blackness retreated from view. She couldn't believe that she had managed to hold her breath for as long as she had. Looking around, she saw that most everyone else had abandoned the effort, too. And small wonder; according to her neighbor's ticking pocket watch, over two minutes had passed.

And yet there was still no sign of Houdini. A trickle of water seeped ominously out from behind the thick burgundy curtains. Was it just her imagination, Benji wondered, or were even the stoic bodyguards starting to look a little uneasy?

. . .

Mama?

The dead woman's lips fluttered. Pennies concealed her familiar blue eyes. Lilies wafted around her like a funeral wreath. Her mouth opened slightly, but no sound emerged.

What is it, Mama? Harry thought desperately. *What are you trying to tell me?*

He reached out for her, only to smack his fingers against the unyielding glass wall of the Torture Cell. His mother's specter faded from view as the jarring impact reminded him of the severity of his situation. With no time to waste, he shook his head to clear his mind and applied the regurgitated pick to the lock of the handcuffs. Given the restraints around his wrists, the angle was complicated, but Harry had mastered this trick ages ago. He hadn't once been billed as the Handcuff King for nothing. There wasn't a lock on earth that he didn't know inside and out.

All he needed was a few more seconds. . . .

. . .

The audience was growing hysterical now. Agitated voices called out from the gallery and stalls. Over three minutes had passed and still Houdini had not emerged from the Chinese Water Torture Cell. In the aisles, men rose to their feet, on the verge of rushing the stage. Time was obviously running out for the imprisoned magician, if it wasn't too late already.

He can do this, Benji thought in an agony of suspense. Pale-faced and trembling, she resisted an urge to chew on her knuckles as she waited with bated breath for her hero to escape from the very jaws of death once more. She reminded herself that Houdini had surely performed this stunt hundreds of times before, on stages all across the world, but, as the seconds dragged on endlessly, fearsome doubts invaded her mind.

It wasn't possible, was it, for one man to stay underwater so long? What if something had gone terribly wrong? What if Houdini was drowning to death at this very minute?

Mr. Sugarman raced onto the stage from the wings, a silver stopwatch clutched in his hand. His ordinarily florid face was ashen. He signaled frantically at an ax-wielding bodyguard, who hastened toward the shrouded tank in obvious alarm. The audience gasped, unsure whether this was all part of the act or not. The bodyguard raised the ax high. . . .

Three loud knocks came behind the curtains, like knuckles rapping against the mahogany lid of the Torture Cell. A signal from Houdini?

The bodyguard lowered his ax. Mr. Sugarman's portly form sagged in relief. The folded drapes fell like ribbons onto the damp stage floor—and there, reclining casually atop the tank, resting his dripping upper body on one elbow, was the Great Houdini. One end of the loose handcuffs dangled from his wrist. Soaked to the skin, but seemingly unscathed by his perilous ordeal, he flashed a gleaming smile. The doleful chords of "Asleep in the Deep" gave way to a triumphant fanfare.

A thunderous roar erupted from the audience. Gasping in relief, over two thousand men, women, and children surged to their feet, giving Houdini a standing ovation that seemed to go on forever. You could practically taste the excitement in the atmosphere; the crowd wasn't so much praising Houdini for his performance as it was rejoicing that he was still alive. Benji stood atop her seat, clapping until her palms burned. All thought of the crucial $10,000 prize fled her brain, at least for the moment.

That's the most fantastic thing I've seen! she thought. *He's amazing!*

Houdini's sparkling eyes singled her out in the crowd. He winked at her as the curtains closed on the greatest performance Benji had ever witnessed.

She thought she would explode with happiness.

· · ·

Sugarman looked primed to explode, Harry thought. The distraught manager was waiting for him in the wings, flushed and indignant. He thrust his stopwatch in his client's face.

Three minutes, forty-seven seconds, Harry noted. *A new record.*

"For crying out loud, Harry!" Sugarman sputtered. "Any longer and you'd be a corpse!"

"A corpse don't earn my kinda money, Mr. Sugarman." Energized by the deafening cheers and applause, Harry paid little attention to his manager's scoldings. Adrenaline coursed through his veins. He never felt more alive than when he had cheated death once more. It was like being born all over again.

Sugarman grabbed onto Harry's arms, as if determined to shake some sense into the other man. "You don't have to do this, Harry," he insisted. "Don't have to push it to the wire every time."

"Yes, I do," Harry replied, less lightly than before. A vision of his mother's ghostly apparition drifted before his mind's eye as he looked Sugarman soberly in the eye. If only the other man knew how close he sometimes came to breaking through to the other side. "Yes, I do."

The cheers of the audience continued to resound throughout the theater, demanding another curtain call. Leaving his clucking manager to his heartburn, Harry bounded back onto the stage. He gave the adoring crowd another star-quality smile as he none-too-humbly took another bow.

His public, Benji included, clapped loud enough to raise the dead.

CHAPTER NINE

———

ELATED BY WHAT SHE HAD JUST WITNESSED, Benji practically flew through the streets of Edinburgh. Her heart was still pounding in her chest; she couldn't have stood still if she'd tried. The whole night seemed magical. Moonlight bathed the familiar streets in enchantment. Her drab, everyday world had been transformed into a thrilling new realm of possibility and excitement. An invigorating wind blew against her beaming face. The orchestra's stirring fanfare resounded inside her brain. She knew somehow that her life would never be the same, all thanks to the Great Houdini.

He's even more marvelous than I imagined!

Her pounding legs couldn't carry her fast enough to outrace her sheer euphoria. She jumped and spun in the air, unable to contain her sky-high spirits. Startled pedestrians looked askance at her antics, but Benji couldn't care less. Those poor souls hadn't been there in the theater tonight, hadn't experienced Houdini in the flesh. How could they hope to understand what she was feeling right now?

She darted into the Princes Street Gardens, seeing, as though for the first time, the sweeping green lawns, leafy groves, and colorful fall foliage. The moving hands of the famous Floral Clock informed her that it was nearly midnight, but she was no Cinderella; tonight's sorcerous spell would not vanish at the stroke of twelve. Defying gravity, she vaulted over neatly pruned shrubs and flowerbeds. The Scott Monument, stretching over two hundred feet above her head, seemed puny compared to the dizzying heights her soul was ascending to. She had just seen a man perform the impossible. What could be more magnificent than that? She couldn't wait to tell her mother all about it.

A train whistled through the park, en route to Waverly Station. The Ross Fountain, its gaudy, gilded glory sparkling in the moonlight, sprayed a towering cascade of water into the sky. Leaving the gardens behind, she sprinted home as fast as she could. She nimbly dodged the tombstones in the derelict cemetery. The ugly gasworks failed to oppress her spirits. A Gypsy encampment waited beyond the graveyard. Cooking fires glowed in front of parked caravans. A skinny nag listlessly grazed on some sparse brown grass and weeds. A couple of mongrel dogs barked at her in greeting. Candlelight shone from the window of the dilapidated stone cottage she and her mother called home. Judging from the flickering glow, Mam was still up, waiting for her.

Good, Benji thought. *I won't be waking her.*

She and her mother had squatter's rights on the crumbling bothy, which had been abandoned by its original tenants well before Benji was born. Located on the outskirts of the city, the two-story cottage had a shingled roof and a splintered pine door that was barely holding on to its hinges. Decaying mortar patched the cracks in the crude stone walls. A thin tendril of smoke rose from the bothy's brick chimney. Mam obviously had a fire going. Benji wondered if there was any supper left. That tasty sandwich was just a fading memory now.

The sound of Benji's racing footsteps drew her mother out of the cottage. She awaited her daughter by the open front door, her arms crossed atop her chest. A fraying shawl, a ragged cardigan, and an old frock protected her from the night's chill. Her face was stern, but the delirious girl overlooked the warning signs in her mother's demeanor.

"I met him, Mam!" she blurted, skidding to a halt. "You should see him! He's got these eyes that just burn all the way through to the back of your head!" Her heart skipped a beat just thinking about it. "He's incredible, Mam!"

A hard slap across the face caught Benji by surprise. "You got *caught*!" her mother hissed.

Without another word, Mam turned on her heels and stormed back into the cottage, leaving a stunned Benji outside in the shadows. Her cheek smarted where her mother had struck her. Angry tears leaked from her eyes. Her magical night evaporated like a disappearing pachyderm. With a single blow, her mother had brought her soaring spirits crashing back down to earth. *It's not fair*, Benji thought bitterly. *Tonight was perfect. Why'd she have to spoil everything?*

Fuming, she trudged into the bothy after her mother. Gas lanterns tried and failed to dispel the murky shadows lurking in the corners of the hovel. The remains of a cooking fire smoldered in the hearth. A kettle boiled atop a wood-burning stove. Stolen theatrical props and costumes cluttered the shelves. An imitation silk carpet, filched from a children's pantomime production of *Ali Baba and the Forty Thieves*, covered a meager portion of the dirt floor. A straw broom was propped up in a corner. Benji's dingy cot rested behind a lattice screen. Her mother's own bed was upstairs in the loft, a mouse scurrying up there before Benji's eyes.

"What did I tell you?" her mother snapped at her as Benji entered. She hurled a pot at the fleeing mouse. "Rule number one! You never get caught . . . *never!*" She shook her head in disgust, as if wondering how she had ever been saddled with such a worthless child. Benji glared back at her. "Well . . . what did you find out? Or were you too busy making eyes at him?"

Benji shrugged petulantly. Why should she waste her breath answering?

She never listens to me anyway.

Her insolent attitude provoked her mother. "Think I like living like this?" Mary gestured furiously at their run-down surroundings. "Think I want to grow old surrounded by grime and filth and wearing somebody else's hand-me-downs?" Years of struggle and humiliation could be heard in her voice. "You should have seen that hotel suite tonight. Fit for a king!" She clenched her fists, obviously tormented by that brief glimpse of luxury. "I want *new* things. I want *nice* things. I want *ten thousand dollars!*"

She turned away from Benji, on the verge of tears. Her mother's naked anguish tore at Benji's heart. For the first time in hours, she wondered what her mam's night had been like. The girl felt a twinge of guilt at the thought of Mam prowling through Houdini's personal things, after the man had been kind enough to treat Benji to his show. But she knew that her mother was only doing what she had to, for both their sakes.

Tentatively, Benji reached out toward her mother, wanting to heal the breach between them. "Did *you* find anything, Mam?"

Mam kept her back to her daughter, but Benji could hear her mother sniffling as she got her unruly emotions back under control. Taking a deep breath, she straightened her spine. Her voice, when she spoke again, was all business.

"Wasn't hardly a single personal thing in the entire suite. Nothing. Like he barely exists." She threw up her hands in frustration. "There was this trunk," she corrected herself. "With his name on it." Her voice took on a more thoughtful tone. She was talking more to herself than Benji now. "Kind of trunk you keep *secrets* in. A big trunk that only takes a tiny wee key."

She turned toward Benji. Her eyes looked hopefully at her daughter, as though perhaps Benji held the answers they needed. "Now where would the 'incredible' Mr. Houdini keep a tiny key like that, eh?"

Benji shrugged again, with less of an attitude this time. She wished she knew, if only to avoid disappointing her mother again, but she didn't have a clue. She hadn't spied a key in Houdini's dressing room.

Sorry, Mam.

Still, Mam wasn't defeated yet. Moving away from the teakettle, she retrieved a newspaper clipping from her purse and handed it to Benji, who inspected the paper in the flickering light of the lanterns. She found herself examining a faded photograph of an old woman in a garden. She didn't recognize the smiling old lady at all.

Who?

"But I got this," Mam explained. "It's his mother." The very same mother, Benji realized, whose last words were the passport to untold riches. Mam reclaimed the photo from Benji's grubby fingers. "It's a start. I'll busk the rest."

Privately, Benji doubted that it would be that easy. She had seen her mother improvise an entire performance out of a few measly scraps of information before, but the usual tricks weren't likely to impress a man who could escape drowning even while locked inside a Chinese Water Torture Cell. She wasn't sure anyone could outwit the Great Houdini.

Not even Mary McGarvie.

CHAPTER TEN

———

"GOOD AFTERNOON, MR. HOUDINI."

An odd, high-pitched voice addressed Harry. He gazed in astonishment. So did Sugarman.

"I have, sir, a secret message from your mother," announced the wooden dummy perched on the knee of a visibly nervous ventriloquist. The dummy's carved features turned toward them with a creak. Its painted visage—with cheeks as red as bloodstains—struck Harry as distinctly sinister. He saw the ventriloquist's lips move slightly. *He's not even terribly good at this,* Harry thought, unimpressed. *I could do better, albeit not with a Scottish accent.*

The amateurish performer winked at his dummy. They wore matching blue caps, tweed jackets, and bow ties. The dummy looked a lot more confident than his partner. "It's in Hungarian, isn't it, Jock?"

Close, but no cigar, Harry thought. He and Sugarman watched the bizarre display from the comfort of two plushly upholstered chairs in the Theater Royale's expensively furnished rehearsal room. Gold trim accented the olive green walls. A pitcher of ice water and a bowl of fruit occupied the antique wooden table between the two men. A chandelier dangled from the elegant plaster moldings on the ceiling, while an authentic Persian carpet cushioned their feet. Sunlight entered the room through the French doors facing the two men. Heavy velvet curtains framed the windows. A large harp occupied one corner, next to a tilted full-length mirror. The ventriloquist and his wooden mouthpiece sat atop a plain wooden chair in the middle of the room. The chair squeaked against the floor whenever he moved.

"Shoulda done your homework, Hamish," Harry said brusquely. "She didn't speak Hungarian. Spoke Yiddish." He gestured toward the door. "Next!"

Jock gave the abashed ventriloquist a dirty look, as if blaming him for the mistake. The pair gloomily exited the rehearsal room while Harry shook his head at the sheer ridiculousness of it all. He had to admit that when he had put out an open call for local psychics and mediums, he had never expected to receive supernatural messages from a carved block of wood.

What next?

The answer turned out to be an obvious vaudevillian who came *tap-dancing* into the room wearing a straw boater and a flashy satin vest. His heels rapped rhythmically against the uncarpeted portion of the floor as he put on an entirely unsolicited display of fancy footwork, before dropping onto his knees à la Al Jolson. He doffed his hat in apparent expectation of a round of applause.

A deathly silence greeted his efforts. Harry and Sugarman traded bewildered looks.

"You're a hoofer," Sugarman said finally.

"Aye, sir!" He jumped to his feet, ready to dance once more. "A hoofer, I am!"

Sugarman tried to determine just what the dancer was doing here. "We're interviewing psychics."

"Think of a number!"

Harry groaned. "Next!"

Hours later, the late-afternoon sun found both men slumped low in their chairs, exhausted by what had proved to be an endless ordeal. The water pitcher had been refilled twice, and the fruit bowl held only a few leftover stems and apple cores, but they were no closer to finding a fit subject for Harry's grand experiment. He had been singularly disappointed by Edinburgh's crop of self-described seers and mystics; most of the aspirants passing through the rehearsal room today had been the usual small-time hustlers and charlatans he ran into everywhere he went, working the same worn-out old tricks. He hadn't even seen a really talented faker, such as Margery, the Davenport Brothers, or the ingenious Rahman Bey. Hours wasted, and all he had to show for it was a sore butt. His bad kidney throbbed painfully.

The door to the rehearsal room opened to admit an unusual sight: two twin girls in matching apricot pinafores. Funereal black ribbons adorned their blond pigtails. No more than ten years old, tops, they stood side by side with solemn expressions upon their eerily identical faces. Their pudgy arms hung stiffly at their sides. They looked more like animated dolls than living children.

Harry sat up in his chair, intrigued despite himself. He couldn't help recalling the infamous Fox sisters, Margaret and Catherine. Those two girls had launched the spiritualist movement in America over eighty years ago when they claimed to receive messages from the Hereafter. In her dotage, one of the sisters finally confessed that they had generated the inexplicable rapping noises by loudly cracking their toes in the dark, but many people still believed the girls to have possessed genuine supernatural powers. Some revered the Fox sisters as modern prophets. Could that be the case with these new girls?

"Message from your mama," the twin on the right began.

Her sister picked up the thread. "Very cold, very cold."

They continued to alternate their pronouncements in an unsettling fashion:

"Misses Little Harry . . ."

"Growing old, growing old."

Sugarman squirmed uncomfortably in his seat. Harry leaned forward, captivated. For the first time all day, a genuine chill ran down his spine. The twins' spooky demeanor made his skin crawl.

"Girls," he challenged them. "Wanna tell me what my mama called me when I was a kid?"

The twins shared a sly look before speaking again. Their girlish voices took on a nasty edge. They chanted faster and faster, still trading off the phrases between them.

"Ezeentsy teentsy figgery fell . . ."

"El, del, dominel . . ."

Suddenly, they spoke in unison. They simultaneously pointed their fingers at Harry.

"Eerie orie, eerie orie . . . you are oot!"

A flash of recognition broke the spell. He scowled at the girls.

"*Macbeth*. Act one, scene one. Am I right?"

What? he thought indignantly. *Just because I never went to college, you think I don't know my Shakespeare?* The girls' thick Glaswegian accents had thrown him off for a moment there, but he had recognized the witches' opening incantation quickly enough. Hell, he had several complete sets of the Bard's work back in his library in Harlem. He sagged back down into his seat, disappointed and disgusted. He was less annoyed at the girls than at himself, for briefly falling for their act. *For a minute or two, I really thought we were onto something.*

Sugarman rose wearily from his chair to shepherd the twins out of the room. One of the girls paused in the door, looking back at Harry. Her large brown eyes met his.

"She'll never forgive you, Harry."

Her words jolted Harry. "What's that?!" he exclaimed, jumping to his feet even as Sugarman hastily shoved the twins out the door. "Forgive me? For what? I never hurt her in my goddamn life!" His mother's face arose from his memory. Pennies covered the loving blue eyes he knew so well. Even in the early days of his career, when he was barely eking out a living, he had always made sure to look after his mother, just as he had promised his father on his deathbed. He had sent the better part of every paycheck to her, even when he and Bess were reduced to stealing potatoes to survive. "What's she talking about, Mr. Sugarman?"

"She's talking ten thousand dollars," his manager said cynically.

His words failed to calm Harry. The twin's accusation hit him like a sucker punch to the gut. *Never forgive me . . . like hell!* What did that pigtailed phony know about the infinite generosity of his mother's spirit? "Why, if God ever permitted an angel to walk this earth, it was my mother!"

"Of course, Harry," Sugarman agreed tactfully.

A rap at the door interrupted Harry's tirade. Sugarman rolled his eyes. He looked inclined to tell the remaining applicants to go away, but the door swung open before the worn-out manager could deny their next visitor admission. Harry settled in for another awful audition, then was pleasantly surprised to behold his underage admirer from the night before. *What's her name again?* He quickly searched his memory. *Benji, that was it.*

Funny name for a girl, he thought. *Wonder if it's a Scottish thing?*

The girl was dressed somewhat less like a tomboy today. A red beret, a knee-length brown dress, and dark wool stockings had replaced the newsboy cap and short pants.

Despite his fatigue, he mustered a friendly smile. "Ah, the psychic's sidekick."

"*Oy vay!*" Sugarman clearly remembered the girl as well. "Mind if I kick our audience in the pants this time?" He started to escort Benji toward the door. "Let's go, kid. Mr. Houdini's had enough for one day."

But Benji wasn't going anywhere. "It's not me. I told you. It's my mam."

On cue, a breathtaking vision appeared in the doorway. Time stopped for Harry as he gazed in wonder at a strikingly beautiful woman with thick black hair and deep brown eyes. She was modestly clad in a long black skirt and pink floral blouse. Her ebony tresses were neatly tied up in a bun, but he could readily imagine them drifting freely about her head and shoulders. Speechless, he stared openly at the lovely newcomer.

Distracted by Benji's stubborn immovability, Sugarman didn't notice the woman at first. Then he followed Harry's rapt gaze to the girl's mother. His eyes widened momentarily, and a concerned look came over his face. Harry wondered if Sugarman was seeing the same thing he was. *How can he not?* he mused. *Just look at her!*

.   .   .

"Forgive this intrusion, Mr. Houdini, Mr. Sugarman."

Mary discreetly took stock of her audience as she entered the room. Their reactions puzzled her. The chubby manager had looked somewhat startled at her appearance, while Houdini himself looked positively entranced. His piercing blue-gray eyes seemed to burn through her, just as Benji said. He hadn't blinked, or scarcely breathed, since he had first laid eyes on her. *What on earth?* she mused. True, she had dressed her best for today, but that hardly explained the man's transfixed state. *Hasn't he ever seen a good-looking woman before?*

This might be easier than she thought.

"My name is Mary McGarvie. We have a psychic act, me and my daughter here." She gestured at Benji, who retreated quietly into the background as she'd been told. "Not such a wonderful act, really. I wear a somewhat . . . revealing . . . costume." She managed an embarrassed blush. "I pretend to look into people's minds. Sometimes I really do."

After giving the matter plenty of thought, she had decided that a touch of candor would be more convincing than any inflated claims of psychic prowess; the trick to being a good medium was to mix a little truth in with the balderdash. Honesty was the best policy . . . to a degree.

"My mother would have called it a travesty, an abuse of a God-given gift. She used hers for healing." She introduced a note of regret into her voice. "Maybe I should have made more of mine, but there's no man at home, you see, and there's bread to be put on the table."

She waited for some response from Houdini, but the man just continued to gape at her as though she were the bloody Second Coming. Hiding her frustration, she tried to get him to open up. *Don't make me do all the work here, mister!*

"Mr. Houdini, I am so sorry. I am so deeply sorry for your loss."

Still as mute as a mannequin, he rose from his seat and crossed the room. He drew back the velvet curtains to let more sunlight in. A golden radiance bathed Mary in its glow. She hoped the light made her look suitably angelic.

"Last night I dreamed a dream," she lied. "I saw someone I've never met, in a garden I've never seen. A lady in a garden. She had hair like silver and she was small and wearing a black dress. She was waving, as if she was beckoning someone to her." She delivered the spiel perfectly, just as she had rehearsed it. "Does that mean anything to you, Mr. Houdini?"

"Means you read the *New York Times*, Mrs. McGarvie," the fat manager said.

Mary realized Mr. Sugarman was going to be a problem. "It was the *Herald Tribune*," she confessed with what she hoped was disarming frankness. Maybe she could win the man over eventually?

"That picture was everywhere," Mr. Sugarman said.

Doubtless Houdini was aware of that as well. The famous showman had yet to utter a word. His handsome face was as inscrutable as the Sphinx. Did he let his manager do all his talking for him? That wasn't what Benji had told her.

"Sometimes it works," she divulged. "Sometimes you have to help it along." She beseeched Houdini with her eyes, pleading for sympathy. He was a fellow performer; surely he understood the importance of putting on a good show. "Is that a sin?"

Houdini didn't answer. He just kept staring at her.

What the devil's the matter with him? Mary was used to men goggling at her, especially when she wore the Princess Kali outfit, but this was different. He wasn't undressing her with his eyes; it was like he were trying to peer into her soul. His intense scrutiny unnerved her, but she tried not to let it get to her. *At least he hasn't thrown me out on my ear yet.*

That was something.

Closing her eyes, she went into her act. She swayed as though she were the one in a trance and not Houdini. She whispered in a deliberately sepulchral tone.

"I read a page unwritten . . . heard words yet unspoken." Her slender arms emulated Theda Bara once more. "But they only seem like shapes and colors to me now."

She swooned, on the verge of losing her balance.

Houdini rushed forward and caught her in his arms. Mary gasped and let out a deep, heart-wrenching sob. Opening her eyes, she looked up into Houdini's blazing orbs, now only inches away from her own. She felt his hushed breath upon her face. His cheeks were flushed with excitement . . . or was it passion? She thought she heard him whisper something beneath his breath.

"I'm sorry, Mr. Houdini," she murmured. "What did you say?"

To her surprise, he was shaking as he helped her regain her balance. His eyes still locked on hers; he reached out and touched her cheek with a trembling hand, as if he almost couldn't believe she was real. Mary had no idea what to make of his actions. None of her schemes, none of her carefully rehearsed speeches, had prepared her for this moment. Her face tingled at his touch.

"No more," he said at last. "It's okay, it's you." A hint of a smile softened his taut expression. "You're the one I've been waiting for."

How about that? Mary thought. She did her best not to smile herself. She had no idea what she had done to provoke such a powerful response from the man, but apparently it had worked. Out of the corner of her eye, she saw Benji watching in amazement. Mr. Sugarman groaned and clutched his enormous gut. Mary was petty enough to enjoy his discomfort at her victory.

We're in.

CHAPTER ELEVEN

———

"You sure you know what you're doing, Harry?"

Sugarman glanced nervously at his employer. The two men stood together on the top floor of the hotel, waiting for the elevator to arrive. Sugarman had been working up the nerve to broach the subject with Harry ever since they had temporarily bid adieu to Mrs. McGarvie and her ragamuffin spawn. Now that he had finally spoken up, he waited apprehensively for Harry's reaction.

"You were there," Harry reminded him. "You saw her. You know what it means."

It means trouble, Sugarman thought. He had known that the moment he first set eyes on the alleged Scottish psychic. But what could he possibly say to Harry about so delicate— and uncomfortable—a matter? Uncharacteristically, he found himself at a loss for words. Acid crawled up his throat.

The elevator arrived. Harry ushered Sugarman into

the lift, but did not step inside himself. The door began to slide shut, but Harry held it back for a moment. "Hey," he teased his manager. "Maybe there's more in heaven and earth than in all your audit books, Mr. Sugarman."

"More than ten thousand dollars?" Sugarman asked.

Unlikely.

Harry let go of the door, and the elevator descended. Sugarman composed himself during the short trip to the ground floor. He smoothed back his brilliantined black hair. The elevator landed with a mild thump. Sugarman took a deep breath. There was no turning back now. For better or for worse.

The lobby of the Scottish Lion was already abuzz with activity. Reporters and newsreel men jostled each other in a roped-off area at the foot of the carpeted grand staircase. A line of hired policemen and hotel employees strained to hold back the impatient horde of ink-stained wretches. Sugarman had to hand it to Harry; this whole psychic talent search was generating a ton of publicity and unpaid advertising. Then again, the Great Houdini had always been a genius when it came to generating headlines. That was a big part of why he was the highest-paid performer in the business.

Who knows? Sugarman thought, sighing in resignation. *Maybe this is a good idea after all?* Then he remembered Mary McGarvie and all his reservations came back with renewed force. *Don't fool yourself,* he thought. *This can't end well.*

Nonetheless, he walked steadfastly across the lobby to join a welcoming party composed of Edinburgh's chief constable, a stocky Scotsman with a walrus mustache, as well as a trio of elderly academics representing the Scottish Society for Psychical Research. The gray beards, spectacles, and bald pates of the latter gentlemen conveyed an irreproachable portrait of sober respectability and scientific authority. *They couldn't look more the part,* Sugarman mused, *if I'd cast them myself.* The involvement of the society, not to mention *Scientific American,* gave Harry's latest brainstorm the aura of legitimacy he so coveted. For himself, Sugarman just hoped that the photos would look good in the papers.

Even more photogenic was the heavy steel safe, constructed of gleaming blue-gray gunmetal, resting upon the stairs. Franz and James, Houdini's overworked assistants/ bodyguards, stood guard over the safe, which had already attracted the attention of the various photographers and newsreel cameramen. The impregnable steel box boasted a state-of-the-art spin-dial lock.

At least Harry's not planning to lock himself in that thing, Sugarman thought. *As far as I know.*

Sugarman, the constable, the experts, and the safe took their positions upon the sweeping staircase. Clamoring like a pack of noisy chimps, reporters surged forward to get as close as they could to the speakers. The impatient scribes hurled questions at the group:

"Where is Mr. Houdini? Will he be making an appearance?"

"Is it true that he has been in contact with his dead mother?"

"Does this concern the ten-thousand-dollar reward? Has anyone claimed the prize?"

"Is the hotel haunted?"

"Does Houdini really believe in ghosts, or is this just a publicity stunt?"

"What's the story, Sugarman?"

The besieged manager declined to answer the shouted queries. Instead he removed a prepared statement from his jacket pocket and waited for the hubbub to subside. The reporters soon took the hint and ceased their braying. They waited silently, their pens poised above their open notepads. Sugarman cleared his throat and proceeded.

"Mr. Harry Houdini announces the most extraordinary experiment ever staged by modern science." Sugarman winced inwardly at the grandiose phrasing. Could he really read this crap? "One that will prove beyond all reasonable doubt the existence of an afterlife."

The reporters applauded the pronouncement, recognizing good copy when they heard it. Sugarman nodded at the chief constable, who was standing a few feet to his right. Epaulets and medals adorned his blue dress uniform. Relishing his moment in the spotlight, the constable held up a paper envelope. The initials H.H. were imprinted on the seal of red wax binding the envelope shut. The crowd waited expectantly for the next twist.

"Sealed in this envelope," Sugarman declared, "are the last words spoken to Mr. Houdini by his dear, departed mother, written down by Mr. Houdini himself. These words are known only to him and have been shared with no one, not even his closest associates."

Sugarman made an effort to deliver the speech with a

straight face, but he needn't have bothered; the fascinated cops, scientists, reporters, and hotel employees were lapping it up. James and Franz stepped aside to let the chief constable approach the metal safe. The cop made a production of placing the sealed envelope in the safe, slamming the door shut, and spinning the lock with gusto. Flash powder exploded as a throng of photographers captured the moment. The newsreel men enthusiastically turned the cranks on their cameras. Impressed reporters applauded the showmanship involved.

"This safe will be lodged in the Royal Bank of Scotland," Sugarman explained, "until the day of the historic Psychic Experiment, which will be conducted under scrupulous scientific conditions in front of the world's press."

He neglected to mention that the centerpiece of this august event was an unemployed music hall performer who was only one step removed from a burlesque dancer. That wouldn't sound quite so "scientific." He prayed that they could somehow get through this ill-advised venture without any trace of scandal. Harry was a married man after all.

"Mr. Houdini intends to contact the departed soul of his beloved mother through a known lady medium, via whom the secret words will be transmitted."

Here's hoping she's only after the ten thousand dollars, Sugarman thought, *and not looking to become the next Mrs. Harry Houdini.* Heaven knew Mary McGarvie wouldn't be the first gold digger, or potential blackmailer, trying to sink her claws into the Great Houdini. Fortunately, Harry, for all the recklessness of his death-defying stunts, had always been smart enough to avoid that kind of jeopardy.

Until now.

He glanced up at the mezzanine overlooking the lobby, where he spied Harry watching the proceedings. Unnoticed as yet by the distracted crowd, Houdini brooded in splendid isolation. His face an inscrutable mask, he resembled a bruised god looking down from on high. Sugarman would have given a week's commission to know exactly what was going through Harry's mind right now. Was he thinking about the Afterlife, Mary McGarvie, his dead mother, or all of the above? What was driving him to continue with this ridiculous charade?

Sugarman felt an ulcer coming on.

.   .   .

"We've died and gone to heaven!" Benji exclaimed. Overwhelmed by the gorgeous hotel suite Houdini had provided for her mother, she bounced up and down upon a king-size brass bed. Spotless white linen served as a trampoline. Plush feather pillows levitated with every bounce. A crystal chandelier swung back and forth. Bouquets of fresh roses and azaleas scented the air. The palatial suite was almost as luxurious as Houdini's own quarters in the penthouse.

Only for the moment, Mary thought cautiously. She paced restlessly across the carpet. Houdini's behavior at the audition still troubled her, although she wasn't precisely sure why. Maybe because she hadn't done anything to warrant such a response? *It wasn't even one of my best performances. Houdini's manager saw right through me.*

Benji bounded off the bed, eager to explore the rest of the suite. Racing into the enormous bathroom, she snatched a bottle of expensive cologne from the marble counter and dashed wildly from room to room, perfuming the already fragrant air. Heedless of her mother's uneasy mood, she sprayed the cologne in front of herself, then ran headlong through the clouds of perfumed mist. She skidded to a halt in front of a large open window displaying a stunning view of Edinburgh Castle.

"Look at the castle, Mam!" Benji darted over to another window and threw back the drapes. Tempting fate, she leaned out of the window. "I can see all the way up Princes Street, all the way to Scott Monument!"

Mary took her word for it. She had bigger things on her mind than a two-hundred-foot-tall pile of greasy black shale. *What exactly is the Great Houdini after?* she fretted. *Just a postmortem chat with his sainted mother, or something more?*

Dropping to the floor, Benji rolled about the thickly piled carpet. She kicked out her arms and legs, practically swimming in it. She looked as if she were making an angel in the snow, just as she used to when she was little.

"It smells like heather!" She buried her face in the carpet, sniffing loudly. "It even smells like heather. And it's all free!"

"Nothing in this world's free!" Mary snapped, losing patience with the girl's foolish naïveté and shortsightedness. She stalked across the suite. Her worried face scowled at the riches surrounding them. "Come Sunday, we don't deliver the 'secret words' our Mr. Houdini wants to hear, this all goes." She savagely indicated the lacy finery, antique furniture, and gilded picture frames, then snapped her fingers loudly. "It vanishes!"

Benji froze in place, caught off guard by her mother's outburst. "But he's taken a real shine to us, Mam!" she protested. The hopeful look on her face almost broke Mary's heart. "The plan's working!"

"That's as may be," Mary hedged, reluctant to look a gift horse in the mouth. "But there's something going on. It was too easy. I didn't have to do a thing."

A knock at the door startled her. Benji went to see who it was, but Mary held up a finger, signaling her to wait. What if it was Houdini himself?

I need to be ready for this.

Mary hurriedly made herself presentable. She tucked a loose curl into place, then straightened her skirt. She cinched her blouse a little tighter at the waist and opened it a little wider at the neck. If Houdini was simply blinded by her charms, she wanted to keep him that way. She struck a dramatic pose by the bed, alluring but not too brazen. *This should do,* she decided. She snapped her fingers at Benji.

Her daughter opened the door to reveal . . . a bellboy.

Mary relaxed, uncertain whether to be relieved or disappointed. Benji sighed and shook her head. Unfazed by their lack of enthusiasm, the gangly youth entered the suite and offered Mary a card on a sterling-silver platter that would have fetched a tidy sum at the pawnshop. "From Mr. Houdini," the bellboy explained. Mary caught him peeking at her décolletage.

Benji swiped the card from the platter, much to the boy's annoyance. He had clearly been instructed to personally deliver the card to Mary. Glaring at the girl, he smartly saluted Mary and took his leave. Benji stuck out her tongue at his retreating back. She handed the card to her mother.

"What's it say, Mam?" Benji was jumping up and down in excitement. She reeked of cologne. "What's it say?"

Mary quickly skimmed the note. "He's inviting me to lunch."

"Mam! This is it!" Benji pirouetted across the room. "This is what we want!"

Mary realized her daughter still had a lot to learn about men and women, and how complicated matters could get between them. She frowned at the card. The terse, business-like invitation offered no clue as to Houdini's true intentions. Not for the first time, Mary wished that she did truly possess the gift.

"Point is, girlie, what does our Mr. Houdini want?"

CHAPTER TWELVE

———

THE EDINBURGH ZOOLOGICAL GARDENS WERE only four miles from the center of the city, yet Benji had never visited them before. Situated on a steep, green hillside in Corstorphine, the sprawling menagerie was the largest zoo in all of Scotland. While her mother met with Houdini, Benji spent the afternoon enthusiastically gawking at the penguins, lions, giraffes, hippos, rhinos, gorillas, chimpanzees, and other exotic animals populating the park. A steam calliope played hurdy-gurdy music loudly enough to be heard all across the zoo. Loud roars and birdcalls punctuated the melody. Benji chomped happily on a caramel apple as she strolled past the monkey cages. A jaunty green beret with a red feather capped her head. She wore a brown woolen jacket over a brand-new blue dress, all courtesy of the Great Houdini's generosity. The shrill screeches of the tiny simians reminded her of the hooting yahoos in the gallery back at McTavish's.

Except that the monkeys were probably smarter.

She halted in front of a large blue cage, captivated by the sight of two small monkeys copulating. A sign on the cage identified the amorous primates as black-tufted marmosets from South America. The male had mounted the female from behind. Wiggling his bright red rear, he thrust repeatedly, while she screeched in either pain or passion. Fascinated, Benji tried to connect the marmosets' frantic activity with various off-color remarks and jokes she had heard backstage at the music hall. Had her mother and father conceived her the same way? Benji found that hard to imagine.

Is that what all the fuss is about?

Mr. Sugarman, who was puffing on a cigar behind her, belatedly realized what the frisky monkeys were up to. "Good Lord!" he exclaimed as he placed a gloved hand over her eyes and hastily steered her away from the cage. Not until her back was safely turned on the alarming spectacle did he uncover her eyes. A uniformed park keeper, carrying a large push broom upon his shoulder, walked by them on his way to the hippo enclosure. Sugarman hollered indignantly at the man.

"There're kids here, right? Women and children!" He pointed back at the offending primates. "You've got male and female in the same cage. There should be some kind of law against it!"

The park keeper shrugged apologetically and continued on. Mr. Sugarman started after him, but Benji tugged on his arm, pulling him away. She led him toward a white-painted footbridge arching over a rippling stream. A gazebo offered shelter from the sun a few yards away. A grand eighteenth-century manor house dated back to the ground's past as a baronial estate. The Zoological Society had acquired the property some years ago. A spinning Ferris wheel crowned the crest of the hill. On this sunny Friday afternoon, scores of families were enjoying the pleasant fall weather. Benji wondered why her mother had never brought her here.

"It's Nature, Mr. Sugarman," she assured him, referring to the monkeys' scandalous behavior. She didn't think she needed to be shielded from such things. *I'm not a child anymore*, she thought. *I'm almost twelve years old.*

Practically a woman.

"Yeah? Well, Nature should learn some decency." He huffed and puffed as they strolled up the bridge. The steep slopes of the hillside zoo had taken a toll on his stamina. He leaned against the railing to catch his breath. Benji handed him her half-eaten caramel apple as she climbed onto the rail. She dangled her legs above the stream.

"Monkeys are just like you and me, Mr. Sugarman," she educated him. Just last year, in fact, the Americans had waged a famous court battle on that very subject, debating Darwin's controversial theory that mankind was descended from apes. Benji had read all about the so-called Monkey Trial in the papers. For herself, she had no trouble accepting that people were just hairless primates. Nothing she had ever witnessed backstage, or in the dingy slums of Edinburgh, made her think otherwise. She remembered the crude Casanova outside the pawnshop, the one who had tried to take liberties with her mother. How different was he from that bare-arsed marmoset pumping away at the female?

How different was Houdini? At this very moment, she recalled, her mother was lunching with the great magician. *"Point is, girlie,"* Mam had asked, *"what does our Mr. Houdini want?"* Benji felt an unexpected stab of jealousy.

"Speak for yourself," Sugarman groused. He eyed her sticky caramel apple with distaste. He clearly did not appreciate having to babysit her today, any more than she felt she needed babysitting. Zoo or no zoo, part of her wished that she could be sharing her mother's lunch with Houdini instead. She took her frustration out on Sugarman.

"You're no different," she accused him. "The Great Houdini says, 'Jump'—you jump. You're just a dancing monkey!"

Sugarman started to wag his finger at her, but Benji didn't stick around for whatever he had to say. Swinging her feet back over the railing, she dropped back onto the bridge and took off down the path. If people were going to treat her like a kid, she might as well act like one. "Let's go look at the Aquarium," she called back over her shoulder. "They've got sharks and underwater tortoises and all sorts!"

Sighing heavily, the put-upon manager trudged after her. He lobbed the gooey remains of her apple into the stream, then tried to wipe the melted caramel from his gloves, but his efforts only made the mess worse. He hollered at her, "Wanna know something, sweetheart?"

Benji stopped and looked back at him defiantly. "What's that, Mr. Sugarman?"

"You're not going to take my Mr. Houdini for that ten grand," he predicted. He lugged his considerable girth up the hill toward the Aquarium.

We'll see about that, Benji thought. *Don't you underestimate my mam.*

Or me.

Smiling sweetly, she skipped up the path.

. . .

A fawning maître d' guided Mary into the elegant hotel dining room. Indulging herself, just for the moment, she enjoyed the star treatment. A red designer dress showed off her figure. A silver fox stole was draped over her bare shoulders. A golden necklace hung around her neck. Her hair and makeup were impeccable. False modesty be damned; she knew she looked sensational.

Houdini rose as she entered the room, his eyes agape. Looking around, she saw that he had apparently reserved the entire dining room for themselves. A table for two, graciously laid out with fine silverware, china, and flowers, occupied the center of the richly appointed chamber. All of the other tables had been shoved up against the cream-colored walls, clearing a space large enough to stage a small circus if one should feel so inclined. Crystal chandeliers hung from the high ceiling. A silver candelabra burned upon the table. Three waiters and a chef stood at attention next to the kitchen door.

The Great Houdini's own private restaurant . . .

"Mrs. McGarvie," he greeted her. "Please forgive the intimacy of our little restaurant. Nosy newshounds are everywhere."

The attentive maître d' pulled out Mary's chair, but she remained standing. She needed a moment to get her bearings. "I never stayed in a grand hotel suite before." She glanced around at the exclusive dining room. "Something to tell the grandchildren."

Remembering that Houdini was childless, she mentally kicked herself. *Was that the wrong thing to say?*

He didn't seem to take offense. "You got the flowers okay?"

"Enough for a wedding," she assured him. It was true; her suite looked like a bloody greenhouse. The overpowering fragrance was almost enough to make one faint. *Should I have mentioned weddings?* she fretted, second-guessing herself again. *What about his wife?*

As far as she knew, Mrs. Houdini was back home in the States. . . .

An awkward moment ensued as they both remained on their feet. The waiters hesitantly approached the table, clutching their menus. They hovered on the periphery.

"Won't you sit down?" he pleaded. "Please, Mrs. McGarvie."

Mary decided to make her concerns plain. "Men don't spend money on flowers just so they can enjoy the smell of them."

"I just meant to be *friendly*, Mrs. McGarvie." He sounded

genuinely shocked that she might have mistaken his intentions. "Are you sure you won't sit down?"

She eyed the candles and flowers suspiciously. "Is this part of the audition?"

"Sit down, please." He sheepishly gestured toward her chair.

Mary still wasn't entirely convinced that he didn't have ulterior motives, but at least she had placed him on the defensive for the time being. Flashing her dark eyes, she finally deigned to sit down. Houdini seated himself across the table from her. The maître d' sighed softly in relief and handed them the menus.

"Champagne for the lady," Houdini ordered. "Best in the house!"

The wine waiter looked overjoyed to be called upon. The maître d' and the other waiters discreetly disappeared. Houdini leaned across the table to whisper to her.

"Listen," he said in low voice, obviously trying to put her at ease. "I was raised in Appleton, Wisconsin. Tiny little town in the middle of nowhere. Sold papers, shined shoes, did conjuring tricks . . . I even did a medium act briefly, when times were hard." He gestured at the ritzy restaurant and its expensive trappings. "This isn't me, all this . . ."

"Really?" She gave him a skeptical look. From what she'd read, he wasn't lying about his humble beginnings, but that had been a long time ago. The Great Houdini had been raking it in for more than a quarter of a century now.

Did he truly understand anymore what it was like to be poor . . . and desperate enough to try almost anything?

He seemed to enjoy being challenged. "You did your research, right? You know everything about me already."

"Not everything," she admitted. *I don't know why you chose me.*

He lifted a silk napkin to reveal a pair of jewel-studded silver earrings, resting in a box atop a small cushion. "A little old-fashioned, maybe," he apologized, "but I like them." He pushed the box toward her. "Allow me."

Mary cautiously examined the earrings as though they might be booby-trapped. Although she prided herself on her ability to read people, she still couldn't get a handle on Houdini. He had seemed sincerely mortified by the suggestion that he was trying to seduce her, yet now he was throwing expensive antique jewelry at her. *What exactly is he after?* Despite her impoverished circumstances, Mary had no intention of becoming any man's kept woman or conquest. Parading before a drooling audience in a sequined harem-girl costume was one thing; selling her body to the highest bidder was something else entirely. *I won't be bought and paid for, not even by the Great Houdini.*

She kept quiet, waiting for him to make the next move. But he just sat back in his chair and smiled. Finally, she had no choice but to break the silence herself. "Mr. Houdini, I'm not a wee girl."

"Harry, please," he insisted.

"What do you want, Mr. Houdini?" she asked him

outright. The same thing as that Romeo in Leith a few weeks back? Or Mr. Fettes at the library?

"I want to treat you as the lady you so clearly are, Mrs. McGarvie." He held up his hands, as if to show her he had nothing up his sleeves. "That's all."

Mary still had her doubts. What magician ever put all his cards on the table?

"That's all?"

"You're special, Mrs. McGarvie," he said so confidently that she almost believed him. She saw her own reflection in his eyes. "You have a gift."

That's what you think, she thought, uncertain how to respond. A wordless moment dragged on for what felt like an eternity. Mary found herself wishing that she were truly everything he seemed to believe her to be. She knew she should agree with him, bolster her psychic credentials, but the usual lines and patter refused to come to her lips. *I don't want to lie to him,* she realized, *but isn't that exactly what I'm here to do?*

They stared at each other in silence.

"Mam!" a high-pitched voice intruded from outside the dining room. Mary heard Benji raising a ruckus at the door. "Where's my mam?"

Mary suppressed a sigh of relief. *Thank heavens,* she thought, grateful for the interruption. *And right on cue.*

A closed door banged open. Benji charged in, shoving her way past the startled maître d'. Mr. Sugarman followed close behind her, visibly short of breath. Flushed and disheveled, he looked as if he had just fought the battle of Waterloo, not merely looked after a mere slip of a girl for a few hours. *That's my Benji,* Mary thought with a touch of pride. *Harder to handle than Madame Girelli's Performing Monkeys.*

"We went on the Big Wheel!" Benji squealed. She raced to her mother's side. "And I was sick on Mr. Sugarman!"

The portly manager dabbed fruitlessly at the dried vomit on his tailored three-piece suit. Mary's nostrils caught a whiff of regurgitated cotton candy, chocolate, and caramel. Distracted by the persistent stain, Sugarman staggered over to the table without bothering to pay his compliments to Mary. Houdini came to his feet and promptly called the other man on his lack of manners. "Back where I come from, Mr. Sugarman," he said stiffly, "we always acknowledge a lady."

Sugarman looked up to take in Mary. His shrewd eyes instantly noted the telltale earrings in their box. Swallowing his pride, he gave Mary a perfunctory bow.

"Mrs. McGarvie!" He assessed her stylish attire. "I hardly recognized you."

She rose and pushed the box with the earrings away. "Mr. Houdini, I don't have the time or the inclination to figure out what it is that you really want. I think I'll just leave you and Mr. Sugarman to your sad games." She turned on her heels and headed for the door. "Benji!"

Her daughter scurried after her.

"No! Mrs. McGarvie, wait!" Flustered, Houdini started to step around the table to chase after her. His hand reached out, but she was already halfway to the door. "Outta my way, Mr. Sugarman." He squeezed past his manager, almost colliding with an oncoming waiter bearing a chilled bottle of champagne. "Mrs. McGarvie! I'm sorry! Forgive me!"

For a second, Mary was afraid that he was going to catch up to her in the lobby, but Sugarman came to her rescue. He laid a restraining hand on Houdini's arm.

"Follow her now, Harry, make a scene, and it'll be all over the papers in the morning." He looked his client squarely in the eyes. "Then where's your great 'scientific' experiment?"

Houdini angrily jerked his arm free. He looked daggers at Sugarman, but did not pursue Mary out the door. He must have known his manager was telling him the truth. Hadn't Houdini already warned her of prying newshounds himself?

Mary swept out of the private dining room into the lobby. Benji hurried to catch up with her at the foot of the grand staircase. She looked up at her mother and whispered:

"Did I get back in time, Mam?"

You bet, Mary thought. For once, the girl's timing was perfect. Poor Mr. Houdini had been thrown completely off-balance, leaving Mary firmly in control of the situation. Benji had maybe even saved Mary from herself, just when she was starting to succumb to their target's blandishments. *He's a charming man*, she conceded. *Maybe too charming*. She reached out and squeezed her daughter's hand. A secret smile played upon her lips.

We'll get that ten thousand dollars yet.

CHAPTER THIRTEEN

───

A LARGE POSTER HUNG UPON THE CLOSED DOOR of the rehearsal room. Torn and curling at the edges, the poster touted THE TANTALISING PRINCESS KALI & HER DUSKY DISCIPLE above a painted portrait of Mary and Benji in their Middle Eastern costumes and makeup. They looked as if they had just stepped out of one of the racier stories in the *Arabian Nights*. Vivid colors gave the poster an eye-catching flair.

Harry's shadow fell across the poster. Impeccably clad in a top hat and tails, he admired the glamorous depiction of Mary McGarvie as a modern Cleopatra. The skimpy outfit flattered her enticing figure. Kohl-lined eyes beckoned him.

His gloved hand gently pushed open the door. Light from the hallway spilled into the darkened chamber. Holding his breath, he entered the silent rehearsal room. A piano and music stand stood idle in one corner. Harry caught a glimpse of his own reflection in a full-length mirror, before

his attention was irresistibly drawn to a few gauzy wisps of
clothing draped over the back of a wooden chair. Glittering
sequins and costume jewelry caught the light from the hall;
even though he had never seen her act, he recognized the
revealing costume Mary wore as Princess Kali.

Unable to help himself, he took hold of the filmy garments and ran them through his hands. His gloved fingers
fondled the delicate fabric. The scent of some exotic perfume still clung to the costume. The intoxicating aroma
stirred his senses, awakening feelings that he had thought
buried with his mother. He inhaled deeply.

A rustle of movement came from an anteroom a few
feet away. A hanging curtain partially concealed the adja-
cent chamber from view. Through the thin muslin, Harry
spied an unmistakably feminine silhouette. Harry's mouth
went dry. Putting the insubstantial clothing back on the
chair, he crept over to the curtain and drew it back just
enough to peer through a crack at . . .

Mary McGarvie in dishabille. Her light cotton slip was
worn and frayed, but incredibly provocative nonetheless.
Laddered white stockings showed off her long legs. Lacy
garters peeked out from beneath the hem of her slip. The
glow of an electric lamp shone through the fabric of her slip
and knickers, exposing her womanly charms. The sloping
curve of her breasts called out to him. He wanted to rest his
head against them forever and let the gentle beating of her
heart lull him into eternal bliss.

How would the Bard have put it? "A consummation devoutly to be
wished."

His breath caught in his throat as she slowly peeled off the torn stockings, revealing the smooth, pink skin underneath. Discarding the old, she produced a pair of new silk stockings, far more sheer and clingy than the workaday stockings she had worn before. She held one of them up before her lips and blew softly into the opening. Inflated by her warm breath, it swelled and billowed like a circus balloon. Her delicate foot slid easily into the waiting stocking, which enveloped her lithe leg like a second skin. Harry's heart was pounding so loudly that he felt sure she would hear it, yet she seemed oblivious to his presence as she effortlessly repeated the procedure with the other stocking. His fingers ached to caress the silken limbs.

Rising from her seat, she opened a nearby wardrobe and took out an old-fashioned white wedding gown, of the sort that would have been fashionable more than sixty years ago. The lacy white chiffon and crinolines held a nostalgic loveliness. A matching headdress and veil accompanied the floor-length dress.

Before his adoring eyes, she donned the pristine gown, which fitted her to a tee. Harry thought he had never seen anything so lovely, not even Bess on their own wedding day. A momentary twinge of guilt troubled his conscience, but he was unable to look away from the captivating vision before him. Mary smiled softly as she admired herself in another full-length mirror. She fitted the antique silver earrings to her ears. They matched the classic wedding gown perfectly.

Wordlessly she turned toward him, at last becoming aware of his presence. Her knowing eyes met his. Had she known he was there, watching, all this time? Her lush red lips opened as though to speak. She whispered softly, but he couldn't hear her over the blood rushing in his ears. He tried to go to her, yet his feet seemed frozen in place. She was only a few feet away, but it might as well have been miles. A helpless longing tormented him.

What is it? he thought. *What are you saying?*

The color gradually drained from the vision before him. Mary's red lips, striking brown eyes, and rosy complexion faded into the faintly sepia-toned shades of an aging photograph. The image grew indistinct and grainy. Harry rubbed his eyes, but the picture continued to blur, until all he could make out was the misty outline of a woman in a wedding dress, framed by the shiny silver mirror behind her.

Wait! he thought desperately. *What's happening? Don't go!*

"Harry!"

He awoke with a start to find himself lying in bed in the Suite Royale of the Scottish Lion Hotel. The pricey sheets and blankets were tangled around him. Flustered and embarrassed, he sat up and looked around to orient himself. Sugarman scowled impatiently at the foot of the bed. Rumpled sheets and silk pajamas mercifully concealed Harry's arousal. He blinked the sleep from his eyes.

"About time!" Sugarman announced. He stomped across the bedroom and pulled open the curtains. Harsh sunlight flooded the room. Harry winced and raised a hand

to shield himself from the glare. The bright light exorcised
the lingering aftereffects of his dream. He threw off the bedclothes and dropped his feet onto the carpet. A custom-
made cushion, which he slept on to reduce the pain from his
injured kidney, rested amidst the disordered sheets.

"What time is it?" he demanded.

Sugarman consulted his pocket watch. "Nine o'clock."

"What?" Harry exclaimed. "You let me sleep till nine
when I'm in training?" He had maintained a rigorous exercise routine for years now, to remain in peak physical condition. He trained constantly, no matter where in the world
he was. His life literally depended on it. "Get yourself a
louder bell, Mr. Sugarman!"

.   .   .

His hair still wet from the shower, Harry joined Sugarman
in the elevator. His sweaty pajamas had been exchanged for
a fresh suit of clothes. Sugarman double-checked his watch
as he recited their itinerary for the morning, as displayed
upon a clipboard.

" 'Gentlemen' of the press, nine thirty. Worshipful
Company of Locksmiths, ten thirty. St. Andrew's Orphanage, noon." He glanced up from his notes. "Want you to
donate a bunch of shoes to the kids."

Sure. Why not? Harry had always made a point of supporting orphanages and children's hospitals wherever he
toured. He often saw to it that blocks of free tickets were
distributed to crippled children and orphans. When he was
a child, his own family had often depended on the charity

of others, so he had always been a soft touch where kids were concerned. *What's a few hundred shoes?*

A framed mirror hung on the wall facing the elevator. Harry frowned at his hair, which was plastered damply to his scalp. He tried to fluff it up with his fingers even as the doors started to close. Just before they shut completely, he caught a glimpse of a furtive figure flitting past toward the empty suite. He recognized the juvenile skulker instantly.

It was Benji.

.   .   .

The girl scampered along the corridor toward Houdini's suite. She stopped outside the door, then glanced up and down the length of the hallway to see if anyone was watching. *Looks like the coast is clear,* she thought. *Just like we planned.*

She rapped lightly on the door, which was ever so slightly ajar. "It's all right, Mam," she whispered in her designated role as lookout. From what she'd overheard, Houdini and his manager had a full day ahead of them. "He's going to be ages."

A firm hand, descending upon her shoulder, contradicted her. Swallowing hard, she looked up guiltily into the stern face of Houdini, who towered over her like an avenging angel. He held a finger to his lips. Benji gulped again. She knew she should call out to her mother, warn her of Houdini's return, but she didn't dare say a word. Mr. Sugarman loomed ominously behind his client. He looked even crosser than Houdini. Benji knew she could expect no mercy from that quarter. Mr. Sugarman probably hadn't forgiven her for throwing up on him yesterday.

That's it, she realized bleakly. Her heart sank all the way down to the basement. *We're buggered but good.*

. . .

Inside the suite, confident that Houdini would not be returning anytime soon, Mary crouched next to the intriguing steamer trunk she had discovered on her previous clandestine search of Houdini's rooms. Instead of a maid's uniform, she wore a new frock and cardigan she had filched from McTavish's dressing rooms. Now that she and Mr. Houdini had been formally introduced, she didn't expect a white cap and apron would fool him anymore.

The trunk still rested at the foot of Houdini's bed. Alas, its sturdy lock was proving harder to open than the door to the Suite Royale. She sorted through a ring of skeleton keys, looking for one that might do the trick. She had tried three keys already, but the lock continued to defeat her efforts. Houdini's initials were engraved above the lock, taunting her. At this rate, she'd never find out what the trunk was hiding.

Come on, you devilish mechanism! I haven't got all day!

She jabbed a fourth key into the lock and gave it a twist. Her ears listened in vain for a satisfying click. The lid of the chest refused to budge.

Bloody hell!

Suddenly, she heard the hallway door swing open. She sprang to her feet, hiding the key ring behind her back only seconds before Houdini appeared in the doorway. His handsome face looked brooding. He scowled at her in disillusionment. Sugarman stood behind him, his pudgy hand resting heavily on Benji's shoulder. "Sorry, Mam," her daughter said contritely. Frightened blue eyes pleaded for forgiveness. "I—"

Houdini slammed the door in Benji's face before she could offer any more apologies or excuses. Despite herself, Mary flinched at the bang of the door. She found herself alone in the bedroom with Houdini. He stepped forward and held out his watch chain. A tiny golden key dangled from the chain.

"Wanna look inside Pandora's box? Take a peek at the real Houdini?" he asked bitterly. He offered her the key. "All yours. No psychic gifts required."

Caught red-handed, Mary turned away. She couldn't meet his eyes.

"No?" he asked. "You disappoint me. Here's me thinking you was the genuine article, solid gold through and through."

For a few seconds, Mary considered throwing in the towel. It seemed as though her play for the $10,000 prize had come to an untimely end. But something in her refused to surrender just yet. Her back to the trunk, she secreted the keys in the folds of her skirt, taking care to keep them from jangling against each other. *Maybe I can still brazen this out,* she thought, *if I just think quickly enough.*

"I was embarrassed to ask," she said sheepishly. Her

cheeks blushed. "I just needed something from you . . . a personal item, a little token, maybe a handkerchief. That's all."

Houdini eyed her warily, seemingly torn between hope and suspicion. Mary sensed that he desperately wanted to believe in her, although she wasn't quite sure why. Was it just that he was determined to carry out his grand psychic experiment, or was there something about her that he couldn't let go of? Something unique?

"It helps me channel the energy, you see," she murmured by way of explanation. Was he buying this at all? "The psychic energy."

His innate skepticism got the better of him. " 'Psychic energy'?" He snorted in disbelief. "You can't do better than that? I've seen hundreds of mediums, crystal gazers, palmists, and spirit guides, and you know what, Mrs. McGarvie? Till somebody proves me wrong, it's all *moonshine*! Con artists and cheap chiselers out to fleece poor, grieving folks looking for a little peace of mind!"

"So that's what this whole charade is all about?" she accused him. Her voice adopted a wounded tone, as though deeply offended by his words. "Proving 'the Great Houdini' wrong?"

Taken off guard by her counterattack, he backed off considerably. A hint of chagrin appeared upon his face. His voice softened somewhat as he awkwardly returned the key to his vest pocket. "I wasn't referring to you personally, Mrs. McGarvie."

I should hope not, she thought sarcastically. She had him on the ropes now. Maybe she wasn't out of this game just yet.

She dabbed at her eyes, feigning hurt feelings.

Houdini fell for it, hook, line, and sinker. He plucked a neatly pressed white handkerchief from his top pocket and humbly offered it to Mary. "To help your psychic energy."

Mary accepted the handkerchief, but she wasn't about to let him off the hook. It was important to keep him on the defensive. "Ten thousand dollars doesn't mean that much to you, does it?" she said defiantly. "It's all just a game."

"Doesn't mean that much?" He objected vigorously to her characterization of him. He gestured forcefully at his king-size bed. "When I was a kid, we used to sleep seven in a bed half that size. My father was a learned man, a great scholar, but he could never make a living in America. I had to go to work at eight years old to help support my family. Trust me, Harry Houdini knows what it means to be cold and hungry and without a dime."

"The difference is, you left all of that behind."

Houdini didn't have a ready answer. He hesitated, at a loss for words, while she sniffled and dried her eyes with his monogrammed silk handkerchief. To her surprise, he burst out laughing. He patted the huge, unmade bed.

"This is the latest in 'slumber science,' I'll have you know." An intentionally humorous tone took the piss out of the moment. "Internally sprung, like me!"

Without warning, he bounced onto the bed. The box springs squeaked beneath his weight. Mary couldn't help being reminded of Benji, jumping up and down on one of the beds in their own luxurious suite. She realized that

Houdini was attempting to break the tension between them by hijacking the scene.

Which means I won.

She relaxed, glad to let Houdini try to get back in her good graces instead of the other way around. A smile came unbidden to her lips. She had to admit he had a way about him; no wonder audiences loved him all across the globe. It would be easy to fall for such a man, if one was inclined to do so.

Watch yourself, Mary, she warned herself. *You're here for the prize money, not a roll in the hay.*

Houdini stopped bouncing. He looked over at her with a nostalgic look upon his face. "You never sleep that peaceful again, do you? Don't think I've slept right since I was nine years old."

"Not at all?" Mary leaned against the big brass bedstead, resting her chin and elbows upon the curved metal bars.

"Not a wink," he insisted. "Not since I got a bed to myself."

A throaty laugh escaped her lips. "You'll have to start inviting people in."

Houdini didn't laugh back. He swung his legs over until he was sitting on the edge of the bed. A wistful tone entered his voice.

"You're right," he admitted. "Can't hardly remember the old days. The *real* days. Like it was somebody else's dream."

His melancholy demeanor touched her heart. She was

surprised to find herself feeling sorry for the fabulously wealthy magician. A crazy idea occurred to her. *What the hell?* she thought. *Nobody says I can't cheer the poor bastard up before fleecing him of his cash.*

"You want to see something real, Mr. Houdini?"

CHAPTER FOURTEEN

THE HIGHLAND LADDIE WAS A COZY, WORKING-class pub down by the docks in Leith. Although it was still early in the evening, the pub was already overflowing with booze, smoke, and a boisterous Saturday-night crowd. Sailors and stevedores mingled with laborers from the nearby gasworks. A fiddler tried gallantly to compete with the raucous din of voices. Tipsy dancers attempted a Scottish reel between the packed tables and benches. Barmaids expertly dodged grabby hands as they catered to the thirsty patrons. A drunk tottered unsteadily toward the men's room. Another sot slumped over the bar, drooling onto the counter. Dirty jokes and shrill laughter echoed off the whitewashed stone walls.

The usual, in other words.

Houdini, Mary, and Benji occupied a snug at the back of the pub. The private room offered a degree of privacy, for those who were willing to pay a little extra for their beer. A pane of frosted glass concealed the trio from the inebriated mob beyond. Houdini and Mary sat next to each other in matching wingback chairs. Benji watched them from across a low coffee table. She still wasn't quite sure what they were doing here, or why her mother had spent the whole day giving Houdini a tour of the "real" Edinburgh, from the decrepit granite tenements of the Old Town to the docks of Leith. How did that fit into their plans to con the magician out of his money? And didn't the Great Houdini have a show to put on tonight?

Benji squirmed uncomfortably in her own chair. Something about this outing wasn't sitting right with her. *At least they didn't stick me with Mr. Sugarman again,* she consoled herself. The chubby manager had grumpily declined to join their sightseeing expedition. *But what's wrong with Mam? She's not acting like herself.*

A barmaid brought them their drinks. Two bitters for the adults and an orange soda for Benji. Without hesitation, Houdini gulped down a pint of coal black beer. Benji couldn't believe her eyes. Harry Houdini *never* drank alcohol, and especially not the night of a show. But there he was, smacking his lips and grinning at her mother. Instead of the formal evening wear he wore onstage, he had on a simple tweed jacket and trousers. A felt cap rested on his lap. He wiped the foam from his lips.

"How am I doing?" he asked.

"You could pass for a native," Mam assured him. She laughed warmly, an unfamiliar sound that immediately set Benji's nerves on edge. She had never heard her mother laugh like that before. *Is she just putting on a show for Mr.*

Houdini, Benji wondered, *or is something happening to her?* The Great Houdini could make an elephant disappear into thin air, Benji recalled. Maybe he could also change her mother into a different person?

Benji didn't like the sound of that.

"Mr. Houdini?" A freckle-faced autograph hound invaded the sanctuary of the snug. He thrust a pen and paper at the star. "Mr. Houdini . . . ?"

Houdini graciously signed the pad.

"Thank you, thank you, Mr. Houdini, sir!" The nameless autograph seeker scurried away, clutching his prize. Houdini shrugged and turned back toward Mam.

" 'When in Rome,' that's what my mom always used to say." He smiled fondly. "Wish you could have met her. You'd have got on like a house on fire!"

"Don't go giving away too much about her," Mam cautioned. "They'll say we cheated."

Was that Mam's plan? Benji speculated. *To get Houdini drunk enough to spill the secret message?* Benji wasn't sure that was such a good idea. *Won't he see through us once he sobers up?*

"Cheat? Not me," he insisted cheerfully. "I'm not like them fakers, Mary. Them cheap chiselers." He gave her a playful wink. "I'm like *you,* just trying to earn an honest dollar."

Out of nowhere, a shining silver dollar appeared in his fingers. Mam silently applauded the sleight of hand. Scandalized by this entire soiree, Benji feigned disinterest, but watched his every move. He tossed the coin in the air, caught it, and flipped it onto the back of his hand. His other hand dropped to cover it.

"Heads or tails?" he challenged Mam.

"You choose," she replied.

Houdini nodded, acceding to the request. "Then I choose neither."

He lifted his hand, but the silver dollar was gone. He smiled at Benji, who smiled back despite herself. Mam laughed, then, out of nowhere, produced a coin of her own. A dull copper penny suddenly rested between her finger and thumb.

"My penny for your dollar," she wagered.

Just like Houdini, she tossed it into the air, caught it, then hid it atop the back of her hand. "Heads or tails?"

"You choose!"

Deferring to pick a side, she lifted her hand. Wonder of wonders, the penny had vanished as well. Or had it? With a cheeky smile, she rotated her hand to reveal the missing penny held against her palm by the tip of her thumb.

"Magic," she declared.

"Magic," he agreed, showing her his own hand. Sure enough, the silver dollar was trapped against his own palm in an identical fashion. "Don't you just love it? Used to practice table magic eight hours a day. Card tricks, rope tricks, sleight of hand . . . you name it. Studied locks and handcuffs for five years solid. Used to run ten miles a day, push weights for two hours, bathed in ice water every morning."

Benji tried to imagine going to such extremes just to learn magic tricks. Why would a person do that?

"Couldn't have had much time for anything else," Mam commented wryly.

"I *made* time," he said passionately, suddenly fired up by the memory of all his past trials and accomplishments. "I was 'Ehrich, Prince of the Air'! Told Mama I'd be a flier one day . . . done that! The first man ever to fly a plane Down Under. Told her I'd be a movie star . . . done that! Produced my own hit movie serials. Swore I'd be the greatest escape artist in the world . . . done that! No cell can hold me. Made all my ambitions come true, grabbed my own piece of immortality."

He leaned closer to Mam, his voice low and intimate. "You're okay. You've got your own little piece of immortality right there." He nodded at Benji, who nursed her soda as she pretended to ignore the growing connection between Houdini and her mother. She felt increasingly like a third wheel. Houdini was talking *about* her, not to her. She was just a conversation piece.

"You don't have children, I can tell." Mam heaved a weary sigh. "Make you old before your time."

Benji bristled at the accusation. *Am I really such a burden?*

"That ain't so," Houdini insisted. "You're the living proof." He rose from his chair and bowed theatrically. " 'The Tantalising and Beautiful Princess Kali,' " he recited from memory, completely skipping over Benji's part in the show. She scowled at the omission. "Sounds like a fun act."

"It's hard graft," Mam sighed. "I fail and we starve."

Houdini could do her one better. "I fail and I die."

He casually dropped his hand onto Mam's arm. She didn't protest. They stared deeply into each other's eyes, to the exclusion of all else. Even Benji could sense the electricity between them. She fumed jealously, watching every touch, every movement, every look that passed between the Great Houdini and her mother. It was obvious that they only had eyes for each other. *I might as well be invisible*, she sulked. *How's that for a vanishing act?*

Houdini's hand brushed over Mam's. She shook her head ruefully. "You don't want to get involved with someone like me."

"Well," he replied, "maybe I do."

The front gates of the Theater Royale burst open. Overwhelmed ushers and usherettes, in snappy gold-fringed uniforms, were swept back by an unruly mob of excited ticket-holders. Pouring into the auditorium and galleries, they competed for the best seats, vaulting and diving between the rows in their eagerness to secure the seats closest to the stage. It was a full house and then some, standing room only. Over two thousand spectators had shown up to experience the Great Houdini in person. Rave reviews and word of mouth regarding the previous night's performance had stoked the crowd's enthusiasm to a fever pitch. The enormous theater's maximum capacity was being pushed to the limit . . . and beyond. Generous bribes assured that the fire marshals looked the other way. The orchestra started warming up in the pit.

Now all we need is the Great Houdini, Sugarman thought. He peered out from the wings at the teeming horde filling the auditorium. Backstage, stagehands readied the lights and props. Franz and James performed a final safety check on the Chinese Water Torture Cell, which was already filled to the brim with fresh water. Harry usually insisted on checking the cell and ankle clamps himself, but Sugarman hadn't laid eyes on his tardy client in hours.

Acid churned in his gut, eliciting a wince of pain. He glanced worriedly at his watch. It was seven thirty-five, less than half an hour to curtain. Sugarman shook his head in disbelief. It wasn't like Harry to call it this close. The Great Houdini *never* missed a performance. In the past, he had always demanded to go on with the show, no matter how sick or exhausted or injured he was. Torn ligaments, ruptured blood vessels, a broken ankle, an upset stomach . . . nothing had stopped him from giving the audience what it had paid for. As far as Sugarman could remember, the only time Harry had *ever* canceled a performance was right after his mother had died.

Has he lost his mind completely? Sugarman fretted. Bad enough that Harry had taken a rain check on today's itinerary in order to play hooky with Mary McGarvie and her brat; Sugarman had spent the entire day making apologies for Harry, while simultaneously arranging for the delivery of three hundred pairs of new shoes to the orphanage. Now Harry's seeming obsession with that scheming Scottish tart was threatening tonight's sizable box office, not to mention inviting an ugly scandal.

Damn it all! Sugarman was at his wit's end where the problem of Mrs. McGarvie was concerned. For a few glorious moments this morning, he had thought the matter resolved when he and Harry had caught the conniving witch snooping about the Suite Royale. But somehow she had turned things around and got her hooks into him even deeper. *Maybe I should have gone with them today,* Sugarman thought, second-guessing himself. *Just to keep an eye on things.*

Dammit, though, he was supposed to be Harry's manager, not his chaperone!

Over by the Torture Cell, Franz Kukol shot Sugarman a quizzical look. No doubt the two assistants were even more baffled by Harry's continuing absence than he was. Sugarman shrugged and threw up his hands to indicate that he didn't have a clue. He anxiously consulted his pocket watch again.

Seven forty-five.

Acid crawled up his esophagus, searing his chest from the inside out. He would have killed for a large glass of milk and a couple of digestive biscuits to settle his stomach. The curtain was scheduled to rise in just fifteen minutes. Already the audience was getting impatient. He could hear them shifting restlessly in their seats, fiddling with their program books. The orchestra started playing the overture.

Morrie Sugarman looked despairingly in the direction of Houdini's vacant dressing room.

Where the hell are you, Harry?

Hand in hand, Mary and Houdini ran through the Princes
Street Gardens. A full moon peeked through the cloudy
night sky. She was surprised to find herself giggling like a
schoolgirl, caught up in some madcap romantic adventure.
Houdini's strong hand warmed hers. Her heart was pounding in her chest. Her cheeks were flushed. Her long black
hair, which had come loose somewhere along the way,
streamed past her shoulders. Benji sprinted circles around
the two adults. Glancing back over her shoulder, Mary saw
the majestic battlements of Edinburgh Castle looming behind them, lit up like something out of a fairy tale. It was as
if she were seeing the familiar castle for the first time. She
had never realized just how beautiful it was.

How have I overlooked that all these years?

The autumn night was cool and breezy. The open overcoat flapped behind her as she raced beside Houdini, who
seemed just as exhilarated as she was. His stamina was amazing; he wasn't even breathing hard. His boyish exuberance
was infectious.

"Where are we going?" she asked breathlessly.

"To the edge!" His eyes aglow with excitement, he
stared upward at something directly ahead. Mary followed
his gaze—and felt a sudden thrill of both fear and anticipation.

The Scott Monument was a soaring tribute to Sir Walter Scott, a native son of Edinburgh's and the legendary author of such classic novels as *Ivanhoe* and *Rob Roy*. Over two
hundred feet tall, it was the largest monument ever to be
erected in honor of a writer. The imposing Gothic tower,

with its ribbed vaults and flying buttresses, was built of local
Binnie shale from the nearby quarries in Linlithgow. Over
the years, the oily shale had acquired a heavy coating of
thick black soot, so that the monument boasted a dark and
somewhat forbidding appearance. Gargoyles and grotesques
adorned the upper reaches of the tower, while dozens of
miniature statuettes, representing characters from Scott's
beloved poetry and prose, resided in separate niches all
along the monument's exterior. Stained-glass windows on
the first floor vividly depicted historic scenes and symbols
from Scottish history. Four heavy stone columns supported
the tower, with a huge marble statue of Scott himself, resting in the space between the columns. The larger-than-life
figure appeared to be hard at work, seated at his desk composing some new epic with an old-fashioned quill pen. His
faithful hound, Maida, rested at his feet.

What are we doing here? Mary wondered, admiring the
Gothic grandeur of the monument. She glanced over at
Houdini's beaming face. *He's not thinking what I think he's think-
ing, is he?*

Benji had spotted their apparent destination as well.
Her adolescent face filled with glee. The girl had been oddly
sulky back at the pub, but had perked up somewhat during
their impromptu dash through the park. Now she looked
almost delirious. Her blue eyes shone like the Chinese lanterns back at the music hall.

Mary couldn't blame her. She was feeling distinctly
giddy herself.

More of Houdini's magic?

Leading the way, Benji ran pell-mell down a tree-lined avenue toward the monument, only to come to a sudden halt. Her face fell as all three of them were confronted by a tall wrought-iron gate topped with painful-looking spikes. A heavy metal chain and padlock sealed the gates shut. It seemed as though their nocturnal adventure had reached its end. Then Benji clearly remembered whom she was with; she gazed up at Houdini hopefully.

His eyes twinkled in the moonlight. Letting go of Mary's hand, he stepped forward and took hold of the lock. His back hid his precise manipulations from view, but the rusty lock quickly surrendered to his magic touch. The padlock flipped open. The chain fell to the ground. The daunting gate swung open before them.

Very slick, Mary thought. Was there nothing the man's nimble fingers couldn't undo? *The police should be thankful he's such a successful performer, 'cause he would have made an unstoppable thief!*

Mischievous grins broke out across their faces as they scampered past the sculpted author into the murky recesses of the silent monument itself. A cigarette lighter appeared in Houdini's hand; the small blue flame cast dancing shadows upon the dark slate walls. A spiral staircase led up toward the pinnacle of the tower. Moonlight filtered through the stained-glass windows above them. Moss clung to the sides of the weathered stone steps.

Holding the lighter aloft, Houdini took off up the staircase, with Benji right on his heels. Mary hesitated, momentarily daunted by the formidable climb ahead. She remembered reading somewhere that it was some 287 steps to the top of the monument. Did she really want to do this?

Why the hell not? Laughing at her own foolhardiness, she chased after the flickering blue flame, taking the steps two at a time. Three sets of racing footsteps echoed within the sepulchral confines of the tower as she raced on up and around the long spiral staircase. Within minutes she had caught up with Benji, but Houdini remained elusively out of sight. All she could see was the incandescent glow of his lighter circling above her until it finally disappeared at the top of the stairs. Mary and Benji sprinted the rest of the way in the dark. By the time they reached the top and emerged out onto an open stone deck, they were both panting and giggling. A stiff wind cooled their sweaty faces.

The top of the monument offered a panoramic view of the city and its surroundings, which was spread out beneath them like a magic carpet. Mary could see all the way from the New Town to Canongate. Moonlight shimmered upon the rippling waters of the Firth of Forth, which stretched across the harbor to Fife. Horse carts and motorcars looked like children's toys from this lofty vantage point. The vertiginous drop to the gardens below filled her with alarm. Only a low stone parapet separated them from a fatal plunge.

"Benji!" she blurted. "Stay away from the edge!"

Thankfully, her daughter didn't need telling where that was concerned. Gasping out loud, her eyes wide with fright, Benji held on to a handrail for all she was worth. White knuckles testified to the strength of her grip. Mary relaxed a little, confident that, for once, the headstrong girl wouldn't be taking any unnecessary chances. *She's not day-dreaming now.*

But where was Houdini?

"The edge of the world!" he called out from somewhere above her. Her heart skipped a beat as she looked upward to see Houdini standing barefoot atop a carved stone gargoyle. The leering sculpture, which served as a drainage spout, jutted out over the edge of the parapet, hundreds of feet above the spiked fence below. He posed confidently at the brink of the precipice, seemingly unconcerned by the peril he was in. One loose stone, one misstep, and he would instantly plunge to his death.

This is no trick, Mary thought, appalled. There were no trapdoors or illusions. The danger was all too genuine. She tore her gaze away from the fearless American daredevil to check on her daughter. Utterly terrified, Benji's face was white as a ghost's.

This is for real.

"Ladies and gentlemen," he announced loudly, as though addressing an invisible audience, "I am to be suspended from the very roof of the heavens with neither net nor harness!" He threw out his arms expansively. "Only a five-strand rope will prevent me from plummeting earthward and dashing my brains to a thousand pieces!"

Mary couldn't look away. Benji looked as if she was about to be sick.

He raised his arms like a man attempting a swallow dive. "And may God have mercy upon my immortal soul!"

"No!" Mary cried out. She frantically reached out for him. *Don't jump!*

Houdini stayed right where he was, poised atop the gargoyle. As if by magic, the wind let up. The heavy clouds dispersed, exposing a glittering sea of stars. The tops of the lower turrets framed him like two sides of a stage. Smiling, he turned toward her and held out his hand.

Mary stared at his outstretched hand. *This can't really be happening.*

Can it?

Caught in his spell, she ventured up onto the parapet. Benji gasped in shock behind her, but Mary barely heard it. Houdini waited for her, his arms outstretched. He leaned forward precariously and she dashed forward to grab on to him. He laughed joyously as she wrapped her arms around his sturdy torso. His own arms enfolded her. They clung together at the edge of a two-hundred-foot drop. His laughter died away as they stared into each other's eyes. Mary was only one step away from falling—in more ways than one.

"It's really dangerous," she advised him.

"A foot in both worlds," he agreed.

Intent on each other, neither of them saw Benji's face harden. Her clenched fists tightened around the cold metal handrail.

All right, Mary thought. *You win.* She stopped fighting it. For so many years she had kept her wounded heart under lock and key, but that hadn't stopped the Great Houdini from getting past all her defenses just as easily as he walked through solid brick walls. She pressed herself against him, feeling the steely frame beneath his casual attire. The masculine scent of him filled her lungs. The walls around her heart vanished into thin air.

She was his.

"Stop time, someone," he murmured softly, for her ears only. Their lips were only inches apart, their breaths mingling. Despite the autumn chill, Mary felt warm all over. Letting go of his waist with one arm, she raised her right hand to his mouth. Her fingers slid between his lips to explore the hot, wet mysteries beyond. He nursed avidly on her fingertips, teasing them with his tongue. She gasped out loud, finding it hard to breathe all of a sudden. A heady sensation threatened her balance.

Behind her, only a few yards away, Benji watched the pair with jealous eyes.

Mary embraced Houdini more tightly, molding her soft body against his sinewy contours. Her mouth found his and she kissed him hungrily.

He pulled away.

To her astonishment, Houdini gently disentangled himself from her arms, as if she were just another challenge to escape from. The night instantly lost its magic. The clouds rolled back, obscuring the stars. Mary felt tricked and humiliated. *What does he want from me?* Her temper flared as she glared at Houdini, fighting back angry tears. She had been ready to give him everything, only to be refused for no reason. Her fists clenched at her sides. *What the hell is he after?*

"Guess I wanna make it last," he said cryptically.

He stepped back from her, out between the tapered ears of the stone gargoyle. Without warning, he spun and leapt into space! Gravity seized him and he fell out of sight.

"No!" Mary let out an ear-piercing scream, the pain of his rejection instantly superseded by pure terror. She threw herself down onto the parapet, expecting to hear his body crash against the ground at any second. *Why?* she thought frantically. *Why did he do it?* Peering fearfully over the edge of the precipice, she braced herself for the gruesome sight of his broken and mangled body lying at the foot of the monument, two hundred feet below. No one, not even the Great Houdini, could survive a fall like that.

But instead of a corpse, she saw Houdini smiling back up at her—from a second parapet merely ten feet below her. He lay on his back, looking quite pleased with himself. Amusement glinted in his eyes as he casually lit a cigarette and blew smoke circles into the air between them. The vaporous rings drifted out over the city below.

Oh, thank God! Mary thought. An overwhelming sense of relief swept away her anger and confusion, at least for the moment. *He's still alive. I haven't lost him.* Gazing down at Houdini, she was overcome by the sheer ridiculousness of the moment. A sudden burst of laughter escaped her lips. The man was impossible, but she hadn't had so much fun in years. *What crazy stunt is he going to pull next?*

Benji came over to see what her mother was chuckling at. Curiosity seemed to conquer the girl's fear of heights as she crept to the edge of the parapet and peeked down at Houdini. Mary was momentarily startled to find Benji at her side; to be honest, she had almost forgotten that her daughter was here. Houdini waved at Benji, but she didn't wave back. Her face held a distinctly sullen expression.

What's the matter with her? Mary wondered. The strangely tight-lipped youngster was like a stranger to her. She couldn't begin to guess what was going through her daughter's head right now. *When did she get so moody all of a sudden?*

.   .   .

The natives were getting restless. Hiding in the wings, Sugarman heard the impatient audience growing more hostile by the moment. Angry voices cried out for Houdini, while the orchestra literally played for time. "Start the bloody show!" someone called out from the gallery. A chorus of additional cries echoed the sentiment. A party in the front rows started stomping their feet, and pretty soon the entire audience joined in. The vast auditorium rocked beneath the pounding feet. "We want Houdini!"

You're not the only ones, Sugarman thought. He consulted his watch for perhaps the thousandth time in the last few hours. It was eight thirty-four; Harry was over a half hour late, something absolutely unprecedented in Sugarman's experience. Had an accident befallen Harry, or had he simply run off for some sordid tryst with Mary McGarvie? *I knew she was trouble.* Having his apprehensions vindicated gave him no pleasure at all. A fresh spurt of acid ate away at the lining of his stomach. *Why couldn't Harry have proven me wrong?*

Backstage, the theater owner caught Sugarman's eye. The distraught Scotsman pointed frantically at his own watch. His panicky eyes demanded that Sugarman do something, before the audience rioted and tore the entire theater apart. Sugarman wondered if the Great Houdini would ever get a booking in Edinburgh again—or anywhere else in the United Kingdom.

He realized that they could stall no longer. If Harry hadn't arrived yet, there was no guarantee that he would be making an appearance anytime soon. Heaven only knew when and if Harry would ever return. The moment had come to accept the unthinkable—and suffer the consequences.

Here goes nothing.

He swallowed hard and strolled reluctantly out onto the stage. The agitated crowd, who didn't know him from Adam, were not inclined to accept him as an adequate substitute for the Great Houdini. Immediately sensing that something was amiss, they unleashed a deafening volley of boos and catcalls. Obscene gestures assailed him. Sugarman's nerve faltered before the angry chorus. He would sooner have faced a swarm of howling ghosts and mediums.

"Ladies and gentlemen!" he shouted over the tumult. He raised his trembling hands in supplication. "I beg your indulgence! The Maestro Houdini has been taken sick with stress-related exhaustion!"

A glass from the theater's canteen smashed against the gilded arch of the proscenium. Sugarman flinched at the crash, stepping backward to avoid a spray of flying glass. Furious shouts, peanuts, and popcorn bombarded him. He backed away from the footlights, retreating from the crowd's violent displeasure. He held up his hands once more in a vain attempt to quiet the mutinous audience.

"There will be a full refund available at the box office by noon tomorrow, ladies and gentlemen!" he assured the irate audience, but the promise did little to mollify the disappointed crowd. The loss of tonight's considerable receipts added injury to insult. "Mr. Houdini sends his deepest regrets."

An egg splattered against his face. Sugarman blinked and sputtered, spitting out pieces of broken eggshell. He irritably wiped the raw yolk and shell fragments from his face with a silk handkerchief. The sticky mess dripped onto his tailored three-piece suit. The long-suffering manager decided he'd had enough.

"Screw you!" he shouted back at the crowd. "And screw him, too!"

He stormed off the stage, fleeing a barrage of flying debris. Eggs, bottles, tomatoes, and other detritus pelted the stage. The strident boos of the audience followed him backstage.

You owe me, Harry, he thought. *Big-time.*

CHAPTER FIFTEEN

———

THE CHINESE WATER TORTURE CELL WAITED
silently upon the stage. Vacant seats and balconies faced the
fiendishly ingenious death trap. The Theater Royale was
empty, its audience and employees long since departed.
Darkness cloaked the many nooks and crannies of the deserted auditorium. Only a single spotlight, perhaps left on
by mistake, shone upon the abandoned Torture Cell. Watery shadows rippled across the floor of the stage.

Benji crept down the aisle toward the stage. Her stealthy
footsteps reverberated throughout the slumbering theater,
but attracted no attention, not even from the night watch-
man out in the lobby. She glanced nostalgically at the front-
row seat she had occupied only two nights before. Passing
by the empty orchestra pit, she clambered onto the stage,
which was at least twice the size of the one she had shared
with her mother at McTavish's Music Hall. Houdini's initials gleamed brightly upon the floor.

A stepladder, left behind by Houdini's assistants, led to

the top of the Torture Cell. Unable to resist the invitation, Benji climbed up the ladder. The mahogany lid of the tank was set firmly in place. She crawled out onto the lid on her hands and knees. The height of the vertical cell, some five feet tall, was nothing compared to the lofty altitude she had achieved atop the Scott Monument earlier that night. A frown came to her face as she recalled Houdini embracing her mother upon the parapet. *It's not fair*, she thought. *I saw him first.*

A trapdoor opened beneath her. Benji plunged into the still water below. Before she could take one last gulp of air, she was immersed in the watery depths of the Chinese Water Torture Cell. The trapdoor snapped shut overhead, locking her in. Her cap flew off her head. Bubbles sprayed from her nostrils as she flailed about in distress, holding on desperately to whatever breath she had left. Her fists pounded uselessly against the thick glass walls of the cell.

She was trapped!

A peculiar sound, like the panting of animals, penetrated her prison. Peering out through the transparent glass, she glimpsed a pair of figures thrashing together right outside the tank. It took her a second to recognize her mother and Houdini, locked in carnal embrace. His bare skin was soaking wet, as if he had just emerged from the cell himself. Princess Kali's wispy garments barely clothed her mother's writhing body. She was down on all fours, her eyes glazed over. He jabbed at her from behind, just like the monkeys at the zoo, while muzzling at Mam's neck. Her mother's face was contorted almost beyond recognition. Unintelligible grunts and moans burst from her lips. Houdini's blazing eyes bulged from their sockets. The veins stood out upon his neck. His face was flushed and perspiring as he feverishly groped her mother's heaving breasts. A loose pair of handcuffs dangled from his wrist.

So *this* is what they had both wanted all along!

Shocked and betrayed, Benji briefly forgot her own dire predicament. Then her nose bumped against the thick glass pane, reminding her that she was still caught inside the Torture Cell. Her cheeks bulged as she struggled to hold on to the last of her air. She hammered at the glass, trying to get her mother's attention, but the frenzied lovers were oblivious to her plight. *Help me, Mam!* she pleaded silently. *I'm right here! Look at me!*

Her lungs burned. She clenched her teeth to keep from inhaling the water all around her. Kicking off from the bottom of the tank, she shoved against the heavy lid, which stubbornly refused to budge. An icy chill came over her as she sank helplessly back to the bottom of the cell. *I'm going to die*, she realized. She was not the Great Houdini; there would be no miraculous escape for her. *I'm drowning right in front of Houdini and my own mother!*

The last thing she would ever hear were the animal cries of their passion.

It's not fair!

An indistinct shape rose up behind her: an angel with flowing red hair. Gossamer, white robes swirled about the heavenly figure. Desperately scraping at the glass, Benji was only vaguely aware of the angel's presence. She couldn't hold her breath any longer. She was all out of air. Bubbles exploded from her lips. Cold water poured down her throat, choking her.

Scarlet locks spread out behind the angel's head like a halo. He reached out for her . . .

Choking, Benji came awake. She sat up in her bed, looking around in surprise. *Thank heavens*, she thought. *It was just a dream.* She eagerly inhaled the perfumed air as she glanced around the darkened hotel suite. The first glimmers of dawn entered the rooms through a pair of open French doors.

She spied her mother standing on the balcony in her nightdress, smoking a cigarette. The rosy sunlight silhouetted her body. A dreamy smile played upon her lips. She had a far-off look in her eyes, one Benji had never before seen. Something was changing her mother. Happiness? *Love?* Benji found the latter hard to believe. Her mother was the least romantic person she had ever met: hardheaded, practical, her feet firmly planted upon the ground. How many times had her mother scolded her for keeping her head in the clouds? Mary McGarvie had no patience for anything as foolishly sentimental as love. Or she didn't used to. Ever since Houdini had entered their lives, Benji didn't even know who her mother was anymore.

Talk about a magic trick!

Mary turned to see Benji watching her. Flicking her cigarette over the edge of the balcony, she joined her daughter in the bed. "Not asleep?"

Vivid images from her dream forced their way into

Benji's mind: Mam and Houdini, fornicating like monkeys in a zoo. She examined her mother's face, looking for evidence that her dream wasn't entirely false. *Just because I dreamt it doesn't mean it isn't true.*

"What happened," she asked suspiciously, "with him?"

Mam didn't bother pretending that she didn't know what Benji meant. "Nothing happened 'with him.'" She looked sadly at Benji, no doubt regretting that her daughter could not have enjoyed a more sheltered childhood. "Harry's a gentleman."

So it was "Harry" now, not "Mr. Houdini." She eyed her mother warily, not entirely sure she believed her. Benji found herself hoping that some ulterior motive was behind her mother's behavior last night, but feared that such was not the case.

"So you didn't get the key, then?" Benji prompted. Maybe this was all a ploy to unlock the secrets of Houdini's steamer trunk?

A long pause did little to allay Benji's fears.

"Not sure I care so much about the key anymore," her mother confessed finally.

Benji couldn't believe her ears. There was no denying it anymore. Her mother had fallen hard for the Great Houdini, and he was maybe falling for her. Benji felt left out again. *It's all about them now,* she thought spitefully. *I'm just in the way.*

She rolled over, turning her back on her mother. She scrunched up her face, refusing to let her mother or anyone else see her cry. Heartbroken, for reasons she wasn't even entirely clear about, she fired back the only way she knew how.

"We're in it for the money, remember," she said harshly. "Not for a roll in the hay like you did with my dad."

She closed her eyes and pretended to go to sleep.

CHAPTER SIXTEEN

——

Sugarman gave Harry hell.

"You dumped on your audience, Harry! You *never* do that . . . rule number one! You taught me that." The incensed manager chewed out his client in the privacy of the suite's king-size bathroom. The memory of last night's debacle was still fresh in his mind. "I'm out there in front of *your* audience, ordinary people who paid good money to see you!"

He paused to see if he was getting through to the other man. A cast-iron exercise bar had been set up at the far end of the bathroom. Stripped to the waist, Harry did chin-ups upon the bar, ignoring his manager's diatribe. His apparent indifference infuriated Sugarman.

"Goddamn it. Twenty years together, Harry, twenty years and God knows how many shows in how many countries, from Sydney to Berlin, and this has never happened . . . never, not once!"

He hurled a newspaper at Harry's feet, reciting the front-page headline as he did so. " 'Harry Houdini Disappears!' " A second newspaper smacked against the floor. " 'Harry Houdini Misses Show!' "

The *Sunday Post, Scottish Sunday Mirror, Scotsman, Daily Record, Herald & Advertiser* . . . the newspapers landed in a heap upon the tiles.

"Harry Houdini screws up!"

Sugarman extracted a telegram from his vest pocket and fumbled with his eyeglasses.

"Harry, this is from your wife! Remember you have a wife?" He waved the telegram in Harry's face. "She's wiring you twice a day and you're going gaga over some shiksa with a cute line in chat!"

The telegram seemed to have no effect on Harry. He mutely wrapped up his chin-up routine and commenced his daily stretches. He bent over and touched his toes in a way Sugarman couldn't have managed if his life had depended on it. Harry's face was a stony mask, betraying no hint of what was going through his mind. He was in another world.

"Harry, this whole 'psychic' thing . . . it's taking over!" Sugarman was near apoplectic; saliva sprayed from his mouth as he shouted at Harry. "You hear me? It's taking over!"

Why didn't Harry realize the danger he was in?

.   .   .

Benji heard Mr. Sugarman yelling at Houdini as she pushed the door open a crack and slipped inside the Suite Royale. As quietly as she could, she closed the door behind her. The manager's loud voice helped to drown out the sound of the lock clicking back into place.

"We've got to sort things out, Harry," Mr. Sugarman scolded his client. "We've got to get our priorities in order."

Benji kept a close eye on the bathroom as she tiptoed through the suite. With luck, the angry manager would be berating Houdini for a while, maybe even long enough for her to find what she was looking for and get out before either of the two men noticed she was here. She quickly scanned the room. Her eyes widened hopefully at the sight of Houdini's waistcoat draped over the back of an elaborately carved antique chair. She darted over to the chair, moving quickly so as not to be spotted by the quarreling men. She offered up a silent prayer of thanksgiving as she escaped their line of sight once more. Her nimble fingers searched the waistcoat, but she could not find Houdini's watch chain, nor the tiny golden key her mother had described.

Where is it? she wondered anxiously. Mam's "psychic demonstration" was scheduled for later today. Time was running out, and they still had no clue as to what the secret message hidden in the envelope was. Their hopes of claiming the $10,000 prize were rapidly slipping away. *This is all Mam's fault,* she thought resentfully. Her mother should have concentrated on getting the key from Houdini, instead of dallying with him in the moonlight. *It's because of her we're in this fix.*

"Okay, Harry!" Mr. Sugarman bellowed. "I quit!"

He stormed out of the bathroom, forcing Benji to swiftly duck behind the chair. She crouched down low and held absolutely still. She didn't even breathe for fear of alerting Mr. Sugarman to her presence. From the sound of things, the cantankerous manager was *not* in a good mood.

"You wanna play poker with me, Morrie?"

Houdini appeared in the doorway, wearing only a pair of cotton drawers. Looking not at all chastened by his manager's lecture, he sternly called the other man's bluff.

"First, I'm 'pushing it to the wire.' Now 'the psychic thing's taking over.' Who put you in charge of the act, Mr. Sugarman? 'Bout time you got *your* priorities sorted."

Mr. Sugarman sighed and stopped in his tracks. He grudgingly turned around to face his unapologetic client. Houdini opened a closet and took out a heavy canvas straitjacket, of the sort used to restrain violent lunatics. Benji shuddered at the sight of the intimidating garment. Houdini's arms disappeared into the jacket's overlong sleeves, which were sewn up at the ends to confine his hands. He crossed his arms atop his chest like an Egyptian mummy.

"Hey," he called out to Sugarman. "Strap me up, will ya?"

Frowning, the manager grabbed the loose ends of the sleeves and knotted them together behind Houdini's back. Leather straps and metal buckles tightened the straitjacket's hold on its captive. Houdini winced as Sugarman pulled the last strap maybe a little too tight.

He did not complain.

"I'm practicing one of my old stunts, one without any risks." Sarcasm tinged Houdini's voice. "That'll sure pull in the crowds, Mr. Sugarman!"

The manager shook his head wearily, obviously tired of fighting with Houdini. He trudged toward the door without looking back. Grimacing, he clutched his chest in pain. Benji guessed that his heartburn was acting up again.

"You're walking like an old man," Houdini mocked him. "Put your shoulders back, ya mustache pete!"

Mustache pete? The slangy American term flew over Benji's head.

Mr. Sugarman didn't even bother to defend himself. He let himself out.

Abandoned without a word, Houdini's face darkened. He stepped back into the bathroom and slammed the door shut.

Benji let out a sigh of relief. Nobody had spotted her! She popped up from behind the chair and resumed her search for the key. Her gaze gravitated toward the locked steamer trunk, before turning toward the suite's various closets and chests of drawers. If not with his suit, where could the key be? *Maybe in the walk-in closet?*

A sudden gasp of pain startled her, almost giving her a heart attack. The agonized cry came from the bathroom. Benji barely recognized Houdini's voice in the hoarse utterance. She stared in alarm at the bathroom door. A pane of frosted glass showed her only the blurry outline of a writhing figure on the other side of the door. Last night's disturbing nightmare came rushing back into her mind:

Houdini mounting her mother, their sweaty bodies thrashing against each other. Animal pants and moans. Faces contorted by pas-

sion. Perspiration glistening upon their skins. Houdini nuzzling on her mother's neck. His hands kneading her sequined breasts . . .

Benji knew she should just keep looking for the key. Whatever was happening in the bathroom was none of her business. But, as further gasps escaped the bathroom, each one more heart-wrenching than the one before, she couldn't stay away. What if Houdini had injured himself? What if he needed her help to escape that ghastly straitjacket? She crept to the bathroom door and peered through the keyhole. *Just a quick peek*, she promised herself, *to make sure he's all right.*

Her unblinking eye bore witness to an astounding sight:

Still trapped in the straitjacket, Houdini hung upside down from an iron bar held up by a solid metal frame. His entire body convulsed as he struggled to escape the constricting garment. Suspended above the floor, his back to the door, he wriggled and squirmed inside the canvas restraint. A pair of leather restraints were clamped around his ankles. His dark hair dangled from his scalp. His face was turned away from her, so that all she could see was the back of his head. Muscular legs stretched above his pinioned torso. The arms of the jacket remained tightly knotted behind him.

Benji couldn't believe her eyes. There was no trickery here, nor any glitzy showbiz trappings. No spotlight illuminated Houdini's battle. No orchestra played over his anguished gasps and grunts of exertion. There was only sweat and pain and raw physical determination. Gritting his teeth against the excruciating torment, Houdini somehow managed to wrench a single arm free. A loud pop, like a gunshot, assaulted Benji's ears as the dislocated limb snapped back into its socket. A mere heartbeat later, he duplicated the arduous feat with his other arm. Tugging the jacket downward over his head, he undid the straps and buckles with his teeth. With one last convulsion, the entire straitjacket fell to the floor below him.

Hiding on the other side of the door, Benji wanted to applaud. In its own way, Houdini's hard-won victory over the straitjacket was more real, more thrilling, than even the infamous Chinese Water Torture escape. Benji couldn't believe that any man would willingly put himself through such a hellish ordeal.

No other man could.

Houdini undid the ankle restraints and dropped down onto the floor. He leapt to his feet and struck a dramatic pose, taking a bow before an imaginary audience. Then, to Benji's dismay, he doubled over in pain. Clutching his stomach, he all but collapsed against a marble counter. A racking cough tore from his lungs. Bright red blood speckled the white tile floor.

What's happening? Benji's mind couldn't accept what she was seeing. The Great Houdini never spit up blood. He was immortal, wasn't he? She stared in horror through the keyhole. *What's wrong with him?*

Still doubled over, he sank weakly toward the floor. As he did so, a bathroom chair was revealed behind him. Draped over the chair was *another* waistcoat, neatly pressed and ready to wear. A golden chain hung upon the jacket. Dangling from the chain, flashing beneath the bathroom lights like a miniature star, was a tiny golden key.

.   .   .

Steam curled up from the tub. Like Venus rising from the sea foam, Mary emerged from an overflowing bubble bath. Her bare feet crossed the cool ceramic tiles. She toweled herself off, then slipped on a red silk kimono. A floral design was printed upon the fabric in metallic gold foil. She slid her feet into a pair of comfy wool slippers.

A radiant smile lit up her face. She hadn't enjoyed anything so luxurious in years; she felt fresh and revitalized. *I could easily get accustomed to that.* She basked in the memory of last night's romantic adventure. Before parting at the end of the evening, Harry had invited her to go dancing this afternoon. She couldn't wait to see him again. Granted, she still didn't know the contents of the famous sealed envelope, but somehow that didn't seem to matter so much anymore. She refused to let thoughts of business spoil such a glorious morning.

Dancing with the Great Houdini. She grinned in anticipation. *Imagine that!*

A thin layer of condensation obscured the bathroom mirror. She wiped away the steamy residue to admire herself in the looking glass. The reflection showed her an attractive woman still very much in the prime of her life. Her lush black hair fell past her shoulders. She pulled open the collar of the kimono to expose the long, smooth line of her neck and a glimpse of a bare shoulder. *Not bad for thirtysome years,* she thought, *and a mother to boot.*

Not bad at all.

There was a knock at the door. *Who?* she wondered. Was Benji back from her scouting mission already? No, the rap was too strong, too emphatic . . . it was the knock of a full-grown man, not her immature young daughter. Perhaps it was Harry himself, unable to wait for their appointment later on?

She started to hurry toward the door, then thought better of it. Smiling slyly, she kept her caller waiting for a moment. She waited patiently for the second knock, then took one last glance in the mirror. Satisfied that she was indeed looking her best, she confidently opened the door. *Here I am,* she thought exuberantly. *Prepare to be dazzled!*

Her smile faded as she discovered Mr. Morrie Sugarman standing in the hall.

Recovering quickly, she concealed her surprise and disappointment. She smiled tightly as she pulled the robe close around her neck. What on earth was the suspicious manager doing at her door this morning?

"Mr. Houdini gets some funny ideas into his head sometimes," Sugarman said. A leather briefcase was gripped in his right hand.

She coolly ushered him in, not about to be intimidated by the scowling Englishman. She guessed that he was referring to last night's escapade in the park. No doubt he hoped to avoid a scandal. "Seven-year itch, Mr. Sugarman," she said blithely. "All marriages go through a rocky patch."

Unless you're smart and kick the worthless bastard out the door like I did.

"Mr. Houdini has a most exceptional marriage," Sugarman declared stiffly. "Mr. and Mrs. Houdini are soul mates. Almost like brother and sister."

"There's the problem, then," she said drily.

Sugarman sniffed indignantly. "That sort of talk give you a thrill, does it?" He looked her up and down with disdain.

Self-righteous ass, Mary thought. *Probably hasn't had a good romp in years.* She crossed her arms atop her chest and looked him squarely in the eye.

"What do you want, Mr. Sugarman?"

He nodded grimly, ready to get down to business. Crossing the suite, he placed the briefcase down on top of the unmade bed. He snapped open the locks without further ado. The lid popped open to reveal stacks of crisp banknotes. A portrait of Sir Walter Scott was engraved on the faces of the hundred-pound notes.

"Know what this is?" he asked. "This is one thousand Scottish pounds. I want you to take it." He looked pointedly at the door. "I want you to disappear."

The neatly stacked banknotes called out to her. She had never seen so much money in one place before. It was an impossible amount, enough to change her and Benji's lives forever. They could move out of their wretched hovel, buy a comfortable home of their own. Benji could get herself a decent education. Princess Kali could retire permanently. Unable to resist, she reached out and touched the money, just to prove to herself that she wasn't seeing things, that it was really there, hers for the taking. All she had to do was leave Harry Houdini behind forever.

Was it worth it?

Sir Walter Scott looked up at her from the tempting banknotes. Mary remembered the Scott Monument in the moonlight. Houdini's hands deftly undoing the lock. A thrilling embrace upon the parapet. The cataclysmic sense of relief when she realized that he hadn't killed himself after all . . .

With effort, she tore her gaze away from the briefcase. She met the scheming manager's eyes once more. "Not sure I want to disappear, Mr. Sugarman."

That was *not* the response he had been expecting. He tried and failed to hide his dismay. His jowly face went pale. Visibly shaken, he nonetheless attempted to regain control of the situation.

"Yeah, you do." He reached out and removed her hand from the money. "What *shtick* you gonna pull to earn you the ten thousand dollars?" He shook his head discouragingly. "Trust me, it's not going to happen. It's *specific* . . . specific words he wants to hear." He spoke slowly, just to make sure she got the message. "Take the money. It's not on offer forever."

Mary considered it. A thousand pounds was far less than $10,000, but this was a sure thing. And a mere thousand pounds was more than she had ever dreamed of making back during her music hall days. She gazed at the money, calculating the odds. Feigning indifference, she scrutinized Sugarman's face. The man's motives seemed obvious, yet Mary sensed that more was here than met the eye. There was something she wasn't seeing yet.

"If I fail Mr. Houdini's challenge, you'll never see me again anyway." She arched a quizzical eyebrow. "Why so worried?"

Sugarman declined to explain. Apparently realizing that she would not be bought off so easily, he snapped the briefcase shut. A nearly physical pang shot through Mary as the precious banknotes disappeared from view. She almost cried out for Sugarman to wait, to accept his offer after all, but somehow she managed to hold her tongue. Her arms hung limply at her sides, her twitching fingers yearning to snatch the case of money back.

I may never have an opportunity like this again.

Briefcase in hand, Sugarman started to head for the door. At the last minute, though, he turned and looked back at her. To her surprise, a wry smile came to his lips. He chuckled to himself, as though at some private joke.

"You're right," he admitted. "You *are* special. You don't know *how* special. You have no idea." A warning tone entered his voice. "But you're going to find out."

Was he trying to frighten her? "You don't scare me, Mr. Sugarman," she said defiantly, her chin held high. "We're going dancing."

"Dancing?" A humorless laugh shook his rotund form. "Oh, it's a *dance* he's taking you on all right." He looked her over sadly. If she didn't know better, she would have sworn that he was actually feeling sorry for her. "You're way out of your depth on this one, Mrs. McGarvie. Believe me."

What does he mean by that? She stared at his back as he exited the suite, leaving her alone with her doubts. Had she really just let a thousand pounds walk out the door? Her eyes brimmed with tears as she prayed that she hadn't just made the biggest mistake of her life. *What's happening to me?* This wasn't her. Mary McGarvie would never have let such a windfall get away, not after scrounging and starving for so many years. All for a married man she barely knew. *Who am I now, and what have I become?*

Nevertheless, the die was cast. She had no choice now but to see this through to the bitter end, for better or for worse. Wiping the tears from her eyes, she bravely mustered a smile.

She had an engagement to go dancing.

CHAPTER SEVENTEEN

———

SHORTLY AFTER NOON, MARY AND BENJI arrived at the hotel's grand ballroom. A sleeveless, burgundy dress clung to Mary's figure. The antique silver earrings glittered upon her ears, having been hand-delivered by a bellboy only an hour before. Her black hair was elegantly done up. Her makeup was immaculate. Beside her, Benji was mortified in a lacy white dress. A bright red carnation was pinned to her front as a corsage. The girl's light brown hair was actually combed for once. She smelled faintly of shampoo.

'Bout time she learned how to act like a lady, Mary thought. Taking Benji firmly by the hand, she led her daughter into the ballroom, where a startling sight met their eyes.

A full ten-piece orchestra occupied the far end of the room. Blindfolds covered the musicians' eyes, but that didn't stop them from playing a lively ragtime melody. On the spacious dance floor, resplendent in a black tuxedo and tails, Houdini danced alone, his arms around an imaginary partner. Mary couldn't help noticing how gracefully he moved, like a professional hoofer. As with their lunch the day before, he and Mary had the room practically to themselves. Off to one side, Sugarman sat at a linen-covered table, glumly puffing on a cigar. An open bottle of champagne rested in an ice bucket atop the table, next to a half-filled glass. Mary wondered what Harry would think if he knew that his overprotective manager had tried to bribe her earlier today. Would he appreciate the risk, the painful sacrifice, she had taken for his sake?

Would Benji?

The blindfolded orchestra, and Harry's solitary waltz, elicited a snicker from the girl. She had been in a sullen mood all morning, and her failure to secure the key to the steamer trunk had not improved her spirits any. Mary hoped this wasn't a preview of what her daughter's adolescence was going to be like. She wasn't sure she had the patience to cope with a sulky teenager full-time. *Was I like this at her age?* Mary could barely remember being that young. *Probably just as well that I didn't tell her about Sugarman's offer.*

The girl's snide laughter alerted Harry to their arrival. He turned toward them, his face lighting up at the sight of Mary. Grinning, he clapped his hands enthusiastically and called out to the band, "Polka! Polka!"

The blinkered musicians obediently launched into an upbeat Bohemian melody. He held out his arms for Mary, who stepped away from Benji to approach him. He tilted his head toward the bizarrely blindfolded orchestra and held a finger to his lips.

"*Ssssh!*" he whispered impishly. "We're all incognito."

Meeting her halfway, he took her in his arms and swept her onto the dance floor before she even had a chance to catch her breath. She felt as if she were being carried away, in more ways than one. Everything was happening so fast!

"Dance!" Harry called out merrily. "Come on, you all gotta dance. Shake a leg, Mr. Sugarman!"

The seated manager eyed Benji dubiously. He looked reluctant to abandon his seat, let alone his booze and cigar. Mary liked to think that she was responsible for driving him to drink. *Serves him right, the scheming Sassanak.*

"Come on," Benji jeered at him, echoing Houdini. "Ya old mustache pete!"

Sugarman stiffened and glowered at the girl suspiciously. *What's that all about?* Mary wondered. With an aggrieved air, he heaved himself to his feet and took custody of Benji, who looked just as disgusted by her choice in partners as he did. They shambled miserably across the hardwood floor. Mary made a mental note to make it up to Benji later. Perhaps a trip to the movies?

At the moment, however, Harry had her in his arms and Mary could think of little else. They galloped across the empty ballroom in 2/4 time, caught up in the music and the emotion. Their feet chased each other around the dance floor. Facing each other in a closed position, they danced cheek to cheek. His right hand held tightly onto her left. His left rested on her hip. A crystal chandelier sparkled overhead. Candles glowed atop the tables surrounding the dance floor.

"Waddaya think?" he asked her, his American accent quite pronounced. "Do people choose the night to do strange things . . . or is it the dark that makes them act funny?"

Mary knew he was referring to their thrilling embrace atop the monument. She answered cautiously, not yet ready to admit just how much that magical encounter had affected her. "It's the night, Harry."

That's the ticket, she thought. *Blame it all on the moonlight.*

"That's right," he agreed readily. From the way he was acting, he seemed to have no doubts or regrets about what had transpired between them. "You can do stuff you wouldn't ever think of doing before. Ask all kinds of questions."

Mary decided to broach a delicate subject, before it was too late to turn back. "There's a couple you never asked last night."

He let go of her briefly and clapped loud enough to get the orchestra's attention. "Fox-trot!"

The band changed tempo, the musicians grinning beneath their blindfolds. Harry embraced Mary again, even tighter than before, and kicked up his heels. The jaunty rhythm and melody of the "Down Home Rag" propelled them around the room. Their faces were only inches apart, their bodies fitting as smoothly together as a hand in a glove—or a key in a lock. Mary's heart was racing, but she refused to let Harry change the subject so easily. There were issues that simply had to be brought out into the open.

"Like . . . men friends," she persisted. "Fathers . . . Mr.

McGarvies . . ." She scrutinized his face, watching carefully
for any sign of jealousy or doubt. "You never asked . . ."

Harry looked back into her eyes. "Maybe I didn't
wanna know."

.   .   .

Lost in a world of their own, neither Houdini nor Mary noticed when Benji and Mr. Sugarman called their own dance
short and slunk back to the table. They sat with their backs
to the wall, watching the fox-trotting couple with equally
morose expressions. Benji found her mother's conduct absolutely indefensible. Had she forgotten that only hours from
now she would be asked to present Houdini's mother's last
words to a skeptical audience of scientists, cops, and reporters? They were about to be exposed as blatant frauds, yet
her mother was wasting time dancing?

Had her brain completely turned to jelly? Or were her
own selfish desires all that mattered now?

Mr. Sugarman looked just as appalled by Houdini's behavior. The foul stench of his cigar offended Benji's nose. He
muttered unhappily, "Haven't seen him this crazy since his
mother died."

It was worse than that, Benji knew. The awful truth was
staring them both in the face.

"That's not crazy," she said sourly. "That's love."

Mr. Sugarman put down his cigar and regarded Benji in
a new light, perhaps recognizing a potential ally. It occurred
to Benji that neither of them wanted this scandalous liaison
between Houdini and her mam to go any further.

But what could they do about it?

. . .

"You're a good dancer," Mary told him.

Apparently his athletic physique and agility were good for something besides breaking out of chains and strait-jackets. He expertly trotted in the distinctive slow-slow-quick-quick rhythm of the dance, maintaining a firm hold on her hand and back. The newfangled sprung floor added an extra bounce to their steps. Mary felt as if she were flying.

"Never danced like this before," he replied.

Mary had her doubts. "I'd have thought you had a girl in every port."

It made sense when you thought about it. The famous Houdini, adored by millions, rich and successful and good-looking on top of it all. He could have any woman he wanted, anywhere in the world. They probably lined up outside the stage door, while his dainty, little wife tended the home fires, thousands of miles away. *Is that all I am to him?* she worried. *Just another stop on his world tour?*

"No," he said firmly, almost as if he were reading her mind. He slowed down enough to give her a good look at his face, which was straight, honest, open. Looking into his eyes, Mary knew in her heart that he was telling her the truth. She wasn't just his latest conquest.

"But you'll be leaving, won't you?" As much as she wanted to surrender to the moment, bitter truths had to be faced. *Whether we like it or not.*

"Montreal," he confessed. "Final date! Then we all go home." He smiled disarmingly, being completely honest with her. They glided atop the polished hardwood. "Chicken soup for dinner."

Her eyes narrowed. "*Mrs.* Houdini make the soup?"

Close enough to kiss, their breaths mingled between them. Their hearts seemed to beat together in 4/4 time. The ragtime music pulsed through their veins.

"Cook makes the soup." He squeezed her hand. "Mrs. Houdini serves it up. You'd like her."

Mary recalled the petite blond ingenue from the photo in Harry's suite. "Don't see us washing the dishes together."

"Maid does the dishes." They slowed to a stop in the middle of the empty dance floor. Serious now, he looked at her head-on. "Things change, Mary."

Like wives? she wondered. Was he talking divorce . . . or some other arrangement? Was she prepared to become the Great Houdini's mistress? Was he willing to leave his delicate little Coney Island sweetheart?

Before she could ask him to elaborate, he clapped his hands once more.

"Tango!"

The orchestra switched gears immediately, playing from memory without benefit of sheet music. He swept her off her feet and into a dramatic promenade. She nestled into the crook of his arm, her head thrown back. The seductive Latin dance, which had been popularized by the late Rudolph Valentino only a few years back, sent her senses reeling. Cheek to cheek, they stalked counterclockwise around their personal ballroom. Mary's blood sang in her veins as the fiery Latin beat carried them away. The music reached a wild crescendo.

"I'm the Great Houdini!" he proclaimed. "I make things the way I want 'em to be!"

If only that were true!

"No," she corrected him. She slipped out of his arms and let him spin away from her. She stood stock-still at the edge of the dance floor. "You can't."

He snaked back to her, refusing to accept that their tango was over. "Oh, I can," he promised. "Believe me. And I will."

"No!" she blurted abruptly. "Stop! Just stop, Harry." She couldn't play this game anymore. The stakes were too high. "This is real. I'm real." Moonlight and false promises weren't enough to live on, not in a world so cruel and un-forgiving. She had learned that the hard way, from Benji's father, but here she was again. What had started out as just another con had become so much more, leaving her naked and vulnerable for the first time in years. Her wounded heart was bleeding all over again. Her voice was hoarse with emotion. "What's happening to me?"

Harry came to a stop before her. Oblivious to the un-folding drama, the orchestra played on, but there would be no more dancing today. Frozen like statues, they faced each other beneath the glittering lights of the chandelier. Fresh tears blurred Mary's sight. Her eyes pleaded for . . . what? To be set free? To lose herself in his arms? To be forgiven for all her deceptions? Everything had seemed so simple before they met. Now she didn't know what she wanted any-more.

Did he?

"What's happening to *us*?" he asked.

Mary knew the answer, even though she had been unable to bring herself to admit it before now.

We're falling in love.

The very idea was more than she could cope with. She backed away from Harry, desperately trying to escape from the irresistible pull of his presence before she disappeared forever down a never-ending whirlpool of heartache and passion. She teetered uncertainly, on the verge of swooning. Her hand went to her head. She felt flushed and feverish.

"I can't dance anymore," she murmured.

Harry held out his hand, offering her his strength and support, but she fled from him as she would from a raging fire. Without another word, she hurried out of the ballroom. She couldn't stay there another minute, not if she ever wanted to be herself again.

Some traps there was no escape from.

. . . .

Benji watched her mother run from Houdini, leaving her behind. She had no idea what was happening. Didn't Mam want to be with Houdini? Then why had she raced from the ballroom like the cops were after her? Benji didn't know whether to follow after her or not. Was this part of the plan? If so, her mother had neglected to tell her.

"Don't worry, sweetheart." Mr. Sugarman leaned across the table toward her. "No future in it." His voice was low and conspiratorial, for her ears alone. "Give me your hand. Got something that might interest you."

He took Benji's hand and softly placed something in

it. It was cold and metallic to the touch. She glanced down at her palm, then looked up at Mr. Sugarman in surprise. Now she was utterly bewildered. Her wide blue eyes questioned his.

Why on earth are you doing this?

. . .

Rapid footsteps caught up with Mary in the corridor outside their rooms. Glancing back over her shoulder, she saw Benji chasing after her. She felt a guilty twinge; in her haste to escape Harry, she had completely forgotten about her daughter. She hoped that Benji wouldn't hold it against her.

Not that I'd blame her, Mary thought. *I haven't been a very attentive mother lately. No wonder she's been pouting.*

Right now, however, Benji looked more excited than annoyed. Her face was aglow. Her eyes were wide as saucers. Breathless, she came rushing up to Mary, a torrent of words spilling from her lips. "Mr. Sugarman doesn't like you," she babbled. "Says you're just a common gold digger."

"You don't listen to *anything* Mr. Sugarman says!" Mary snapped. The man wouldn't be so callous as to tell Benji about his attempt to buy them both off, would he? She didn't want to have to explain to her daughter why she had turned down a thousand pounds, especially when she wasn't entirely sure she could explain it to herself. Sugarman needed to keep his big mouth shut. "Got it?"

Benji blinked in surprise, taken aback by her mother's outburst. She took a deep breath and started over again. "No, Mam," she explained. "Mr. Sugarman's on *our* side."

What? Now it was Mary's turn to look confused.

Benji held out her hand. Her mother's eyes widened in shock.

Resting in the girl's palm, reflecting the glow of the hall lights, was a tiny golden key.

CHAPTER EIGHTEEN

───

THE STEAMER TRUNK, WITH ALL ITS SECRETS,
awaited them. Mary contemplated the locked trunk,
while Benji drew the drapes. The sudden lack of sunlight imbued the suite with the funereal gloom of a mau-
soleum. Mary felt like a body snatcher, about to unearth
the buried mysteries of Harry's past. Maybe some secrets
were better left undisturbed? She couldn't help wondering why Sugarman had slipped Benji the key. *What's his
angle?*

Key in hand, she hesitated before trying the lock.

"Go on, Mam," Benji urged her. The girl joined Mary
in front of the trunk.

Mary knelt down on the carpet. There was no turning
back now, not with ten thousand American dollars at stake.
Harry's initials were engraved above the keyhole. Mary
traced the letters with her fingertip. Taking a deep breath,
she inserted the tiny golden key into the lock. A satisfying
click confirmed that the key had worked perfectly.

All right, Harry, she thought. *Let's see what you have hiding up your sleeve.*

Benji helped her lift the reinforced lid of the trunk. They both looked inside. It took Mary's eyes a moment to adjust to the murky shadows, but then she beheld the exposed contents of the trunk.

Time stood still. A sharp intake of breath broke the silence.

Trembling, Mary lifted an antique wedding gown from the trunk. The starched white chiffon and crinolines looked as if they dated back to the previous century. A veil and headdress had also carefully been preserved. Dried flower petals fell from the dress onto the floor. A fusty odor clung to the ancient gown.

But that wasn't all the trunk contained. Putting down the gown, Mary rescued a framed photograph from the bottom of the luggage. The faded, sepia-toned print captured a beautiful young bride on her wedding day, wearing the same gown Mary had just liberated from captivity. Old-fashioned silver earrings complemented the bride's natural beauty. Mary's hand went instantly to her own ears, where the same earrings now dangled.

But the silver earrings weren't the only things that Mary recognized.

The woman's attractive features, her dark eyes, and lustrous dark hair belonged to the same face Mary saw in the mirror every day.

A sickening feeling came over Mary as she realized that she was the spitting image of the woman in the photo.

"*It's his mother,*" she whispered in shock. She was staring at a portrait of the young Cecilia Weiss.

Benji saw the resemblance as well. "She looks like you, Mam."

All the blood drained from Mary's face. She didn't know how to react. Of all the things she had hoped to find in the enigmatic steamer trunk, her own mirror image was the last thing she had expected. *This can't be happening,* she thought. It was like some sort of bizarre nightmare or hallucination. Everything she thought she knew about Harry and herself had suddenly been turned upside down. *What does this mean?*

"Like I said, Mrs. McGarvie. Way out of your depth."

She looked around to see Sugarman standing behind them. Thrown for a loop by the telltale photograph, Mary hadn't even heard him come in. Benji watched her mother with a worried expression; for the first time in days, Mary thought she saw a touch of compassion in her daughter's blue eyes.

"Mr. Houdini was closer to his mother than most sons even dream of," Sugarman informed her. "You should have seen him after she died. He visited her grave every night for months. Fifteen minutes after midnight, the very moment of her death. It's still the last place he visits every time he leaves the country, and the first place he goes to as soon as he returns." Sugarman looked Mary over and shook his head in disbelief. "You're a dead ringer for her when she was young. Took my breath away the first time I saw you."

Mary remembered Houdini's rapt expression when they first met, the way he had stared at her all throughout her audition. She finally realized why he had chosen her for his experiment, why he couldn't seem to let her go. *I look just like her.*

Jolted to her core, Mary stared numbly at the photo. There were no words to describe what she was feeling just now. *I thought he loved me, like a man loves a woman.* But that was not what this had been all about. This was something darker and more disturbing. Her entire body trembled in shock. She felt as though she had been run over by a hearse.

Sugarman plucked the photograph from her limp fingers. He placed it back in the trunk, along with the antiquated wedding dress, and turned the key to lock the trunk once more. "Maybe all this does something for you," he insinuated. His piggish eyes gazed down on her in judgment.

She felt sick to her stomach. Nausea gripped her as she recalled their passionate embrace atop the monument. She replayed every moment in her mind, every smile and tender moment. Her gorge rose. A plaintive whimper issued from her lips.

Sugarman observed her discomfort. "I thought you show people were, you know, more open-minded?" He slipped the key into the pocket of his waistcoat.

His contemptuous tone ignited Mary's temper. A cold fury mercifully overcame her initial shock. She rose slowly to her feet and turned to face the heartless manager. Something curdled inside her, perhaps the last vestiges of a silly romantic fantasy from which she had awoken only just in time. Sadder but wiser, the old Mary McGarvie reasserted itself. Her face hardened.

"We're here for the star prize, Mr. Sugarman."

His jaw dropped, thoroughly nonplussed. Mary smirked. If he had been expecting this . . . upsetting . . . revelation to send her packing, he had severely underestimated her fortitude and resolve. More than ever now, she was determined to beat the Great Houdini at his own game. How dare he toy with her emotions to satisfy some twisted obsession. Dr. Freud would have a field day with Harry.

"But . . . you need the *words*," Sugarman sputtered. "You need his mother's dying words."

Benji reached up to comfort her. "It doesn't matter, Mam."

Mary savagely shoved her daughter away, rejecting her touch. She wasn't sure if the girl truly grasped the full implications of their discovery, but there was no way a mere child could understand the searing pain and anger Mary was experiencing right now. As if by magic, her love for Harry had been transformed into a white-hot yearning for revenge. No one, not even Benji's bastard of a father, had hurt her like this before. He had to pay . . . and dearly.

"I'll put on his mam's pinny if I have to," Mary snarled. "I'll dress him, feed him, *clean* him. Whatever it takes." She spelled it out for Sugarman, plain as day. "You want me gone? You better help me, Mr. Sugarman." She looked him over with a knowing eye. "If anyone knows the words, *you* do."

He didn't deny it. Instead he seemed to eye her with a

grudging respect. "Win the ten grand and you disappear, right?"

"That was always the deal," Mary assured him. *Although I let my foolish heart get the better of me for a spell there.*

Sugarman sighed. He sounded weary unto death of all the intrigue and melodrama that had plagued Houdini's stint in Edinburgh. "Used to be a nice guy," he reminisced. "Can you believe it? I got old and mean."

Happens to us all, Mary thought unsympathetically. *Some of us just wise up faster than others.*

He slumped down into the nearest chair. "There aren't any words," he confessed. "At least Harry Houdini never heard any. He was doing a show when his mother died," he muttered ruefully. "Talks like he was there. Gives you every detail, makes himself weep. I've heard it a million times, but it's all hogwash." He looked up at Mary. "His big regret? His deepest guilt? The moment his mother needed him most . . . *he wasn't there.*"

Mary was astonished. She hadn't thought it possible for Houdini to flummox her any further, not after what she'd discovered in the locked trunk, but she barely believed her ears. All this time his grand psychic experiment had been nothing but a hoax. There was no secret message to be discovered. It was all a pointless charade.

Just like our "romance," she thought bitterly. *Nothing but smoke and mirrors.*

She had thought she was conning him, but he had been making fools of everyone all along. But to what end? To lure unsuspecting "psychics" into a trap, exposing them in their deceptions? Or was this entire exercise a genuine attempt to find the one true medium who could grant him what he truly craved: a reunion with his long-dead mother?

He doesn't want me. He never did.

He just wants his mommy back.

Benji looked up at her. Confusion was written all over her face. Mary felt sorry for the girl. These were deep waters they were swimming in, too deep for a child her age to ever comprehend, no matter how worldly or wise beyond her years. It was almost more than Mary's own mind could cope with. They were beyond ordinary passion here. Houdini's oedipal fixation skirted the edge of madness.

He wants a message from his mother? she thought. *Very well.*

But it's going to cost him. . . .

CHAPTER NINETEEN

———

REPRESENTING THE SCOTTISH SOCIETY FOR Psychical Research, the female scientist reminded Benji of every prim schoolmistress she had ever known. Her silver hair was done up in a bun. A pair of spectacles rested on the bridge of her nose. Clad in conservative tweeds and brogues, she presented Mam with an all-too-familiar wedding gown. Benji silently watched the transaction from the corner of their suite.

"Mr. Houdini asks that you wear his mother's wedding dress, madam," their visitor explained. "In order to help channel the psychic energy, you understand."

Benji was amazed that so educated a lady could fall for such shit. It was as Mam always said, most people positively wanted to be fooled. Doctors and professors and such were no exception. In fact, sometimes they were easier to con than most.

Mam gave no evidence that she had ever laid eyes on the ancient gown before. Accepting the dress, she waited patiently for the other woman to leave the suite. She kept the gown at arm's length from her body, touching as little of the lacy fabric as possible. With the female scientist's back turned toward her, she recoiled from the gown as she would from a rotting corpse.

The door clicked shut, leaving them alone in the suite.

"Look at it, child!" Mam spat, unable to keep quiet a minute longer. "Look at it! He doesn't want me. The little boy wants his mammy!"

Benji could tell that, beneath the fury, this act was tearing her mom apart. This wasn't like conning the punters at the music hall for a few pence a ticket; the strain of overcoming her own revulsion was costing Mam dear. Benji was starting to wish that she had never heard of Harry Houdini or the $10,000. "We shouldn't do it, Mam. We'll be all right, you and me."

"No, we won't be all right," Mam snapped. She hurled the detested wedding gown onto the bed. "We'll be *poor*. And poor people aren't all right. They're angry and cheated and old before their time!"

Distraught, she buried her face in her hands. Violent sobs shook her body. Benji crept timidly toward her mother, uncertain how to console her. Despite their differences, she hated to see Mam suffering like this. She reached out her hand, wanting to comfort her mother somehow, but she hesitated at the last minute. What if Mam didn't want to be touched? Her mother had been acting so strangely lately that Benji had no idea how she might react. She reluctantly withdrew her hand.

"Mary?"

Houdini appeared in the doorway. Benji had thought the door to the suite was locked, but perhaps that didn't matter; a locked door was hardly likely to keep the Great Houdini out anyway. He gazed at Mam from the doorway, making no effort to come any closer. Concern and trepidation showed upon his tense face. He had looked more comfortable facing the Chinese Water Torture Cell.

What's he doing here? Benji fretted. *Does he know we peeked inside the trunk?*

She was impressed with the speed at which Mam pulled herself together. She discreetly wiped a tear from her eye as she confronted the magician, her chin held high. Her dark eyes flashed with anger. Scorn dripped from her voice.

"Come to see Mama?"

He flinched at her harsh rebuke, but offered no heartfelt denials. His silence spoke volumes. Recovering from the attack, he came forward and offered Mam an envelope.

"The money's yours," he said.

Mam glared at the envelope with disdain. "Mr. Sugarman already tried to buy me."

He did? Benji thought, confused. *When was that?* Her mother hadn't breathed a word of any previous offer to her. The unexpected revelation made the girl uneasy; what else wasn't Mam telling her? Visions of copulating monkeys flashed through her brain. Part of her didn't quite understand why her mother didn't just take the money. Wasn't that why they were here? Was her mother going to let a fortune slip away out of wounded pride? Say it wasn't so!

"It's the whole ten grand," Houdini promised. "A personal check. You don't have to do a thing." He pressed the envelope into Mam's hand. "Take it. Get yourself a new life." He smiled sadly. "That's what I'd do."

Benji held her breath. *Do it!* she thought. *Take the money! We can get on a train and go anywhere we want. We can leave all of this behind!*

Her mother exploded instead. "How can you be so stupid!" she shouted at Houdini, driving him backward toward the door. Her face was livid with rage. Benji had never seen her so angry, not even when McTavish had fired her. "Don't you understand? It's not about the money anymore."

Love, Benji thought, scowling. *It's all about love now.*

A nervous cough interrupted the ugly scene. Clearly embarrassed, the female researcher stood in the doorway. To avoid meeting anyone's eyes, she pretended to examine a schedule of the afternoon's proceedings. No doubt she thought that she had walked in on a lover's quarrel, which wasn't far from the truth. Blushing, the scandalized spook hunter cleared her throat.

"Mr. Houdini, Mrs. McGarvie, please. They're waiting."

It was time to face the music—unless Mam accepted the money right here and now. Benji anxiously watched her mother's face. *Do it,* she pleaded silently. *Put an end to this before it's too late!*

Her mother tore the envelope in two.

Benji gasped out loud. Her eyes bugged out in horror.

The torn halves of the envelope fell upon the floor, taking all of Benji's hopes for the future with them. *You've ruined it*, she thought spitefully. She felt an abiding disgust for the entire adult world. *You've ruined everything*.

She didn't know whom to blame more, Houdini or her mother.

They both seemed to have gone completely mad.

.   .   .

The gunmetal safe was wheeled into the ballroom by two straining policemen. The chief constable, decked out once more in his full dress uniform, led a silent procession of Edinburgh's finest, along with a delegation of sober-faced representatives from the Royal Bank of Scotland. A half dozen officers escorted the safe to ensure that it wasn't tampered with. The conservative pin-striped suits of the bankers contrasted with the bobby helmets and buttoned-down, blue tunics of the policemen. Their deliberate pace echoed upon the hardwood floor.

The procession was met by a panel from the psychical research society. The committee was led by Dr. Samuel Knox, a gray-bearded professor from the University of Edinburgh, who stood stiffly at attention before a long oak table at which two chairs were set. Houdini's personal assistants flanked the table. The rest of the ballroom was filled to capacity by an impatient throng of journalists, photographers, radio announcers, newsreel crews, and local dignitaries. Empty seats in the front row were reserved for the Scottish scientists and other participants. An editor from *Scientific American* magazine had already claimed a ringside seat. Arc lights flared, illuminating the empty table in the center of the room. The packed chamber was abuzz with excitement. A hubbub of voices rose from the crowd. Jaded reporters took bets on the outcome of the experiment. If the Great Houdini was looking for publicity, he had gotten it in spades.

Marching as though in a military exercise, the police escort took their positions as the heavy safe was deposited upon the tabletop. The weight of the safe caused the table to creak loudly, but it did not buckle under the load, much to the disappointment of some of the photographers, who were hoping for a touch of slapstick to enliven the stodgy affair. Technicians in white lab jackets checked an impressive array of equipment that had been set up expressly to monitor today's experiment. Mercury thermometers measured the ambient temperature. Barometers tracked minute fluctuations in the air pressure. A psychrometer charted the relative humidity. Microphones were on hand to amplify any inexplicable auditory phenomena. Glass canisters stood ready to capture any possible ectoplasmic emissions. Tesla coils generated an electromagnetic field. Dials whirred. Electrodes flashed. Static crackled. The air smelled faintly of ozone.

The chief constable turned toward the learned professor, making sure that the photographers got his good side. "The safe is untouched," he announced dramatically, savoring his moment in the spotlight. He placed a hand over his heart. "You have my word."

Professor Knox solemnly acknowledged the constable's

testimony. He introduced his various distinguished comrades to the press, who were more interested in when exactly Houdini was expected to show up. Curious eyes awaited their first glimpse of the mysterious "lady medium" who was supposed to be the centerpiece of the experiment. Despite their best efforts, the assembled journalists had been unable to determine the name of the lady in question. At Houdini's insistence, the identity of the medium remained a closely guarded secret. False rumors circulated that the infamous Margery had traveled all the way to Scotland for a rematch with Houdini. Few reporters, though, took this story seriously. Hadn't Houdini already exposed Margery as a hoax?

So who was this new lady?

The demonstration was scheduled to take place promptly at three in the afternoon, but the appointed hour came and went with no sign of either Houdini or the medium. The waiting assemblage grew restless as minutes dragged by. The heat of so many bodies raised the temperature in the ballroom to a stultifying degree. Male reporters tugged on their collars. A handful of lady journalists fanned themselves with their notepads. An annoyed columnist started a slow handclap, until a stern glare from the chief constable shut him down. Irritated voices arose from the crowd of reporters. Didn't Houdini realize they had deadlines to make? Was he just trying to prolong the suspense or what?

"What gives?" someone called out. "Where's Houdini?"

"Please, gentlemen, ladies." Professor Knox attempted to soothe the restive spectators, while exchanging apprehensive looks with his colleagues. He tugged nervously on his beard. "I beg your patience. I'm sure Mr. Houdini will be along shortly."

.   .   .

Let's get this over with, Harry thought.

He marched across the lobby toward the ballroom. Sugarman followed behind him, the Judas. In his heart, Harry had no doubt that it was his manager who had tipped Mary off about her remarkable resemblance to his mother. *Probably thought that would break us up*, Harry guessed. *Well, maybe he got what he wanted.*

His confident stride belied the confusion he felt inside. He knew he should be tightly focused on today's experiment—the eyes of the entire world would be upon him—yet he felt distracted and out of sorts. His thoughts were in turmoil, his heart in conflict. He could still hear Mary's harsh words to him, still see the undeniable pain and humiliation in her eyes. *I never meant to hurt you*, he thought guiltily. *I never intended any of this. I just thought that you were the one. The one who could finally give me the answer.*

Maybe she still could? Despite everything?

"Mr. Houdini!" A young man in an overcoat stepped in front of him, disturbing Harry's reverie. The brash interloper held a notepad and pencil before him. "What do you hope to gain from this experiment?"

It took Harry a moment to recognize the man as one of the reporters who had greeted him upon his arrival in Edinburgh. Was that really only three days ago? He felt as if he had lived an entire lifetime since meeting Mary. The rest of his life paled in comparison.

"Right, the psychic reporter . . ."

The journalist grinned, pleased that the Great Houdini had remembered him. The impromptu interview attracted a circle of hotel guests and employees. "We know the truth before it happens, isn't that right, Mr. Houdini?"

"Not this time!" Harry declared. His showman's instincts kicked in automatically. "This experiment is nothing less than a battle between Love and Death, gentlemen. Is Death final, or will Love triumph? Place your bets, please!"

Only a fool would bet against Harry Houdini . . . except maybe Harry himself.

Will she really be able to do it? he wondered. For once, he didn't know how the show would end. *Does she even want to after what I did to her?*

He pressed forward. Reluctantly, the crowd parted to let him pass.

Either Death or Love awaited him.

.   .   .

The crowd in the ballroom was on the verge of revolt. They rose from their seats, clamoring for the experiment to begin. Professor Knox snuck a peek at his pocket watch. It was nearly three fifteen. Houdini or no Houdini, he realized that he couldn't stall any longer.

How did I get talked into this fiasco? he thought irritably. *I should have known better than to place our society's reputation in the hands of some showman from the States.*

The bright lights reflected off the thick lenses of his spectacles as he stepped forward, fumbling nervously with his notes. He raised his hand for silence. The bumptious minions of the press did not respond as readily as the obedient students in his classroom, but, within minutes, the noisy hullabaloo had quieted to a muffled rumbling. He signaled the various technicians that it was time to begin. The lights of the chandeliers dimmed. A sound recordist tweaked a knob. A newsreel photographer cranked his camera.

"Ladies and gentlemen, fellow investigators." Reading aloud from the notes, he commenced his opening statement. "The aim of the Scottish Society for Psychical Research is to evaluate the evidence for the paranormal under the strictest scientific conditions." He attempted to lighten the mood somewhat. "I can assure you, ladies and gentlemen, no phantom escapes us!"

He paused for a laugh, which was not forthcoming. Stony faces greeted his witticism. No one even cracked a smile. The utter failure of the jest momentarily threw him off his stride, but he quickly regained his composure. He gestured grandly at the substantial collection of advanced scientific apparatus assembled around the testing table.

"Temperature, humidity, and air pressure are all noted at precise intervals. Sound is recorded, flash photographs will be taken, any physical evidence will be carefully collected and catalogued, while on occasion. . . ."

A mocking voice interrupted his prepared remarks. "Okay, prof, you did it," a reporter in the third row heckled him. "I'm in a deep, deep sleep."

The scribe's impertinent wisecrack got the laughter Knox's own joke had failed to elicit. The professor found himself the target of a barrage of derisive laughter and jeers. His face reddened in indignation. Flustered, he tried to resume his presentation.

"As I was saying . . ."

No one was interested. "Where is Houdini?" another reporter demanded. A chorus of irritated voices took up the cry.

"Where is Houdini?"

CHAPTER TWENTY

S OUNDS LIKE MY CUE, H ARRY THOUGHT.

Excited voices and a smattering of applause welcomed him as he strode into the ballroom, doing his best to conceal his anxiety over Mary. Sugarman trudged glumly behind him. Houdini waved at the audience and indicated for them to take their seats. He cordially shook the professor's hand. *What was his name again?* Harry wondered. *Cox? Knox? Something like that?* It wasn't like him to forget such details. Ordinarily, he had an exceptional memory. *I can name every act I ever shared a bill with.*

The professor took a reserved seat in the front row. Sugarman sat down beside him, wryly observing the scene. The chief constable, his officers, and Harry's assistants receded into the background, leaving Harry center stage. He felt very much at home before the audience. All that was missing was an orchestra and footlights.

He stepped forward to address the crowd.

"When my dear mother lay dying, departing this earth

for a better place, she spoke her last sweet words to me, her devoted son. Those words are engraved forever upon my heart." He placed his palm over his chest. "My heart, ladies and gentlemen."

In truth, he had been performing at the Circus Beketow in Copenhagen when he received word that his mother had been stricken with a stroke. Although he had immediately caught the first boat back to America, canceling his European tour, he was already too late. His mother was dead by the time he returned to New York. According to his brother and sister, who had kept vigil over her deathbed, Cecilia Weiss had spent her final hours desperately trying to impart some vital message to Harry, but her stroke had kept her from getting the words out. *If only I'd been there,* he thought, *perhaps I could have figured out what she was trying to say.* He had spent every day of the last thirteen years agonizing over what she had wanted so much to tell him. Was she trying to forgive him for not being there at the end? Did she know how much he cherished her? *I should have never embarked on that tour of Europe. I knew she was ill.*

The chilling pronouncement of the sinister blond twin echoed in his mind:

"She'll never forgive you, Harry."

Repressing a shudder, he continued his spiel. By now, the well-rehearsed lies came easily to his lips:

"Those words are also written on a slip of paper that has been in the safekeeping of your own Royal Bank of Scotland." Patriotic murmurs of approval emanated from the audience; no doubt they felt honored that their native institution had been entrusted with so weighty a responsibility. The seated bankers puffed out their chests. "Those words are known *only to me*. If our medium's gift is genuine, the esteemed Mrs. McGarvie shall receive those last words from the Other Side and transmit them to us today."

Despite everything, including Mary's dubious history as a music hall mentalist, Harry still clung to the hope that she held some special connection to his mother's spirit. He had felt as much the moment she had first walked into the audition room. Surely their meeting was no random coincidence, nor the deep bond they so obviously shared? Destiny seemed to have drawn them together, the events of the last few days all leading up to this last crucial test.

What were you trying to tell me, Mama? Is there really an afterlife?

Perhaps today he would finally learn the answer.

There was a rustle at the doorway. All heads turned as Mary entered the ballroom, dazzling in the perfectly preserved white wedding dress. The silver earrings sparkled like diamonds. Audience members jostled each other and craned their necks to get a better look at the gorgeous medium. Flash powder exploded brightly. Reporters scribbled madly in their notebooks. The movie camera swiveled to capture Mary's entrance. Benji, uncharacteristically pretty in a sunny pink pinafore, held her mother's train. The girl looked as though she would sooner have faced a firing squad. Harry caught snatches of excited chatter from the press:

"All right! She's a looker!"

"Anybody catch that name? McGarvie, right? With a *G*?"

"What's with the bridal getup? I thought this was a spook show, not a wedding!"

"Look over here, doll! Smile for the cameras!"

"Who's the little girl?"

Nobody seemed to recognize Mary as Princess Kali, late of McTavish's Palace. *Probably just as well*, Harry thought. Scientific American *would not approve.*

Even though he had known what to expect, he found himself unprepared for the heart-stopping sight of Mary in his mother's wedding gown. It was as though the framed photograph in his trunk had suddenly come to life. His mouth went as dry as Prohibition. He wiped his sweaty palms on his trousers. Although he had attended literally hundreds of séances over the last few years, this was the first time he had ever felt as though he were looking at a ghost.

Mama?

Raising a hand to hush the noisy racket, he presented her to the audience. "Mrs. Mary McGarvie of Edinburgh." The crowd held back their applause, waiting to see if the so-called medium would come through with the secret message. Before the watchful eyes of the assemblage, Harry ushered Mary to one of the empty chairs at the oak table. He furtively examined her face, hoping to discern just what she was feeling right now. Was she still angry? Hurt? Confused? Her inscrutable features betrayed no hint of her true emotions. She was a pro, just like him.

Then she spotted Sugarman out of the corner of her eye. Just for an instance, a murderous look shot from her dark eyes before her carefully composed mask slipped back into place. She took her place at the table. Her lovely face looked almost mystically serene. Her tranquil appearance was a testament to her skills as an actress; the divine Sarah Bernhardt could not have been more convincing.

Practically unnoticed, Benji took a seat to the right of Sugarman. All eyes were on Harry and his beautiful costar. The entire ballroom seemed to hold its breath. You could have heard a pin drop—or even a tiny golden key.

"There is no trickery here," Harry declared. The words were directed at the audience, but meant for Mary as well. He gave her a meaningful look, offering her a way out. *It's not too late*, his eyes said silently. *You don't have to do this if you don't want to.* "Mrs. McGarvie, are you ready?"

The look she gave him back was hard and unforgiving. She nodded grimly, not even deigning to speak. Harry felt both thrilled and terrified that his grand experiment was going to proceed as planned. There was no turning back now. He soberly took his seat across from her. The glare of the arc lights cast half of him in shadow, half in the spotlight. His eyes were fixed on her to the exclusion of all else.

Please, he prayed. *Grant me the Answer I seek. Don't let her be a fraud like all the others.*

Mary glared at him one last time, then closed her eyes. He could hear her breathing get deeper and deeper. He recalled the trance she had entered during that first audition three days ago, when she had swayed and swooned into his arms. As before, a dreamy look transformed her features. In the audience, skeptics and believers alike watched in rapt fascination.

Her lips fluttered softly. Harry remembered the taste of her kiss. The memory blurred with the recollection of his mother's own gentle kisses.

"Mama?" he entreated. "Can you hear me? Dear little mother?"

At first, she said nothing. Then Mary's mouth opened. Harry leaned forward anxiously, caught in an unbearable torment of suspense. "Mama?" he whispered hoarsely. "Please try, Mama." His throat tightened. "Ehrich's here. Your good boy's here."

Mary's eyes blinked open. They looked into his own expectant gray-blue orbs. His entire body was tense with anticipation. His knuckles whitened as he tightly gripped the edge of the table. *What is it?* he thought frantically. *What's the answer?*

"Mama?"

She shook her head. A look of profound pity and regret replaced her "entranced" visage. "I'm sorry," she said. "I can't do this . . . and I can't take your money."

The spell was broken. Bedlam erupted in the crowded ballroom. The psychic researchers and chief constable looked appalled. The reporters jumped to their feet and started hurling questions at both Mary and Houdini. Everyone was talking at once.

No! Wait! Harry panicked. His anguished mind refused to accept what was happening. *You can't stop now! I've waited too long already!* He fought an urge to grab Mary by the shoulders. *You're supposed to be the one!*

Mary clumsily rose from the table, almost knocking over her chair in her haste to get out of the spotlight. Ignoring the shouting of the crowd, she hurriedly looked about for the nearest exit. Her eyes shone wetly in the glare of exploding flashes from the photographers. Harry himself was nearly blinded by the blazing onslaught. Floating blue spots obscured his vision.

Surging forward, the frenzied journalists blocked her escape. Harry's assistants struggled to hold back the crowd, while the dumbfounded policemen looked at each other in bewilderment, uncertain how to proceed. The chief constable, who looked as if he suddenly wanted to be anywhere else, tried to conceal his mortified face from the cameras. Red-faced bankers shouted angry accusations at the stage. Professor Knox shook his head and stared abjectly at the floor. Sugarman grimaced and clutched his stomach. The entire situation was spiraling out of control.

A sudden, violent thumping halted the chaos. People paused and looked about in confusion. Harry's red-rimmed eyes zoomed in on the source of the disturbance:

Benji.

In the front row of the audience, all but forgotten in the tumult, the girl shook violently in her seat. She seemed to be in the grip of some sort of epileptic seizure. Her eyes were shut, much as her mother's had been. Her mouth hung slackly open. The legs of her chair bounced loudly atop the hardwood floor as she shuddered and kicked uncontrollably. Her blank expression was that of one in a trance. Her lips fluttered. Foam speckled the corners of her mouth.

"Wait! Wait!" Harry called out. He pointed frantically at Benji, calling her to the crowd's attention. He rushed toward the seemingly mesmerized child. The throng of reporters parted to let him through, not wanting to get in the way of the extreme drama of the moment. A quick-witted technician swung a spotlight on the stricken girl. Her head lolled atop her shoulders. Seated beside her, Sugarman lurched to his feet and backed away from Benji. He looked totally flabbergasted, and not a little spooked.

Harry reached Benji. He gazed down at her with a thunderstruck expression. He had no idea what was happening or why. *Benji?* Never in a million years would he have expected Mary's tomboy daughter to manifest spiritual gifts of her own. *Why her? Why now? I don't understand!*

All he knew was that something truly uncanny was taking place, right before his eyes. Benji's breathing grew shallow. Her eyelids opened by only a crack. The orbs beneath them rolled upward so that only the whites could be seen. Her jaws twitched as she began speaking in tongues:

"*Guter Junge, braver Junge Ehrich, Ehrich mein gutes Kind, mein lieber Ehrich.*"

Harry's blood ran cold. All the hairs on his body rose up in alarm. Little Benji McGarvie, Princess Kali's "Dusky Disciple," born and raised in the streets of Edinburgh, Scotland, was speaking Yiddish, just as his mother used to. Her voice acquired a distinct Hungarian accent. The loving endearments stirred precious memories.

"Let me through!" Mary forced her way through the crowd to her daughter's side. She knelt beside Benji and looked at Harry with wide, terrified eyes. "What is it? What's wrong?"

He could tell from Mary's petrified expression that this was no act. She was genuinely confused and frightened by her child's condition. He didn't know what to tell her. Judging from her agitated state, nothing like this had ever happened to Benji before.

What was that quote from the Book of Isaiah again? "And a little child shall lead them."

Another violent spasm jolted Benji. Her chair smacked against the floor even louder than before. The noisy banging elicited startled gasps from the onlookers. By now everyone in the ballroom was straining to see what was going on. The entire audience had been rendered speechless by the disturbing spectacle.

"Ehrich!" Benji cried out. "Ehrich! Ehrich!"

There was no mistaking those familiar cadences. Harry dropped to his knees.

"It's her," he whispered.

An arc light popped overhead, further dimming the lights. Eerie shadows fell over the unearthly scene. Jaded reporters crossed themselves. Goose bumps broke out throughout the audience. Hushed voices whimpered in dread as otherworldly forces appeared to invade the ballroom. The temperature dropped several degrees. The female scientist hugged herself to keep from shivering. A valiant sound recordist swung a boom mike toward Benji. Alert technicians checked the readings on their equipment. Recording needles flickered erratically.

"Where are you?" the girl's unnatural voice echoed in the hushed atmosphere of the haunted ballroom. "Where are you, Ehrich?"

"Here!" Harry answered urgently. He clasped Benji's hand. Her flesh felt cold and clammy to the touch. "I'm here, Mama. I'm here!"

"Ehrich! My good boy!" Benji's tiny body stiffened, as though suddenly afflicted with rigor mortis. "I need you! I need you! Come, Ehrich! Come to Mama!"

Tears sprang to Harry's eyes as he visualized his mother lying on her deathbed thirteen years ago, her withered body calling out to him in vain. According to his siblings, she had lingered for nearly three days, paralyzed, before finally slipping away, fifteen minutes after midnight. How she must have suffered in those final hours! How she must have wondered where he was!

"Your mama love you so much," Benji cooed. Her distorted voice took on an unnerving singsong quality, like the voices of the spooky blond twins three days ago. "Your mama so alone . . . so afraid!" Her head jerked from side to side, looking blindly for something beyond her sight. Her tiny hands reached out. "Ehrich! Ehrich!"

"I'm here, Mama!" He squeezed Benji's hand, holding on to it as tightly as the clamps that held his ankles during the Chinese Water Torture Escape. Tears blurred his vision. "I'm here!"

She couldn't seem to hear him. "Where is my Ehrich?" she moaned piteously. "Why you not come to me?"

Her desperate entreaties tore at his heart, dragging thirteen years of guilt out into the open. "I was on tour, Mama! I had shows to do!" He remembered the last time he had seen his mother alive, at the pier in Hoboken as he was embarking for Europe. It had been harder than usual to say good-bye; he had kept coming back down the gangplank to embrace her one last time, as if part of him had somehow known that he would never see her again. In the end, he had been the very last person to board the steamer. He had waved at her from the prow until her small, slight figure had finally disappeared into the distance. "Oh, God! Forgive me! I'm sorry! I'm so sorry." Defying Jewish tradition, his siblings had delayed her burial until he made it back to New York. He had found her shrunken body laid out in the parlor of his town house in Harlem. Her pale and lifeless face haunted him to this day. "Forgive me, Mama!"

"She'll never forgive you, Harry."

Only a hand's breadth away, Mary was focused entirely on her daughter. Mary's face was a whirl of conflicting emotions: guilt, fear, incomprehension. Childless, Harry could only imagine what the panic-stricken mother was going through right now.

"Where are you, Ehrich?" Benji screeched. "Where is my child? I can't see you!" Her plaintive cries grew more shrill by the moment. "Mama can't see you, Ehrich! Mama can't see you!"

"I tried to get there!" Harry barely saw Benji anymore; in his mind, he was at his mother's deathbed, pleading for forgiveness. The sheer injustice of it all still drove him to despair even after all these years; he had taken care of his mother his entire adult life, just as he had promised his dying father, only to abandon her when it really mattered. He wrung his hands. "I tried. I was just too damn late!"

His hysterical apologies seemed to go unheard by the possessed girl, who thrashed against the back of her chair as another brutal convulsion seized her. Mary threw her arms around Benji, clasping her tightly in an effort to still her fragile body. Harry pulled at his hair and howled in agony. The entire audience recoiled from the dreadful scene before them; it was like something out of a Greek tragedy.

Oedipus, perhaps.

With surprising strength, Benji broke free from her mother's embrace. Her hand grabbed Harry's arm, her nails digging into his flesh. Her eyes opened wide. Crazed, bloodshot orbs stared into his own. The Eastern European accent suddenly vanishing, she hissed at Harry with a fierce messianic fervor:

"He's waiting for you! The angel with the fire-red hair. Got wings, too! Clock says noon . . . sun goes black!" She threw out her arm, pointing at some invisible specter hovering above them. Following her gaze, Harry saw nothing but the burned-out arc lights. "Watch out! Here he comes!"

A final shudder passed through her body. Blinking, she came out of her trance. Releasing her death grip on Harry's arm, she withdrew her hand. Benji trembled from head to toe, her adolescent body soaked in sweat. Tears streamed down Mary's face as she tenderly stroked her daughter's hair. Benji rocked against her mother, sucking her thumb. For the first time, they truly looked like mother and daughter. Benji sobbed against Mary's shoulder.

It's over, Harry realized. His mother's spirit, if that was indeed what had animated the girl, had departed. The secret of his mother's deathbed pleas remained intact, while Benji's last cryptic utterances posed yet another mystery. He was alone again, and more in the dark than ever before. *Was that really you, Mama?*

He knelt upon the floor, utterly drained and devastated. His chin drooped onto his chest. He stared numbly at the scuffed wooden floor. Tears flooded his eyes. Inner tremors shook his entire body. The world he knew had been blown to pieces. He had nothing more up his sleeve.

"Mr. Houdini!" The professor—Knox?—emerged from the crowd of appalled spectators. He seemed intent on salvaging the situation somehow, perhaps to preserve the honor of his distinguished society. "Mr. Houdini? Can you make an official confirmation?"

Harry couldn't speak. The professor's queries seemed to come from a thousand miles away, barely impinging on his turbulent thoughts and emotions. It seemed to Harry that he had lost everything: his mother, Mary, maybe even his mind. He had always harbored a secret fear that his intense obsessions would someday drive him insane. Small wonder he had been fascinated by straitjackets and lunatic asylums. Deep down inside, he had never truly recovered from his mother's death. Mary had been his last chance to finally make peace with himself over what had happened thirteen years ago. But instead his very soul had been blasted apart. He knew he would never escape that heartbreaking voice for as long as he lived.

"*Where is my Ehrich! Why you not come to me?*"

He moaned in agony.

"Mr. Houdini?" The professor tried once more to rouse Harry from his stupor, then abandoned the effort. He turned toward the forgotten safe. "The envelope!"

His face ashen, the chief constable carried out his duty with much less enthusiasm than before. He reluctantly entered the combination and, without dramatic flourishes, opened the door of the safe. It took him a moment or two to work up the nerve to extract the sealed envelope. He gripped the envelope by the corner, as though the harmless paper sleeve would singe his fingertips if he held on to it too long. With an audible sigh of relief, he hurriedly handed the envelope to the professor.

The bearded academic also handled the envelope as though it were a ticking bomb. He swallowed hard and broke the wax seal. A frown showed through his beard as he read the enclosed missive. Lifting his glasses, he peered closer at the note to confirm the awful truth. He cleared his throat and turned to face the audience.

"The paper is blank," he announced.

He raised the document aloft, displaying a clear white expanse of paper. "There are no words!"

Startled gasps burst from the spectators. Bewildered faces looked to Harry for answers. *I'll bet they're confused*, he thought. Mustering what little remained of his strength, he rose to face the inquisitive throng. The showman in him felt he owed his public some explanation. Besides, he had no more secrets, not anymore. Benji's inexplicable display had exposed his greatest failure for all the world to see. He had nothing more to hide.

"To my eternal shame," he confessed, "I was not there when my mother died. I was too late." His hoarse, quavery voice lacked its usual confidant bravado. Tear-filled eyes looked heavenward. "I never got there in time, Mama! I'm sorry!" His voice cracked completely. "Forgive me, Mama! Forgive me!"

An awkward, almost embarrassed silence followed Harry's emotional breakdown. The reporters and other spectators stared at Harry as though they barely recognized him. Who was this distraught, weeping figure before them? Surely not the Great Houdini. Everyone knew that Harry Houdini was unstoppable, indomitable, immortal. He laughed in the face of dime-store mediums and their cheap theatrics. So who was this shattered wreck of a man . . . and what sort of headline would this make?

Hungry for another angle, they swamped Mary and Benji instead. A tidal wave of shouting journalists and scientists engulfed the mother and child. They bombarded the pair with questions, competing with each other to steal Mary's attention away from Benji.

"Mrs. McGarvie! Did you know your daughter was a psychic?"

"What's the girl's name?"

"Where's her father?"

"Why don't you want Mr. Houdini's money?"

"Did you know that there was no message in the envelope? Was that why you refused to continue the experiment?"

Harry found himself standing off to one side, ignored by the crowd. Sugarman elbowed his way through the disorderly crush to reach him. He looked like an overfed salmon fighting his way upstream. Concern showed on the manager's face.

"Harry?" He had to raise his voice to be heard over the uproar. "You okay, Harry?"

Only vaguely aware of Sugarman's presence, Harry watched as Mary attempted to escape the ravening horde. Holding on tightly to Benji, she fled toward the doorway, only to be pursued by a mob of interested parties. Just for a moment, she glanced back over her shoulder at Harry. Their eyes met across a sea of jostling bodies. Was it just wishful thinking on his part, or did he see a further touch of pity in her eyes? Then she was swept away by the press of bodies, disappearing from his sight just as his mother had when his ship had pulled away from the pier so many years ago. Harry felt doubly bereft, as if he had just lost the love of his life for the second time.

A hush fell over the ballroom. Empty chairs faced the oak table and the vacant safe. Electronic apparatus hummed and buzzed in the background. The violated envelope lay upon the floor, forgotten and trampled upon. Not unlike Harry.

"Are you okay?" Sugarman repeated. He eyed Harry worriedly.

Okay? Harry found the question laughable. He was far from okay.

He doubted that he would ever be okay again.

CHAPTER TWENTY-ONE

—

TWO HUNDRED AND EIGHTY-SEVEN STEPS. THE last time Harry had climbed to the top of the Scott Monument, he had fairly flown up the long spiral staircase. He had been giddy with excitement, intoxicated by the magic of the night and Mary McGarvie's invigorating company. He hadn't felt so young in years, certainly not since the early years with Bess, before his mother grew old and frail. Edinburgh had been a fairy wonderland, the Princes Street Gardens a second Eden. Death and sorrow could not touch him. Gravity was just another illusion.

Tonight was different.

It was after midnight. His show at the Theater Royale had ended years ago. Still shaken by this afternoon's disastrous séance, he had barely been able to drag himself through the performance. He had recited his usual patter in a fog, just going through the motions. For a few crucial moments, during the Chinese Water Torture Cell stunt, he had almost decided *not* to escape, to let the suffocating water win at last.

Only his pride and professionalism had kept him from suc-
cumbing to the suicidal impulse. His legend was all he had
left; he would not want it said that the Great Houdini died
by accident. How his spiritualist enemies would laugh if he
drowned in one of his own ingenious contraptions.

Only a coffin will ever hold me.

He trudged wearily up the steps. Pale moonlight illuminated the patriotic stained-glass windows. Unable to
sleep, he had wandered the slumbering city for hours ...
until his restless feet and fevered mind had finally brought
him back to the towering Gothic monument. Dark and
foreboding, it struck him as the perfect stage for the Great
Houdini's final escape.

Up and up he went, his steps echoing inside the deserted tower like a funeral drum. His pace quickened as he
neared the top. A tiny blue flame danced atop his upraised
cigarette lighter, lighting his path. The weathered stone
staircase gave way to steps of metal and then of wood. His
face was drawn and gaunt. His hollow eyes were turned upward toward the peak of the monument. His black formal
attire was more than suitable for a funeral. He counted
down the steps as he climbed steadily onward. His pace
quickened as he neared the top.

Two hundred and eighty-five ...

Two hundred and eighty-six ...

Two hundred and eighty-seven.

And here we are.

At last he emerged onto the top landing, two hundred
feet up. It was a cold, clear night. Stars glittered overhead

like cheap costume jewelry. All of Edinburgh was spread out beneath him. An autumn wind whistled past his ears. He thought he heard his mother's voice in the wind, calling out to him.

"Where are you, Ehrich? Where is my child?"

Was his mother truly reaching out from beyond? Perhaps there was only one way to know for sure, one that did not require the intervention of mediums or supernatural entities. The only wonder was that he had waited so long before finding out the answer for himself.

Is there really an Afterlife? Let's get this settled once and for all.

His face devoid of emotion, Harry stepped up onto the same stone parapet upon which he had embraced Mary yesterday night. The memory of that transitory taste of bliss was not enough to deter him. A pair of carved stone griffins, crouched at opposite ends of the parapet, were his only audience. He strode out onto a leering gargoyle like a condemned man walking the plank. He stared out into the night, which beckoned to him seductively. Gravity waited to end his cares forever.

He felt as though his soul were weighed down by heavy chains. His heart was imprisoned within a sunless dungeon. But no hidden panels or concealed lockpicks could free him this time. Trapped in a never-ending hell of guilt and remorse, there was only one means of escape left to him.

I'm coming, Mama, he thought. *We'll be together soon.*

Poised upon the brink of oblivion, he threw out his arms just as he had the night before. If he leaped far enough, he would easily clear the lower parapet this time around.

There would be no miraculous death-defying feat. Neither Mary nor Benji were on hand to rejoice in his survival. He wondered if either of them would truly mourn his death. Thousands of miles away, back in America, a magnificent bronze coffin awaited his mortal remains. He had already made arrangements to have himself buried beside his mother.

He spied a clock tower in the distance. It was almost twelve fifteen, the exact moment of his mother's death. The time had come. He whispered softly to an invisible audience.

"May God have mercy upon my immortal soul."

His life did not flash before his eyes.

Only Mary's face . . .

.   .   .

A dog barked in the night, somewhere outside Mary's cottage. She frowned at the noise, afraid that it would wake Benji.

Exhausted by her bizarre ordeal, the girl was sound asleep in her tiny cot at the rear of the bothy. She had spoken little since her fit at the séance, and Mary had been too busy getting her away from the voracious reporters and scientists to talk to Benji about what had happened. For several hectic minutes there, Mary had thought that the baying mob would never let them go, but she had eventually managed to flag down a cab outside the hotel and escape the frantic scene. The fare had consumed the last of her ready cash. By the time they had finally made it back to their miserable hovel on the outskirts of town, Benji had been dead to the world. Mary hadn't had the heart to wake her.

The poor wee thing! Will she ever be the same again?

In truth, Mary felt utterly fatigued as well. The embers of a dying fire illuminated her wan complexion. The crumpled wedding gown lay in a heap upon the floor; she had changed into a red cotton robe as soon as she had tucked Benji into bed, but the fusty odor of the ancient gown still clung to her skin. She sat wearily at the rough-hewn wooden table. Spread out in front of her was pile after pile of crisp $100 bills. The money had been delivered by messenger hours ago. She didn't have to count the stacked greenbacks to know that they added up to exactly $10,000.

It didn't seem nearly enough for what she and Benji had been through.

A chilly breeze entered the cottage, stirring up the feeble orange flames in the fireplace. Mary looked up to see Harry standing in the open doorway. Beyond him, she caught a glimpse of the nearby cemetery and gasworks. Her brow knitted, but she didn't react in surprise. *I should have known this wasn't over yet*, she thought. *How do you escape from an escape artist?*

"Thanks for the money," she said bitterly. "Or have you come to take it back?"

He stood awkwardly upon the threshold. His formal evening wear was rumpled and disheveled. The black suit looked as if it had been through the wars. "I thought you said it wasn't about the money?"

"Well, look what you've done to me!" she accused him. He had already broken her heart. How dare he question her motives now!

Not waiting for an invitation, he stepped tentatively inside the bothy. He showed no interest in their tawdry surroundings. His haunted gaze was centered only on her. "All I did was make you fall in love."

Mary laughed harshly. "Don't flatter yourself."

"I made a mistake," he apologized. "I'm sorry."

"Oh, that's all fine, then!" She couldn't believe the nerve of him. "Mama forgives you. Now get out!" She rose angrily to her feet, her fists clenched at her sides. The discarded white gown lay on the floor between them. "That wasn't love. That was infatuation. That was . . ." Consumed with fury, she struggled to find the right words. "That was just another dance. I'm not sure. Was it a polka or a foxtrot?"

He tried to reply, but she didn't want to hear it. Spittle sprayed from her lips as she railed at him sarcastically. "Another fling! That's right, just another fling!" Her eyes narrowed as she went in for the kill. "Except that it never quite happened, did it? And why was that?"

Talk about a magician, she thought. *Somehow he screwed me without ever taking my clothes off!*

"I'd never been there before," he stammered. Confusion was written all over his face, as if he could barely put what he was feeling into words. "I didn't understand what was happening."

He approached her, holding out his hands.

"Don't touch me!" she snapped. The last thing she wanted now were those tricky hands of his coming anywhere near her. There had been too much of that already.

"I didn't mean that." He retreated hastily, an abashed expression on his face. "That's not what I want."

"So what *does* the Great Houdini want?" she demanded. " 'Cause you don't want me." Her voice was cold and matter-of-fact. "I'm not your little darling wife." She shot a dirty look at the gown on the floor. "I'm not your mama!"

He trembled before her. Sweat beaded upon his brow. He looked as if he might pass out at any moment. "Mary . . . I'm afraid."

His obvious distress and vulnerability caught her somewhat by surprise. This mere-mortal frailty was not exactly what she expected from the fearless Harry Houdini, the wealthy and successful star of stage and screen. Her white-hot rage cooled slightly, supplanted by extreme puzzlement.

"Afraid of what? Afraid of me?"

What remained of his composure shattered like a broken mirror. "I'm afraid of myself." Tears of anguish poured down his face. "Of what I feel for you . . . what I want." His eyes were filled with yearning. "I love you, Mary, but . . . it's . . . it's shameful."

"Shameful?" She was incredulous. "Who taught you that?"

His mother? His dainty little wife? Mary tried to make sense of what she was hearing. Had Harry's intense filial devotion to his mother become so entangled with his more amorous passions that lovemaking itself struck him as unnatural and taboo? Sugarman was right; she was way out of her depth here. She was no psychiatrist; she couldn't begin to fathom the tangled intricacies of Harry's unconscious mind.

"It's how things are," Harry murmured weakly. He stared at his feet. His mother's wedding gown lay only a few feet away. "It's how they've always been."

Her heart melted, drowning the last of her rage. "It's not shameful, Harry. It's what men and women do." Her voice adopted a gentler tone. "It's what keeps the winter at bay. And it keeps the loneliness at bay. And sometimes," she said wistfully, "if you're lucky, down there amongst the sweaty sheets, there's the tiniest bit of human love."

She caught her breath, surprised by her own words. Until this moment, she hadn't known that, deep in her heart, she still believed all that. The admission drained the last of her strength. With no more anger to sustain her, her legs felt as flimsy as Princess Kali's costume. She reached out and grabbed on to the wobbly tabletop to steady herself. A stack of $100 bills toppled over. The loose bills were strewn across the table.

"Ever find it?" Harry asked her. "That tiny bit of love?"

Mary remembered Benji's father, then shook her head sadly. "Never. Not once . . . I washed the sheets."

"That's what I figured." Harry smiled ruefully and turned to leave.

To her astonishment, she found she couldn't let him go. "Harry . . . ?"

He slowly spun around to face her once more. He threw up his hands in surrender, as if he didn't see the point. A hopeless laugh escaped his lips. Love was one feat the Great Houdini had never mastered.

"They say it's easy," she said. "They say it's like falling."

"No falling's easy," he quipped. "Not sure I got the nerve."

The irony of the situation, that the world's greatest daredevil and escapist was terrified of falling in love, was not lost on her. But she knew exactly how he felt. Jumping off a bridge while bound in chains, or escaping from a strait-jacket hundreds of feet above the pavement, was nothing compared to truly opening up your heart to another person. That was the ultimate death-defying act.

"Me neither," she confessed.

Before her courage could fail her, she crossed the room and joined him by the door. She drew the door closed and locked it. The dying fire crackled in the hearth. Her own bed waited upstairs, only a short climb away.

"Know what it was that made me fall for you? I mean, *really* you?" His ardent eyes devoured her and she could tell that he was genuinely seeing her, not some maternal figment from his past. "You looked so fierce when you threw the earrings back in my face that first time. A fighter!"

Mary blushed. "I never much liked me."

"Well, I do."

She believed him. He wasn't just spouting ballyhoo to

sucker a gullible mark. She took his hand and pressed it against her cheek. Despite the cold outside, his flesh was surprisingly warm. No wonder he could survive being dropped into icy rivers. His blood was hot enough to keep him warm.

He claimed her other hand and raised her palm to his lips. She felt the tender touch of his kiss. By now, they were both trembling, and not from any autumn draft. Beneath her ratty cotton robe, her bare flesh was alive with anticipation. "It's easy, isn't it?"

"Just like falling," he agreed.

He took her in his arms and kissed her. Mary's heart pounded as she hungrily kissed him back. She wrapped her arms around him and didn't let go. The depth of her passion overwhelmed her. Her head was spinning, her senses on fire. This was the kiss she had always been waiting for, even if she had somehow forgotten that over the years. The kiss she had needed all her life. She knew without a doubt that Harry felt exactly the same.

Gasping for breath, they finally came apart. Harry's face was flushed and radiant, not at all like the lonely, pathetic scarecrow who had invaded her home only minutes ago. She had never seen him so vibrant, not even that night on the monument. For the moment at least, his awful demons seemed to have fled him. Mary felt her own blood rushing through her veins. The fatigue of earlier was replaced by desire. Her eyes gleamed in the firelight.

"Again," she urged him. "Do it again."

. . .

Out of darkness, an indistinct figure drew nearer. Golden wings flapped above the shadowy apparition. An ephemeral snow-white robe stood out against the empty black void. The figure came closer and closer. A crimson halo seemed to crown the spirit's head.

In her pitiful cot, buried beneath the fraying covers, Benji tossed and turned in her sleep. Animalistic gasps and moans, barely loud enough to hear, insinuated themselves into her dreams. Perspiration bathed her face. Her head rocked from side to side atop her pillow. Sweat plastered her slack brown bangs to her forehead. Her limbs twitched spasmodically. She raised her hands to defend herself against an otherworldly visitor only she could see.

Gilded feathers brushed against her face. An avenging angel hovered over her, filling the sky. Flowing red tresses framed the face of the spirit, which Benji couldn't quite make out. A heavenly glow blurred her vision. Somewhere in the distance, voices cried out in warning. She felt a sudden sharp pain in her stomach. . . .

CHAPTER TWENTY-TWO

THE FIRST RAYS OF DAWN ENTERED THE COT-
tage, waking Mary from the deepest sleep she had enjoyed
in years. Tangled in the bedclothes, she opened her eyes to
the diffused yellow sunlight. She stretched luxuriously beneath the sheets, feeling renewed and refreshed. A deep
yawn filled her lungs. For once, she greeted the day with
anticipation and not simmering resentment at her lot in life.
Memories of last night's rapturous lovemaking brought a
smile to her lips. She reached for Harry, but found only a
shallow depression in the bed beside her. A mystified frown
appeared on her face. Her hand explored the empty depression. It was still warm.

"Harry?"

She sat up and looked around the cramped loft that
served as her bedchamber. Had the great magician pulled
another vanishing act? For a second, Mary feared that
Harry had slipped away in the night, leaving her alone and
abandoned. Then she spotted his clothes strewn on the floor

around the bed, lying crumpled on the rough wooden planks along with her red robe, right where she and Harry had cast the excess garments as they had eagerly dragged each other toward the waiting bed. The empty apparel presented Mary with a puzzle. Where could Harry have got to without his clothes?

Bewildered, she stumbled out of bed. The fire in the hearth downstairs had died out hours ago, and the chilly October morning held a hint of winter. Goose bumps broke out across her bare skin; she threw on Harry's black frock coat to shield her from the cold. Fern-shaped layers of ice frosted the bedroom window. Mary scraped the ice away and peered outside. She blinked in surprise at what she spied.

What the devil . . . ?

Not bothering to put on anything else, she hurried down the stairs to the ground floor. A quick glance assured her that Benji was still out like a light. Mary was inclined to let the girl sleep as long as she liked today, after her harrowing ordeal yesterday. The front door was unlocked and Mary ran out of the bothy into the rocky, weed-filled yard outdoors. A damp fog clung to the earth. The ground beneath her feet was wet with dew. Her breath misted before her lips. She shuddered and pulled Harry's coat tightly about her. A rooster crowed somewhere in the vicinity of the nearby Gypsy caravan. The drifting fog obscured her view of the distant gasworks and its smokestacks. A marble angel watched over the graveyard.

Harry was strolling a few yards away, as naked as the

day he was born. His bare feet splashed through a puddle of icy water, but he didn't even seem to notice. His tousled hair needed a comb. His magnificent physique was exposed for all the world to see, no ticket required. He tread across the frozen ground as if he were walking on water. He gazed at the misty yellow sunrise in wonder, as if he had never seen one before.

You would never have guessed that he was over fifty years old.

Mary shook her head in disbelief, laughing all the while. She ran toward him. "Just what do you think you are doing?"

Hearing her voice, he spun around and threw out his arms. An exuberant grin stretched from ear to ear. He seemed completely unashamed of his nakedness. *And why should he be?* Mary thought. She admired his sinewy physique and washboard stomach.

" 'And with one bound,' " he proclaimed, as though quoting from some melodramatic pulp novel, " 'he was free!' "

He looked as if he meant it, too. She had never seen him looking so relaxed and carefree. Even at the pub and atop the Scott Monument, some secret sorrow had kept him from fully surrendering to the moment. She remembered how he had pulled back from her upon the parapet, choosing to leap out into space rather than deal with the powerful attraction between them. Judging from his jubilant attitude this morning, he wouldn't make that choice again.

This time he chose her.

Shivering, she wrapped herself and the coat around him. She basked in the comfort of his embrace, sharing the warmth of her own body with him. They swaddled themselves against the frigid dawn. Even though her toes were freezing, Mary never wanted to let go.

"You'll catch your death!" she warned him. *Good Lord,* she thought, *now I really do sound like his mother!*

"Quite the reverse," he insisted. His eyes sparkled joyfully. He squeezed her tightly enough to lift her off her feet. "Quite the reverse!"

His mouth found hers and they lost themselves in another precious moment together. Chains of guilt and poverty no longer weighed them down. Walls of deception dissolved into thin air. Suspicion was transformed into absolute trust and intimacy.

They were free.

At least for now . . .

· · ·

The black Rolls-Royce looked more than a little out of place on the neglected dirt road approaching Mary's cottage. The Phantom's powerful engine purred relentlessly. The ground crunched beneath its wheels as it cruised like a shark toward the dilapidated hovel. It luminous headlights tore through the fog. Watching from the doorway, wearing his rumpled black suit, Harry wished that he could somehow make the chauffeur-driven limousine disappear into the ether. Alas, that was beyond even the Great Houdini's powers. Nor could he make time stop forever, no matter how much he might have liked to.

His life had found him.

The limo came to a stop in front of the bothy. A passenger door swung open and Sugarman emerged. He sighed and shook his head at the rustic setting. Holding the door open, he maintained a discreet distance from the cottage.

No need to make him come in after me, Harry thought. *I owe the poor bastard that much for everything I've put him through the last few days.* He had privately forgiven the manager for spilling his secrets to Mary. In the end, everything had turned out better than Harry could ever have imagined. *Besides, if I know Sugarman, his ulcer has already punished him enough this trip.*

Resigned and at ease, Harry stepped out of the cottage. Mary followed closely behind him. Benji sat on a stoop outside the bothy, practicing her juggling. Harry had tried to speak to her earlier, but the girl had been withdrawn and distant all morning. Did she resent what had transpired between him and her mother, or was she simply upset that he was leaving? Harry still didn't entirely understand what had happened to the girl at the séance yesterday, but perhaps some mysteries were better left unexplored. Thanks to Mary, he didn't need to wallow in the past anymore. *I'm ready to live now.*

Without being too obvious about it, Sugarman consulted his watch. Their boat left for Canada in a couple of hours; no doubt the act was already packed up and ready to go. Sugarman watched Harry with an anxious expression. The manager looked as if he had his doubts as to whether Harry was actually coming with them.

Don't worry, Morrie, Harry thought. *Never let it be said that the Great Houdini disappointed his fans.* He had contractual and financial obligations as well; after all, he still had a wife, employees, and various relatives to support, not to mention all the retired magicians and vaudevillians he quietly provided for on the side. Mr. Okata would be expecting his pension check. *And I just gave away ten thousand dollars to a deserving mother and child.*

Not caring who was watching, he tenderly kissed Mary's palm. Her enchanted brown eyes captivated him once. "What happens now?" he asked her softly.

They both knew the answer. Mary maintained a brave front, although her voice cracked a little. "You go to Montreal. You do your show."

"Last one. The last time."

"No." She held up her hand to silence him. "No promises."

They had not spoken of divorce or the future. Neither of them had wanted to spend the little time they had left discussing the discouraging realities of their situation. Harry knew he should feel guilty for cheating on Bess, but, in truth, he hadn't been much of a husband to her for years, especially since his mother died. His career—and his grief—had always come first. She deserved better than the obsessed spook-chaser he had become, especially now that he was truly in love with another woman. Perhaps the kindest thing he could do would be to let her free. Maybe someone could bring joy into her life the same way Mary had rescued him from despair.

It was ironic; he had always billed himself as a "self-liberator," but, in the end, he had needed another person to finally escape from the dungeon walls that had imprisoned his heart for so long. He didn't regret a minute of what had happened last night. Mary was indeed the answer he had been looking for all these years. He gave her back a smile that was just as stoically courageous as hers.

"We're free, ain't that right?"

He glanced over at Sugarman. The manager's foot tapped impatiently upon the ground outside the Phantom. Harry started toward the limo, only to have Mary throw her arms around him. She passionately kissed his eyes, his ears, his mouth. She held on to him tightly, unwilling to let him go. Overcome with emotion, he returned her embrace. She felt his strong arms hug her to him. His bare face pressed against hers. He whispered into her ear:

"You saved me, Mrs. McGarvie."

She rested her head on his shoulder. "You saved yourself, Mr. Houdini."

"Harry?" Sugarman called out sheepishly.

The anxious manager sounded as if he couldn't cope with the uncertainty much longer. Harry figured Sugarman was probably more worried now than he was whenever his client was lowered into the Chinese Water Torture Cell. Harry usually dragged the drowning escape out to four minutes just to prolong the suspense. He was tempted to do the same thing this time.

Instead he reluctantly pulled away from Mary, who finally let him go.

"You saved me, too," she whispered.

He gave her one last kiss, then somehow managed to tear himself away from her. Leaving her was harder than any escape he had ever attempted before. Mary silently watched him go. As he passed the stoop, Harry paused long enough to say good-bye to Benji. The girl didn't look away from the balls she was juggling. Her unsmiling expression didn't change. Her mouth was sealed tighter than the envelope in the safe.

"Lost your voice again, huh?" Harry smiled down at the scowling tomboy. "Where'd you last hear it?" Just as he had in his dressing room when they'd first met, he dipped his hand into his top pocket and pretended to extract the missing voice. He lobbed it back to her. "Look after your mama for me."

Despite herself, a hint of a smile appeared on Benji's face. Harry was glad to see that he hadn't hurt the girl's feelings completely. She seemed like a good kid. Too bad she had been put through a wringer the last few days.

He looked back at Mary and waved his hand in farewell.

"Bye, angel. . . ."

. . .

Mary watched Harry disappear into the Rolls-Royce. Holding the door, Sugarman remained outside the limo for a moment. He and Mary regarded each other across the rocky ground. She wondered if Harry's faithful manager could see the change in him this morning, and whether Sugarman would be disposed to acknowledge that she had played some part in helping Harry overcome the ghosts that had tormented him for so long. Ultimately, it didn't really matter what Sugarman thought of her, but she liked to think that she had proven herself to be more than the deceitful gold digger he had first taken her for . . . even if he hadn't been entirely wrong at first. A lot had happened over the last four days, perhaps more than the ubiquitous Mr. Sugarman realized. *I'm not the person I was before.*

And neither was Harry.

Sugarman eyed her through the fog. Mary fully expected him to sneer in her direction. Instead he paused and grudgingly tipped his hat in respect.

How about that? she thought. *Will wonders never cease?*

Sugarman got into the limo and closed the door behind him. Moments later, the Rolls-Royce pulled away from the cottage and sped toward the harbor. Mary's heart caught in her throat as the black limousine vanished into the swirling mist. She stood there staring, even after there was nothing more to see than a foggy stretch of road. Was part of her hoping that the limo would turn around and come back for her? She shook her head sadly. She knew better than that.

Good-bye, Harry.

Benji came up beside her. She juggled the practice balls from hand to hand. To Mary's surprise, the girl suddenly spoke in a familiar *mittel*-European accent:

" 'Angel with fire-red hair. Clock says noon! Watch out! Here he comes!' " Benji spat onto the ground. Her face and voice were hard and unforgiving. The foreign accent went away. "Just gave him what he wanted. It was easy." She looked up at her mother in disgust. "You're going soft, you are."

Mary stared down at her daughter. Instead of Benji, she saw a smaller, more embittered version of herself ... before Harry unlocked her heart.

"It's like Mr. Sugarman said," Benji snarled. "It's all just showbiz mumbo jumbo." She let the balls crash down into the dirt. "All we've got is what we can touch and see."

The spite in the girl's tone startled Mary. Was this because of her spending the night with Harry? She'd suspected that Benji had a schoolgirl crush on Harry, but she had never expected this level of jealousy. Had she broken Benji's heart by "stealing" the Great Houdini from her? Or had she simply done too good a job of teaching Benji how cold and cruel the world could be?

"That's my girl," she said bleakly.

The warm glow left over from the night before cooled somewhat. Mary's spirits sank. How tragic would it be if she had overcome her own bitterness only by crushing Benji's dreams? Mary fretted over the daughter's cynical tone and expression. *How could I let this happen to her right beneath my nose?*

Had they won the $10,000 at the cost of her daughter's heart?

MONTREAL

CHAPTER TWENTY-THREE

———

MONTREAL WELCOMES HARRY HOUDINI READ
the enormous banner stretched across the regal facade of the
Princess Theater. An eager crowd surged toward the approaching Rolls-Royce. Ghosts, skeletons, witches, and
other fiends pressed their faces against the limo's window.
Wide eyes peered out from behind the grotesque makeup
and masks. Excited voices shouted in both French and English. Streamers, balloons, and firecrackers greeted Houdini's arrival. Painted jack-o'-lanterns adorned the banner.

It was October 31, 1926. Halloween.

Seated beside Harry, Sugarman scowled at the ghoulish
faces outside the limo. He moved to lower the blinds, but
Harry restrained him. He grinned back at the costumed
revelers, enjoying the show. The bogus ghosts amused rather
than troubled him. These were the only sort of spooks he
wanted to see anymore. Their gleeful spirits were infectious.

"Let 'em get a good look, Mr. Sugarman."

A photographer's flash went off outside, blinding Harry.

·   ·   ·

Mary tried to keep from blinking as the flash powder ignited.

She stood to one side, while Benji posed in front of the dilapidated cottage in which they had once lived, before trading in the bothy for more comfortable digs in New Town. She and Benji were both stylishly (and expensively) dressed in the latest fashions. Mary wore a smart three-piece suit of knitted jersey. Benji was tucked snugly into a cashmere sweater and a fetching plaid skirt. Photographers snapped multiple shots of the girl. Benji's unearthly performance a few weeks back was still big news. LOCAL GIRL AMAZES HOUDINI! the headlines had screamed the next day. Now a somewhat smaller crowd of journalists had convened for a follow-up story on how the great magician's generosity had changed their lives. Did any of the gathered reporters and photographers have any idea of all that had really taken place during Houdini's most recent visit to Edinburgh?

I'd wager not, she thought.

A biting cold wind nipped at her cheeks. Mary wondered what the weather was like in Montreal. Glancing back at the cottage, she experienced a bittersweet pang, recalling the night she and Harry had spent together beneath that leaky roof. It had only been a single night, but they had made the most of it. She counted herself lucky to have had even those few hours. It was more than some people found in a lifetime. *Forget séances and mediums,* she thought. *Only love offers a true taste of Heaven.*

Relishing her moment in the spotlight, Benji smiled for the cameras, while a smirking reporter coached her. No doubt he thought a story on Scotland's youngest and most famous medium was perfect Halloween fare.

"Give us the look," the newsman urged. "You know, the psychic look." Benji obliged by looking soulfully up at the sky. A beatific expression lit up her girlish features. "That's it! Like you just got the message direct from Heaven! That's the one!"

Mary recognized the look from her old Princess Kali act. Apparently, Benji was the headliner these days. Mary tried to see the humor in it, but couldn't help being troubled by how easily the fraudulent routine came to her young daughter. A cloud passed before the sun, and a sudden pall fell over Mary's spirits. Her limbs trembled. A dizzy spell threatened her balance. Mary frowned and placed a hand to her forehead. All the blood drained from her face.

What's happening to me?

A dull roar filled her ears. She glanced around in confusion, but could not discern the source of the mysterious hubbub. The roar grew louder inside her skull, drowning out the inane chatter of the reporters and the pop of the exploding flash powder. It was as if an entire crowd of people were cheering somewhere in the distance. If she concentrated, she could almost make out the words, or at least the language. Was that actually *French* she heard?

.   .   .   .

The opulent lobby of the Princess Theater had been extensively decorated for Halloween. Spun-cotton cobwebs draped the elaborately carved walnut railings. Paper cutouts of witches and black cats adorned the Italian-marble columns. A white-sheeted specter hung from the chandelier, casting his shadow on the Venetian-mosaic floor. Grinning jack-o'-lanterns occupied niches throughout the lobby. A papier-mâché skeleton perched atop a stunning art deco clock mounted above the front entrance.

It was four minutes to noon.

A mob of fans and journalists poured through the revolving door to witness Houdini in person. Dressed in his best black suit, Harry turned to address the crowd. Sunlight beamed down on him from the lobby's high glass windows. The myriad voices echoed strangely in the spacious chamber. Among the usual throng of reporters and photographers, Harry spotted a handful of colorful trick-or-treaters. A bald-headed ghoul with pointed ears and jagged fangs was obviously inspired by that *Nosferatu* movie a few years back. A shapely woman in a skimpy Cleopatra outfit inspired fantasies of Mary as Princess Kali. How were she and Benji faring back in Scotland? It would be nearly sunset there, he realized. *Will I ever see them again?*

Sugarman, Franz, and James fought a losing battle to keep the crowd under control. The bodyguards knew better than to get too rough with either the press or Harry's adoring fans. This was his public after all; they depended on them for their livelihood. Microphones were thrust in Harry's face. He raised his hand to wave to the crowd.

"*Bonjour*, Montreal!"

Cheers and laughter answered his salutation. He had always made a point of addressing international audiences in their native tongue. It invariably won him plenty of goodwill, no matter how atrocious his accent!

A fresh-faced young man, whose varsity sweater and baggy trousers pegged him as a college boy, rushed forward to meet him. Franz and James moved swiftly to intercept him, but Harry waved them off. A few days ago, he had delivered a lecture on the evils of phony spiritualists to a packed auditorium at nearby McGill University. Afterward, the impressed students had given him a standing ovation. Harry doubted that he had anything to fear from this collegiate admirer.

"Hi, Mr. Houdini!" the beaming youth greeted him in English, obviously thrilled by the opportunity to speak with the famous magician. "My name's Smiley. Sam Smiley. I'm a student at the college here, studying Business Management."

Harry shook Smiley's hand. "Business Management, eh?" He shot a smile at Sugarman, sharing a private joke. *Beats the University of Hard Knocks, I guess.*

"My friend Gordon here wants to shake your hand, too, Mr. Houdini." Smiley gestured toward a second youth near the front of the audience. He was beefy, with the broad shoulders and thick neck of a linebacker. The sky blue uniform of the Royal Canadian Air Force marked him as a military man. The brim of a felt cap shadowed his features.

Why not? Harry thought. He nodded, and Gordon

stepped forward to join them. Well over six feet tall, the strapping youth had a good three inches on Houdini. He looked older than his friend, perhaps in his late twenties, and had a florid complexion. Freckles spotted his face.

"Pleased to meet you, Mr. H.," Gordon said. Like his friend, he spoke English with an affected Oxford accent. He grinned knowingly. "You're a man who can take a punch, right?"

Harry glanced at the man's RCAF uniform . . . and froze in surprise. A pair of miniature metal wings were pinned above the man's front pocket. Air force wings. Benji's eerie prophecy flashed through his brain:

"He's waiting for you! The angel with fire-red hair. Got wings, too."

"Mr. Houdini can take any man's punch," Smiley boasted to his burly friend. "Isn't that right, Mr. Houdini?"

Sugarman didn't like where this was going. "Get these kids out of here!" he bellowed at Harry's bodyguards. Franz and James looked to Harry for confirmation of the order. But Harry was barely paying attention. Benji's ominous warning echoed inside his skull as he lifted his eyes toward the art deco clock above the revolving doors. The minute hand raced around the clock face as the hour hand ticked toward twelve. Everything seemed to be happening very fast.

"Clock says noon, sun goes black."

"I said, 'Isn't that right, Mr. Houdini?' " Smiley repeated.

Outside, a cloud passed overhead. The sunbeam coming through the window vanished. A shadow fell over Harry. A melancholy gloom invaded the lobby. Distracted, Harry finally registered that Smiley was asking him something.

"What did you say?"

The clock struck twelve.

"Watch out! Here he comes!"

"Trick or treat?" Gordon said. Before Harry had a chance to tighten his abdominal muscles, the looming airman drove his fist into Harry's unprepared gut. One, two, three . . . repeated blows slammed into his stomach. Harry gasped and staggered backward, clutching his abdomen. A sharp pain exploded inside him.

·   ·   ·

Three thousand miles and five time zones away, Mary suddenly felt as though she had been kicked in the stomach. She reeled backward against the cold stone wall of the cottage. Her heart started racing like a runaway train. An icy chill invaded her to the marrow. Her face went as white as chalk.

The photo shoot was over. A chartered limo waited to convey them back to their elegant new home. Benji was already by the car, treating the press to some final remarks. No one paid much attention to Mary as she gasped and struggled to catch her breath. Her skin turned pale and clammy. A cold sweat broke out over her body.

"No . . . ," she whispered. An awful certainty came over her that something terrible was happening. Inside her skull, she heard the flapping of mighty wings. She tasted blood upon her lips. An agonized face flashed before her eyes.

Harry!

J. Gordon Whitehead tossed his cap in the air, exposing a mop of bright red hair. He clasped his hands above his head. "Yes!" he crowed triumphantly. "Houdini's down and out! KO'd in the first round!"

His pal Smiley slapped him on the back. It wasn't everybody who could take down the Great Houdini. Photo flashes burst like gunshots. The two youths laughed at their victory, until the heavy hands of the bodyguards descended on their shoulders. Franz Kukol and James Vickery dragged the startled boys away from Harry, who looked as if he was about to topple over. He grimaced in pain.

"Get back! Get back!" Sugarman shouted at the dumbfounded crowd. He ran up behind Harry and caught him before he hit the floor. Harry coughed up blood onto the expensive mosaic floor. His face was pale as death.

The magician's obvious physical distress wiped the smiles from the students' faces. "I didn't hit him so hard!" Gordon protested. Both men stared at the injured man in dismay. Their jaws fell open. Smiley chewed on his knuckles. Gordon started sweating profusely.

"Someone get a bloody doctor!" Sugarman shouted. He carefully lowered Harry onto the floor, cradling his head. Harry spit more blood onto the floor as he continued to clutch his stomach. The pain was indescribable, even worse than when he had ruptured his kidney back in Detroit. His entire belly felt as if it were on fire. Harry figured most men would have blacked out by now, but he had trained himself to cope with all but the most severe pain and discomfort. At the moment, that was no blessing. His bloodshot eyes looked up at Sugarman's anxious face.

"Saw that one coming," he said drily.

Did the manager remember Benji's cryptic warning? Or did he still think that Mary and her daughter had conned them out of the $10,000? Harry was starting to think that the possessed girl had earned the money fair and square.

"You're going to be all right, Harry." Sugarman's panicky expression belied his words.

Harry shook his head. "I don't think so, Morrie. This time I keep falling." Harry remembered standing atop the Scott Monument, poised to jump. At the last minute, only the memory of Mary's lovely face, and an overpowering need to see her one last time, had kept him from going through with the fatal plunge. But apparently his farewell tour could not be extended indefinitely. The curtain was about to fall for good.

Sugarman blurted out a confession. "I told them, Harry. God forgive me, I told them all that stuff about your mother!"

With the last of his strength, Harry reached up and gave Sugarman's hand a reassuring pat. "I know you did," he said gently. But that didn't mean that everything Benji had said in the séance was a lie. Not everything was a fraud and an illusion. Mary had shown him that. He could die happy knowing that he had mastered the greatest feat of all before exiting the stage. Even if only for one night.

Blood trickled from the corner of his mouth. He managed a wry smile. He hoped the crowd in the lobby appreciated having front-row seats to the Great Houdini's final escape. Too bad there wasn't a fanfare. "Catch me."

His lifeless body slumped against the floor.

.   .   .

"Catch me."

The voice whispered in her ear as clear as a bell. Mary stumbled and threw out her hand to steady herself against the wall of the cottage. The world momentarily spun around her. The ground seemed to shift beneath her feet. Her eyes glistened moistly. The phantom pain in her gut evaporated as quickly as it had come. She felt her entire world get a little colder.

Harry, she realized. *He's gone.*

She slumped against the wall, barely able to stay on her feet. She buried her face in her hands. No more voices echoed inside her skull, only the memory of Harry's final message. Unlike Harry and his mother, she would never have to wonder what he had said at the end, or question whom he was thinking of in his final moments.

"Catch me."

Over by the limousine, Benji finally noticed that something was amiss with her mother. A look of genuine fright replaced the polished facade she was putting on for the press. Leaving the reporters and cameras behind, she ran across the rocky yard to Mary.

"Mam? What is it?"

Tears flooded Mary's face. An overwhelming sense of loss overcame her, rendering her incapable of speech. How could she ever explain to her daughter what she was feeling now, how she knew deep in her heart that the Great Houdini would never return to Edinburgh in this lifetime? It sounded insane, she knew, but she would have staked her life on it. There could be no doubt.

Harry was dead.

"What's wrong, Mam?"

Mary could only sob in reply.

CHAPTER TWENTY-FOUR

A NEWSREEL PRECEDED THE FEATURE ATTRAC-
tion. Today's scheduled matinee was *The Black Pirate* with
Douglas Fairbanks, but Benji was in no mood for swash-
buckling adventure. It was the newsreel she and Mam had
come to see. Seated in the darkened theater, her teary eyes
glued to the screen, Benji watched silently as her own
ad-libbed prophecy came true.

HARRY HOUDINI'S HIGH NOON!
THE FINAL CURTAIN!

Jerky images depicted two distraught young men being
hauled away by the police. The sweaty-faced youths ges-
ticulated frantically while mouthing apologies. An intrusive close-up captured the miniature wings on the larger
student's air force uniform. His fair hair and freckles were
emblazoned on Benji's memory forever. Tears welled up in
her eyes.

HARRY HOUDINI RECEIVES FATAL PUNCH
FROM RED-HAIRED PRANKSTER

The papers said that Houdini had died of a ruptured appendix. Doctors speculated that the organ had already been badly infected before Whitehead's brutal punches burst the swollen appendix. In the end, no charges had been pressed against the repentant airman and his cohort. In the subsequent weeks, Whitehead had shunned the press, disappearing into obscurity. Benji found she bore no grudge against the unwitting instrument of Houdini's demise ... which she herself had predicted weeks before.

Not for the first time, Benji wondered from whence her fatal warning had come that fateful afternoon in the ballroom of the Scottish Lion Hotel. She had thought that she had simply pulled the words out of her imagination, using bits and pieces of a half-forgotten nightmare. But now she didn't know what to believe. Had higher powers spoken through her somehow? Had her dreams been more than dreams? Maybe the world was more mysterious—and wondrous—than she had ever thought before. Maybe it wasn't all just crude tricks and hocus-pocus.

Benji wanted to think so.

THE WORLD MOURNS THE GREAT HOUDINI

Flickering news footage, accompanied by the organist's rendition of Chopin's "Funeral March," captured heartbreaking scenes of grief. Hundreds of people wept openly as Houdini's coffin was borne through Grand Central Station after finally arriving back home in New York City. Thousands crowded the broad avenues outside his funeral, blocking traffic. At a tidy gravesite in Queens, next to a marble monument to Cecilia Weiss, a somber representative of the Society of American Magicians broke a magic wand in half over Houdini's coffin. A bearded rabbi read a prayer. Houdini's widow, veiled in black, collapsed and needed to be helped away by Mr. Sugarman.

Benji knew how she felt.

Tears fell from her eyes as she began to weep openly. Her mother reached out and gently squeezed Benji's hand. She turned and hugged her daughter for the first time in years. Benji heard her mother sobbing as well. They clung together desperately, comforting each other as never before. Just as their competing feelings for Houdini had once divided them, their shared grief now brought them closer together.

It was, perhaps, the great magician's final miracle.

HARRY HOUDINI!
MAGICIAN! WONDER WORKER!

Harry appeared upon the silver screen, preserved forever in his prime. Nattily clad in his formal attire, he posed upon a stage before closed velvet curtains. Proud and confident, he laughed and waved at an eternal audience, ready to triumph over whatever death-defying challenges lay ahead. Nothing could ever bind him, perhaps not even the grave. The Great Houdini was indeed immortal.

This was exactly how Benji wanted to remember him.

Closing her eyes, she snuggled into her mother's loving embrace. Mary stroked her hair.

.   .   .

Somewhere, beyond the curtains and the footlights, Harry leapt from a stage that jutted out over all of eternity. His arms spread like wings as he dived into a clear blue sky. Gravity released him as an invisible orchestra struck a soaring chord that would last forever.

He was free.

BIBLIOGRAPHY

There is no shortage of books and websites about the Great Houdini. Below is a sampling of some of the resources I consulted in writing this book:

Chaykin, Howard, and John Francis Moore. *Batman/Houdini: The Devil's Workshop*. New York: DC Comics, 1993.

Cobb, Vicki. *Harry Houdini*. New York: DK Publishing, 2005.

Cox, Clinton. *Houdini: Master of Illusion*. New York: Scholastic Press, 2001.

Fitzsimmons, Raymund. *Death and the Magician: The Mystery of Houdini*. New York: Atheneum, 1981.

Fleischmann, Sid. *Escape!: The Story of the Great Houdini*. New York: Greenwillow Books, 2006.

Kalush, William, and Larry Sloman. *The Secret Life of Houdini: The Making of America's First Superhero*. New York: Atria Books, 2006.

Shatner, William, and Michael Tobias. *Believe*. New York: Berkley, 1992.

Shavelson, Melville. *The Great Houdinis!* Greenwich, CT: Fawcett Publications, 1976.

Sutherland, Tui T. *Who Was Harry Houdini?* New York: Grosset & Dunlap, 2002.

ACKNOWLEDGMENTS

When my editor first teased me with the possibility of writing a historical novel based on an upcoming motion picture, I had no idea that the movie in question was about the Great Houdini. As I've always been fascinated by Houdini, I was thrilled to discover that I would be spending several weeks exploring the life and history of the world's most famous stage magician.

Thanks to my editor at Pocket Books, Ed Schlesinger, for thinking of me, and to my agents, Russ Galen and Ann Behar, for making it happen. I also have to thank Myriad Pictures for providing me with a generous assortment of photos from the film as well as an advance copy of the movie trailer. The Oxford Public Library helped me track down several useful books on Houdini, including many of those listed in the bibliography.

Finally, as always, I have to thank Karen Palinko for supporting me on the home front, along with our ever-growing family of four-legged housemates: Alex, Churchill, Henry, Sophie, and Lyla. (Check out my website for some frankly adorable photos of the whole gang.)

ABOUT THE AUTHOR

—

GREG COX is the author of several previous movie noveli-
zations, including *Ghost Rider*, *Daredevil*, *Underworld*, and
Underworld: Evolution. He has also written books and short
stories based on such popular series as *Alias*, *Batman*, *Buffy*,
Infinite Crisis, *Iron Man*, *Fantastic Four*, *Farscape*, *52*, *The 4400*,
Roswell, *Star Trek*, *Underworld*, *Xena*, and *X-Men*. His official
website is www.gregcox-author.com.

He lives in Oxford, Pennsylvania.